P9-EJK-616

8 2006

out of patience

out of patience

BRIAN MEEHL

DELACORTE PRESS

Published by
Delacorte Press
an imprint of
Random House Children's Books
a division of Random House, Inc.
New York

Visit us on the Web! www.randomhouse.com/kids
Educators and librarians, for a variety of teaching tools, visit us at
www.randomhouse.com/teachers

Library of Congress Cataloging-in-Publication Data
Meehl, Brian.
    Out of Patience / Brian Meehl.
      p.   cm.
    Summary: Twelve-year-old Jake Waters cannot wait to escape the small town of Patience, Kansas, until the arrival of a cursed toilet plunger causes him to reevaluate his feelings toward his family and its history.
      ISBN: 0-385-73299-6 (hardcover)—ISBN: 0-385-90320-0 (Gibraltar Library Binding)
      ISBN-13: 978-0-385-73299-4 (hardcover)—ISBN-13: 978-0-385-90320-2 (Gibraltar Library Binding)
      [1. Family—Fiction. 2. Self-perception—Fiction. 3. City and town life—Fiction.] I. Title.
    PZ7.M5128170ut 2006
    [Fic]—dc22
2005013873

The text of this book is set in 12-point Goudy O.S.
Book design by Trish P. Watts
Printed in the United States of America
10 9 8 7 6 5 4 3 2 1
First Edition
BVG

For my mother and father,
who introduced me to toilets
and so many other wonderful things

1 it came from above

Like most twelve-year-olds, Jake Waters was a collector of head bonks. He'd gotten most of the standard ones. From the one you get when you're learning to walk—the coffee-table uppercut—to the one you get when there's nine gloves on a baseball field and only one ball to catch—the who's-got-it confusion-cracker.

But in the long history of head bonks, this was a first.

Jake didn't see it coming because he was wearing his KSF baseball hat pulled down low. It bounced off his head and flopped on the burnt-out grass. The sudden blow was startling, but not as surprising as what delivered it.

A toilet plunger.

As he rubbed his head and stared at the plunger lying on the yellow grass, lightning almost struck twice. Another toilet plunger pogo-sticked off the ground. His eyes shot upward as two more plungers sailed out the window, arcing toward him like rubber-tipped missiles. This was no freak accident. This was a full-fledged plunger attack. He dropped his bike and scurried out of range. More plungers shot out the window and flopped on the grass.

Then the plunger barrage stopped.

He squinted at the upstairs window as his father's voice drifted out. It was surprisingly calm for a man whose toilet plunger collection had just been chucked out the window. "Are you finished?"

The woman who answered seemed insulted by the pass-the-ketchup ease of the question. "No!" she exploded.

It was Jake's stepmother, Wanda.

Then his father shouted, "Not that!"

A new object spun out the window. It looked like a super-sized Frisbee. It skipped off the porch roof and landed in the tumbleweed hedge the wind had a way of planting around the house. It was a dark wooden toilet seat.

Jake looked up as his father's back blocked the window. He was wearing his usual blue T-shirt with WATERS & SON PLUMBING on the back. "That's enough," he said.

"You got that right, bub!" Wanda spit the last word like she wished she had one more plunger. The one she wanted to drive through his heart.

Jake heard her clomp loudly down the stairs in her clogs. For the three years Wanda had been his stepmother, he remembered her being more loud than not. It wasn't her fault. She was from a loud city: Las Vegas. She met Jim Waters while he was in Vegas at a weeklong plumbers' convention. They got married before the end of the week.

The screen door blew open. Wanda stomped out on the

porch, lugging a big suitcase and a boom box almost as big as the suitcase. She wore blue jean cutoffs and a tank top with curlicue pink letters: THE MIRAGE. It was the name of the casino in Vegas where she had been a showgirl.

She spotted Jake in the yard and pulled up short. "Why aren't you at the game?"

"I left my glove on the porch," he said.

"I was gonna come say goodbye there." She bumped her suitcase down the porch steps. "Sorry, Jake, I was hoping you wouldn't have to see this. I was hoping *I* wouldn't have to see this."

Jake wasn't sure what to do. His father had taught him to help women carry heavy things. But asking your stepmother if you could help her with her suitcase when she was leaving didn't seem like a good idea. She looked mad enough as it was. He decided to do the thing that had worked for six generations of Waters men. When in doubt, don't move.

Wanda lurched by him, then dropped the suitcase and the boom box behind her battered red Mustang. She stabbed the trunk with a key. "Aren't you gonna ask me?"

Jake blinked. "Ask you what?"

"Why I'm leaving the most worthless man I've ever married. And believe me, I've married some worthless men."

"Why?" It wasn't the first time he'd heard her rank his father among what she referred to as the Three Stooges.

"He did it again," she declared.

"What?"

"What he promised he'd never do."

This was one of the things Jake wasn't going to miss if Wanda was really leaving for good this time. Asking her a direct question was like doing a search on Wanda.com and getting a dozen pop-ups. He tried again, even though he knew the answer was several pop-ups away. "What did he promise he'd never do again?"

She glared at him. "Are you gonna help me with these or stand there like a stump?"

That was pop-up number two. But Jake was glad to finally have a reason to move. He grabbed the suitcase and hefted it into the trunk. Then he wedged the boom box next to it. He barely got his hands out before she slammed the trunk.

"He got on eBay again," she blurted, getting to the point in record time. "I just found out he used the grocery money to buy another one of them plungers!" She flailed her hands at the plungers scattered in the yard. "I mean, what kind of man collects useless old toilet plungers?"

The kind of man who did appeared behind the screen door in the shade of the porch.

"I don't know much about cooking and being a mother," she shouted toward the house. "But the best cook in the world can't turn a plunger into a pot roast!" She grabbed Jake's shoulders and locked on his eyes.

He tried to meet her fiery gaze, but he couldn't stop staring at the purple vein bulging in her forehead.

Her voice softened. "Jake, listen to me, and listen good."

Her vein deflated. He found her eyes. They were different from the eyes he'd seen all summer. They weren't sad or angry anymore. They were filled with the bright clarity of someone who'd wrestled her demons and won. Her demons included fourteen plungers and an old wooden toilet seat.

"I want you to do two things," she declared. "You run yourself to the nearest mental hospital and get your daddy some help. When he's safely locked up, learn to drive, and then you do what no Waters man has done in a hundred 'n' forty years. Get out of this dried-up cow pie of a town."

Jake knew there was a lot he was going to miss about Wanda too. Her loud music. Her leftover-spaghetti-scrambled eggs, which were much better than they sounded. And she told great stories about other parts of the country. Big cities like Las Vegas and Los Angeles. She'd even traveled to foreign cities. She had stories about Tijuana and Acapulco.

Wanda squeezed his shoulders. "Promise me, Jake. You're gonna get outta here and see the world."

"I promise," he whispered.

Her red lips stretched into a smile. "Good. And when you get your goin' agoin', you come 'n' see me in Vegas."

2   jim waters

Jake watched the red Mustang hurry down the street and turn left. Then it disappeared behind the tallest building for miles around, the abandoned grain elevator. He listened to the squawk of worn-out springs as the Mustang bumped over the railroad tracks, and the gun of the engine as Wanda made her break for Highway 40.

Wanda wasn't doing anything special. She was doing the most popular activity in Patience, Kansas, for well over a century. Leaving.

Jake didn't hold it against her. In fact, if his father hadn't been watching, he might have jumped into her Mustang and gone with her. Promising Wanda to get his goin' agoin' was something he'd promised himself already.

At the beginning of the summer, on his twelfth birthday, Jake Waters had made a vow. He was going to be the first J. Waters not to die in Patience, Kansas.

He didn't know if any of the other five J. Waterses who came before him had made such a vow. If they did, they

6

didn't live up to it. The first four J. Waterses—Jeremiah, Jud, Jack, and Joseph—had all moved over to the cemetery on Temperance Street. It was the only street in town attracting new residents, but the welcome wagon was a hearse.

Then there was J. Waters number five. Jake's father. His name was James, but everyone called him Jim.

Jim wasn't as ready for the nuthouse as Wanda claimed. Yes, he had a front yard littered with antique toilet plungers. Yes, he was picking them up like it was as normal as picking melons. But he wasn't crazy. He was just, as the old-timers say, a half-bubble off plumb.

Jim Waters was made of head, hands, feet, and length. He had a shock of swept-back hair, graying at the sides. Some say he looked like the guy on the twenty-dollar bill. Andrew Jackson. That's as far as the similarity went. Andrew Jackson never wore a ratty baseball cap with the Waters & Son Plumbing logo on it. The logo was a monkey wrench crossed over a toilet plunger.

Jake moved toward the house and plucked a plunger off the grass.

"Careful," Jim cautioned, "that's antique rubber."

"I know."

Jake knew all about the plungers. When each one was made, by what manufacturer, and where each one fit in the evolution of toilet accessories. It was an unfortunate side effect of listening to his father go on about the horde of antique bathroom stuff that clogged two upper rooms in the Waters house, and, as Wanda said, "spilled onto the walls upstairs and down."

Jim's defense of what he called his sensational sanitary-ware and the "nuggets of toilet knowledge" that hung on the walls was simple. "History is in the eye of the beholder." His dream was to open what was going to put Patience, Kansas, back on the map. The American Toilet Museum. The ATM.

Having a father whose greatest ambition was opening a toilet museum wasn't a walk in the park. It was more like walking around with a toilet paper streamer stuck to your shoe. But Jake had resigned himself to the embarrassment and the teasing that came with his father's potty museum pipe dream.

Sometimes it even had an upside. Like the time in school when they were studying Ancient Egypt and Jake aced a report in which he asked, "After you go to the afterlife, do you still go to the bathroom?" Jake knew the ancient Egyptians believed you did. Along with everything they stuffed in a pharaoh's tomb for use in the next life, they also installed a bathroom. Even dead pharaohs need the proper facilities.

Jake picked up another plunger and watched his father inspect one of his treasures: a Delux Declogger, manufactured by Sioux City Suction Cups, circa 1930. "Dad, did you really buy another plunger on eBay?"

Jim squinted at the business end of the Delux Declogger. "Some people just don't have a vision of the future."

Jake took that as a yes and came to Wanda's defense. "Wanda has a vision of the future too. It's called Las Vegas."

Jim scooped up another plunger. "Yeah, but how long will it last?"

His father had a point. Wanda had left before and then come back. "You think she'll come back this time?"

"I don't know. She's never taken her boom box before." Jim threw his son a reassuring smile. "You know, Jake, sometimes things have to get worse before they get better."

"Dad, everyone in the family's been saying that for a zillion years and things have only gotten worse. What if there is no better? What if there's only worse?"

Jim lifted the plunger like a king raising his scepter. "*Ad Astra per Aspera.*"

"Yeah-yeah, I know." It was his father's favorite Latin expression, which, like knowing everything about a Delux Declogger, had lodged in Jake's brain. "To the stars through difficulty."

"Thatta boy." Jim grinned. "Now get goin' or you're gonna miss the game. I'll be there as soon as I round up these strays and get 'em back to the herd."

Jake carried two plungers up to the porch, set them down, and grabbed his baseball glove off the old tin box sitting next to the door. It was a milk delivery box from the era when milkmen delivered fresh milk to your door. That was another thing about Waters men. They never threw anything away that was perfectly good even though what it was good for had come and gone ages ago. *Why throw away a perfectly good telegraph machine? We might need it someday.* Jim claimed the family was blessed with the "preservation gene." Jake thought it was more like the pathetic pack rat gene.

As Jake thumped down the steps he wished his father was as good at holding on to Wanda as he was at holding on to useless junk. He lifted his mountain bike off the burnt grass, then worked his glove onto a handlebar. He felt a hand on his shoulder and glanced up.

"Are you all right?" Jim asked.

Jake stared at the bouquet of plungers cradled in his father's arm. He resisted the urge to toss the question right back. *Are you all right?*

The truth was Jake wasn't sure how to feel about Wanda leaving. That's the thing about people who leave and come back, then leave and come back. It's like someone who says goodbye, then gets stuck in a revolving door. Your feelings get stuck there too. You don't know what's coming or going.

So Jake did what felt right considering the circumstances. He shot his father a Wanda pop-up. "Depends on how I hit 'em today. Ask me after the game."

3 endurance street

As Jake pedaled away from the house, a feeling finally welled up inside him. He knew exactly what it was.

Envy.

If Wanda had really left for good this time, she'd just done what he could only dream of. Look at Endurance Street for the last time.

The street was nothing like the perfect streets he saw on television. TV streets had two rows of neat houses, with bright green yards and kids playing all over the place. The only thing Endurance Street had in common with TV Street USA was the strip of concrete down the middle. Instead of rows of neat houses, Jake's street was a messy jumble of buildings. There were a few original wooden houses jutting up like bleached bones from another era. Except for the Waters place, these old houses were empty, home to wood rats, spiderwebs, and windwhistle. Plunked down among the skeleton houses were a couple of doublewide trailer homes and a huge metal equipment shed.

The street's crazy quilt of yards was equally pathetic. Some yards were balding patches of cinnamon brown grass. Mini–dust bowls waiting to happen. Others had become salvage yards, home to herds of rusting farm equipment and vehicles. But the ones that were the farthest from TV Street were the abandoned lots where buffalo grass chewed at the fraying edge of town. A motionless windmill rose up from one. An oil-pumping jack perched on another. It looked like a huge iron bird with its rusty beak stuck in the ground.

Endurance Street was on its way to what the old-timers call go-back land. But Jake knew it was more than buffalo grass and broken dreams gnawing away at Patience. There was something else slowly grinding the town back into the prairie.

The curse.

Jake braked to a stop at the corner of Endurance and Courage Street. He wasn't checking for cars. There was so little traffic all the town's stop signs had been replaced with yield signs some time ago. He stopped because he had a choice. He could turn right and go to his baseball game, or he could turn left and follow Wanda. All he had to do was cross the railroad tracks, ride the flat mile out to Highway 40, dump his bike, and hitch a ride west. In a couple dozen miles he'd be in Colorado. On his way to Las Vegas. *Ad Astra per Aspera.* To the stars through difficulty.

But it wasn't just Wanda that had him thinking. The temptation to run away often waited for him at the corner of Endurance and Courage. And not because Courage was the street that led out of town. It was the abandoned house squatting on the corner. It was home to Jake's worst nightmare.

The nightmare went like this. He's eighteen and finally leaving town. He climbs on a brand-new Harley, waves to his father, and thunders down the street. He stops at the corner of Endurance and Courage. He looks into town one last time. That's when it happens. The house on the corner lunges out of the ground and grabs him. He tries to break loose, but it's no use. The house swallows him like a snake sucking down a frog.

Jake wasn't a half-bubble off plumb for having such a weird nightmare. The house *was* scary. It was sunk halfway into the ground. It had a regular sloped roof, but the gutters were so low you could walk up and look down into them. The windows were half buried. They looked like eyes peering out of the earth. It was called a dugout house, and it was sunk in the ground for good reason. For protection against the blistering heat and tornadoes of western Kansas.

But in his nightmare it was more than a dugout. It was a coffin. A hungry casket waiting to snatch him, throw on the lid, and bang in the nails. That's why he called it the coffin house.

He sometimes wondered if his nightmare was connected to the town's curse. After all, the curse was all about destroying the town, and his nightmare was all about destroying him. There was another unavoidable connection. Jake was related to the curse. It was his great-great-great-grandfather Jeremiah who started it all.

But Jake wasn't a huge believer in the sins of the great-great-great-grandfathers being visited on their great-great-great-grandsons. In fact, the story of the curse had been stirred in the storyteller's pot for so many generations, it was hard to tell what was real and what had been thrown in the stew to spice it up. Like the whole thing about the Plunger of Destiny. Even though his father denied it, Jake knew that something as silly as a Plunger of Destiny was just some storyteller overspicing the stew.

"Hey, Jake!"

He jumped and turned toward a girl riding a bike over the tracks. She had earth-colored skin, and her long black hair fanned out behind her KSF baseball cap. Like Jake, she was wearing a KSF baseball uniform. A Louisville Slugger lay across her handlebars.

Jake threw her a quick wave. "Hey, Cricket."

Her real name was Nisira Rashid, but most people called her Sira or used her nickname, Cricket.

Sira coasted past him and looped a circle in the empty intersection. "What's the matter, forget which way the field is?"

Jake pushed off toward town. "No, I was figuring out how to take the lead in Game 5 of the World Series."

"Yeah, right," she scoffed as she swooped by him. "Nobody's taking the lead if we miss our first at bat."

He pedaled to catch up. "Hey, with only eight players it's not like they're gonna start without us."

"Eight, oh-eight," she shouted over her shoulder. "In 1908, the Kansas legislature passed a law against eating snakes in public."

"No way," he said as he caught up to her.

"It's a fact. There were these performers called geeks who bit the heads off snakes in sideshows. So the people decided, 'All right, that's it, the next person who eats a snake in public is going to jail.' "

Jake rolled his eyes. This was how Cricket got her nickname. She jumped from one subject to another faster than a cricket in a grass fire. She could also jump faster and farther than anyone on the baseball field.

"Where do you get this stuff?"

Cricket grinned. "It takes a lot of butt travel, Jake."

"Butt travel?"

"Reading. You should try it sometime."

He frowned. "We've still got two weeks of summer. When school starts, I'll butt travel."

4   nisira rashid

Sira wasn't originally from Kansas. She was born in Karachi, Pakistan. The Cricket of Karachi was her full nickname. When she was four years old, her family moved to Patience after they bought the Tumbleweed Motel out on the highway.

Being a Pakistani-American in Kansas made Sira a little different, but that was only the beginning. Compared to the other kids in Patience—all eight of them—she was the master of different. For one, she liked school. At the moment, she was obsessed with her over-the-summer school project. She called it "Kansas: 100 Years of Freaky & Fascinating Facts." Here's how it worked. For every number from zero to ninety-nine, she had to memorize a fact about Kansas, or Patience, that corresponded with the years '00 to '99. When she wasn't playing baseball or helping her parents at the motel, she was on the hunt for her next freaky or fascinating fact.

There was one other thing that made her different. She was the only person Jake knew who thought it was cool to grow up in a town with its own curse.

The two of them rode toward an old brick gas station with a drive-thru canopy. Its faded sign read PATIENCE SERVICE STATION. It was the perfect name because patience was what you needed to buy gas there. The tanks had been empty for years. The only pump left was a rusty air pump. The hose was long gone, but the gauge still promised thirty-two pounds of air pressure.

Sira swerved under the canopy and coasted past the air pump. " '32," she announced. "In 1932, the worst grasshopper plague in Kansas history wiped out every crop in the state."

"You told me that one already," Jake protested.

She sped up behind him. "Don't you want to help me memorize them?"

"Sure, as much as I wanna stare at the sun till I go blind."

"Okay, Tweener, how's *your* summer project going?"

Tweener was Jake's nickname. One of the reasons he got it was because he was good at hitting the ball in the gaps between the infielders.

He leaned back and rode with no hands. "I'm not a big believer in multitasking. I'll start it after I win the World Series of Workup."

"Too bad." She stood up on her pedals. "That means you won't be starting it till *next* summer." She took off at a sprint.

Jake raced after her.

Sira wasn't his best friend. How could she be? She was a girl. But she was the only person he'd told about his vow to get out of Patience. He figured she would understand. She had plans to get out too.

Her plan went like this. College, join the CIA, become a spy, save Pakistan and India from having a nuclear war, win the Nobel Peace Prize, but then not show up at the ceremony because she couldn't blow her cover as a spy. She was still deciding who to send in her place.

Sira thought it was a terrific plan. What could possibly go wrong?

When Jake teased her about shooting for the moon, she said at least she was shooting for something, which was more than he was doing. He argued that there were different kinds of escape plans. Hers was a step-by-step plan, like a staircase that took you farther and farther out of Patience. It was easy having a step-by-step plan when you had parents who wanted you to do something with your life. But when you were the sixth J. Waters to be born there, and the family business had been Waters & Son Plumbing for more than fifty years, getting out wasn't some step-by-step staircase thing. It was more like sneaking out a window in the middle of the night.

Jake's plan went like this. Grow up. Get out. On a Harley. He even had a name for it. OOPS. Short for Out of Patience Someday.

He thought it was a terrific plan. What could possibly go wrong?

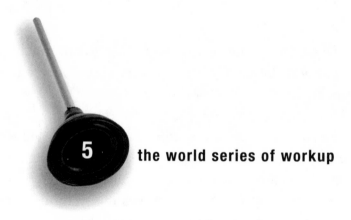

5 the world series of workup

At one time, the baseball field on the north edge of town had an official name. Now everyone just called it Mange Field.

The outfield was an expanse of seared crabgrass with three bald patches where generations of outfielders had done the boredom shuffle. The dirt infield was spotted with dark islands of henbit, a straggly weed with long tendrils. Even though the wire backstop was corroded and rusty, it had an encouraging lean toward first base. The two chicken-wire dugouts still had plywood roofs to keep out the rain, but they couldn't keep out the tumbleweed. It didn't matter. With only eight players in the KSF Workup League, no one ever sat down.

Sira and Jake skidded their bikes in the dirt behind the backstop. The six other contenders for the World Series of Workup were warming up in the field.

A big, sturdy-looking kid with a broad smile shouted from first base. "Rule book says there's a 10-point penalty for being late." Howie Knight turned to the pitcher's mound and the only grown-up on the field. "Isn't that right, Dad?"

Howie's father, Marvin Knight, was the coach, pitcher, umpire, and sponsor of the KSF Workup League. He was a short, thickset man with a large head that made his baseball hat look too small. He checked his watch and made the call. "No penalty for missing warm-ups, but they'll miss batting practice." He waved at Jake and Sira. "Take the field, end of the rotation. One more batter, and Game 5 begins."

Jake trotted past Howie at first base. "Hey, I thought you wanted me to come in second."

Howie gave him a friendly whack on the back with his glove. "I wasn't after you, buddy. It's the girl that's gotta go down."

"I heard that, Howie," Mrs. Knight called from the small set of bleachers behind the first-base line.

"What? What did I say?" he protested.

Mrs. Knight shook a scolding finger. "Play to win, Howie, not to see someone else lose."

"Okay, but remember this is war!" Howie shook his fist at the sky. "Waa-waa-waaaaarrrrr!"

Reaching the bald spot in right field, Jake smiled at Howie's antics. Jake knew how much his best friend wanted to win. The summer before, Howie "Kapowie" Knight had lost the World Series of Workup to Tommy "the Crushman" Conners by one point. This was Howie's year. Especially since the Crushman had moved away. There was only one problem. The Cricket of Karachi. For

Howie, goofing off was his way of avoiding his biggest nightmare. Losing to a girl.

Mr. Knight threw a few more pitches to the freckle-faced little girl at home plate. She hit a weak grounder back to the mound.

"Good work, Rosie." Mr. Knight pumped his fist in encouragement. "Save your best stuff for the game. All right, Workup Wildcats, bring it in for the lineup."

For those of you who have never played workup, or even heard of it before, here's how it works for eight players.

THE KSF WORKUP LEAGUE RULEBOOK:

1) The game starts with one batter, four infielders, and three outfielders. Coach Knight pitches to everyone, covers home, and umps the game.

2) When a batter gets on base, the players rotate so the first baseman becomes the next batter. The infield moves over one position. The left fielder moves to third base, the center fielder moves to left, and the right fielder moves to center. That leaves right field *empty*. Right field becomes foul territory. To make the right calls, two additional foul lines cut the outfield into wedges of left, center, and right field.

3) If three batters get on base, which leaves the entire outfield empty, the outfield becomes foul territory. Anything hit over the heads of the infielders is a foul ball. However, anything hit over the outfield fence in normal fair territory is still a home run.

4) Batters bat until they're put out. A batter gets points each time they get a hit. A single is worth 1 point, a double 2 points, a triple 3 points, a home run 5 points. Once a

batter is put out, they return to the field wherever the end of the rotation is.

5) Committing an error costs players 12 years old and older 1 point. Players under 12 are not penalized for an error.

6) The game lasts until 54 outs are made. At which point, the player with the most points wins.

RULES FOR THE WORKUP WORLD SERIES:

7) The lineup for Game 1 is youngest to oldest. The lineups for Games 2–7 start with the player with the lowest score batting first, then moving up until the player with the highest score bats last.

8) The World Series is 7 games over 7 days.

9) Whoever has the highest score at the end of Game 7 is the new World Series of Workup Champion.

10) And don't forget, during each game, when the horn sounds once, it's time for the KSF Seventh-Inning Stench. When the horn sounds twice, the Seventh-Inning Stench is over.

Keeping track of the scores of eight different players was complicated. That's why Mrs. Knight always brought her laptop. She tracked all the scores, statistics, and number of outs.

As the players ran in from the field, a few parents arrived and sat in the bleachers. Reading from her laptop, Mrs. Knight announced the standings going into Game 5. "Rosie Kinney, who's *doubled* her four-game total from last year, has six points."

Everyone applauded. Rosie turned red.

"Rosie starts in the batter's box," declared Mr. Knight.

And so it went, from the lowest score to the highest, with Mrs. Knight adding uplifting comments for the players with low scores. The last three players had the highest scores and were sent to the outfield. Jake took left field. He was in third place with 47 points. Sira took center and was in second place with 52. Howie was in right with the lead after four games. 54 points.

"Ladies and gents," Mr. Knight announced from the mound. "This is Game 5 in the KSF World Series of Workup."

A dozen spectators applauded. A cowbell rang from the third-base side of the field.

The bell ringer was on the other side of Faith Street, sitting in the shade of her sagging porch. Mrs. Bickers always watched the games from her porch. She called it her luxury box. Mrs. Bickers had the lungs of an opera singer. Besides using her bell and a voice that could reach Nebraska, she hit a gong every time someone was put out. "Let's go, Wildcats!" she bellowed.

The first six outs of the game went quickly.

Jim Waters arrived in his Waters & Son Plumbing van as Jake came to bat. As he took a seat in the bleachers, Jake ripped a line drive between the third baseman and the shortstop. He raced to second for a standup double and pumped his fist.

Jim echoed his fist pump. "Way to dig it out, Tweener-beaner!"

Jake grinned from second base.

His father had given him the name Tweener. Not just because he was good at hitting in the gaps. Tweener had been the nickname of Jake's mother when she played soft-ball in high school and college. Jim liked to remind Jake that he got all his jock genes from his mother, and if he ever went fishing for jock genes in the Waters family gene pool he'd come home empty-handed.

"A two-bagger," Mr. Knight called as Mrs. Knight added two points to Jake's score.

Sira was up next.

"C'mon, Cricket!" shouted Mrs. Bickers. "Take it yard!"

Besides being up on the lingo for hitting a home run, Mrs. Bickers was Sira's biggest fan. Way back when she was a kid and Patience had a real baseball league, girls weren't allowed to play. Mrs. Bickers was rooting for Sira to settle an old score.

Sira did her bit for the cause by smacking Mr. Knight's second pitch over the right field fence. The fans cheered. Mrs. Bickers shook her bell and shouted, "Thatta way, Cricket! The rooster crows, the hen delivers!"

Jim, who was sitting behind Sira's father, tapped Mr. Rashid on the shoulder. "It's the World Series, Zain. Where's Bhamini?" Bhamini was Sira's mother.

"Someone's got to keep the motel open," Mr. Rashid answered in his clipped, singsongy accent. "After all, it is the high season."

Jim laughed. "Sure it's the high season. Yesterday it broke a hundred, and it'll do the same today."

As Sira crossed the plate and Jake came to bat again after being driven in by her homer, Mrs. Knight turned to the two men. "Speaking of missing women, Jim, where's Wanda?"

"That's right," Mr. Rashid added, "I saw Wanda out on the highway, and she was burning the rubber. Why such a hurry?"

Jim smiled at Mr. Rashid's sometimes less-than-perfect mastery of American expressions. "The reason she was burning rubber," he corrected, "was because one of her grandparents got sick. She had to get to Vegas."

"Oh dear," Mrs. Knight said with forced concern. "Was it the same grandparent who took sick last winter?"

Jim answered her haughty look with a serious nod. "Same one. Turns out his allergy to flashing neon has gotten worse."

Before Mrs. Knight could throw him a comeback, a voice knifed across the field. "Hey, scorekeep!" From her porch, Mrs. Bickers punched a gnarled hand into the sunlight. "Don't forget to give Cricket five big ones!"

As Mrs. Knight turned back to her laptop, Jake hit a hard grounder to Howie at first. He fielded the ball, tagged the bag, and trotted toward home.

"All right, Kapowie!" Mrs. Knight cheered. "Show us your stuff!"

For the next hour, Sira and Howie traded the lead back and forth. After 46 outs, and three hits in a row from Sira, she had a six-point lead. Jake was still in third place but well behind Sira and Howie. The World Series of Workup was beginning to look like the match-up everyone had anticipated. A head-to-head battle between Howie Kapowie and the Cricket of Karachi.

With eight outs left in the game, Rosie hit a ground ball back to Mr. Knight. He mysteriously bobbled the ball, and

Rosie beat the throw to first. "A single for Rosie," he shouted as Rosie got her first point of the game.

That brought Howie in to bat again. Everyone shifted over, leaving right field empty and foul territory. Mr. Knight threw a fastball down the middle. Howie hit a blast into right field. It looked long enough to be an over-the-fence home run, but it hit the wooden snow fence with a loud thwack and bounced back into the field.

"Foul ball," Mr. Knight ruled.

Howie fought the urge to slam his bat in the dirt. "Gimme another just like that."

As Howie stepped into the batter's box, the distant growl of diesel engines rode in on the wind. Howie crouched in his stance. "C'mon, Dad, hurry up." The diesels grew louder.

Mr. Knight started his windup, but the blast of a truck horn stopped him.

"The horn!" Rosie shouted from first base. "Seventh-Inning Stench!"

Mrs. Bickers rang her cowbell. "Seventh-Inning Stench!"

6 the seventh-inning stench

Howie chopped his bat in the dirt and glared at his father. "Why didn't you throw it?"

As players trotted in, Mr. Knight shot him a stern look. "Rule Number Ten, Howard. 'When the horn sounds, it's time.' "

Players ran to a water cooler and grabbed a drink before the trucks got closer. Mrs. Knight punched keys as she uploaded music on her laptop. Parents stood up. Some stretched, a few checked pagers or cell phones. Then they were all engulfed by a sour, rancid, nose-twisting stink.

The first notes of "Take Me Out to the Ball Game" swelled from Mrs. Knight's laptop.

A BRIEF HISTORY
OF THE SEVENTH-INNING STENCH:

- At first, every Workup League game had a seventh-inning *stretch*.

- It usually came about eleven in the morning.
- About the same time, Mr. Knight's KSF dump trucks made their first delivery to KSF.
- KSF stood for Knight's Soil & Fertilizer farm.
- The trucks were coming from big feedlots where they fatten up thousands of cattle.
- The trucks were filled with what binge-eating cattle do best.
- Make manure.
- Manure is the key ingredient in making Knight's soil and fertilizer.
- Rotting manure stinks.
- Bad.
- Kids started changing the words when they sang "Take Me Out to the Ball Game."
- It soon became "Take Me Out to the Stink Farm."
- The seventh-inning stretch was officially changed to the Seventh-Inning Stench.

As the big trucks with their containers full of manure turned off Courage Street and rumbled past the field, they delivered the full, eye-watering force of their fly-buzzing stench. The players and fans wrinkled their noses and sang.

> *Take me out to the stink farm,*
> *Take me out to the cloud.*
> *Buy me some cow pies and buff'lo chips,*
> *I don't care if I'm up to my hips.*
> *Let me root, root, root in the Knight soil,*

It's a smell with a charm.
For it's one, two, three whiffs, you're out,
At the old stink farm.

"Over the Rainbow" it wasn't.

While the Seventh-Inning Stench was in good fun, it was also a tribute to Knight's Soil & Fertilizer. KSF was the biggest employer left in town. Actually, except for Gas & Goodies out on the highway, it was the only employer.

The last truck growled by and gave a double horn blast. The Seventh-Inning Stench was officially over. As the south wind swept the odor off the field, Mr. Knight swept off home plate.

Howie was still at bat. Mr. Knight wound up and gave him another fastball. But Howie's rhythm had been thrown off by the break. He hit a grounder to second and got thrown out. Mrs. Bickers sounded her gong.

Howie was still six points behind Sira. If he didn't rack up some points in his last at bat, she would have the lead going into Game 6. Something no girl had ever done in the World Series of Workup.

As Jake rotated in from left field to third base, he saw a cloud of dust rising on the empty horizon. It was a vehicle driving in from the north. As it came closer he saw it was a brown UPS van. The crack of ball on bat snapped him back to the game. A hot grounder shot toward his left, he stabbed at it. The ball ricocheted off his glove into the outfield.

"Hey, Tweener," Howie yelled from center field. "You forgot to wipe your eyes after the Stench."

Mrs. Bickers gave a rude quack on a duck call—her sound effect for an error. Mrs. Knight charged Jake with an error and he lost a point.

He shrugged it off and glanced toward the bleachers.

His father waggled a long finger toward the sky. It was his to-the-stars-through-difficulty gesture. Then he slid off the bleachers and strode toward his van.

Jake wondered where he was going. Maybe he'd gotten an emergency call on his cell phone. As another batter came up, he decided to concentrate on the game before he lost another point.

7   dust devil

Mrs. Knight read from her laptop. "At the end of Game 5, the new leader is Sira Rashid, with 68 points."

During the applause and Mrs. Bickers's clanging bell, Sira turned to Jake. "1868," she whispered, "Bill Cody and Bill Comstock had a buffalo hunting contest to decide who deserved the name Buffalo Bill. In eight hours, Cody shot sixty-nine buffalo to Comstock's forty-six, and Cody became Buffalo Bill Cody."

"Whoop," Jake said flatly. He wasn't in the mood to hear any of her freaky and not-so-fascinating facts. After his error, and a terrible day at the plate, he had slipped to fourth place.

She gave him a friendly elbow. "Hey, I'm just trying to get your mind off the game." As Mrs. Knight read the other scores, Sira recited more freaky and fascinating facts.

Jake wanted to plug his ears but his hands were too busy

clapping for the other players. It was one of Mr. Knight's rules. Applaud your fellow players. He said it built self-esteem. Jake went along with it but didn't believe it. How could a man who collected cow manure for a living know anything about self-esteem?

Mrs. Knight gave out the last score. "Even though she had only one hit today, Rosie's still way ahead of her score from last year, with a whopping seven points."

As everyone clapped, Jake braced for Sira's next dopey fact. It didn't come. "What's the matter?" he muttered. "Nothing happen in oh-seven?"

She frowned. "Kansas had a drought of freaky and fascinating facts. But trust me, I'll find one."

"All right, Workup Wildcats," Mr. Knight announced. "Tomorrow, warm-ups at eight-thirty sharp. Game time, nine on the button." He glanced toward Jake and Sira. "Don't be late or I might take a closer look at the rule book."

As the crowd dispersed, Sira punched Jake in the arm. "Oh-nine, 1909, Kansas hosted the first International Horseshoe Pitching Contest."

"Why me?" he groaned as Howie closed in on them.

Howie threw a friendly arm over Jake's shoulder. "Did you see that, buddy?"

"See what?"

"How I let Cricket get ahead because she's a girl."

Jake chuckled. "Right, and I suppose you're such a nice guy you're gonna let her win the Series too."

"Nah." Howie grinned as he went toe to toe with Sira. "Tomorrow," he growled like a wrestler from the WWE, "it's the Cricket of Karachi vs. Howie Kapowie. We're goin' head to head, and the Cricket's goin' down!"

"That's right," she teased as she danced around him. "Down to first, down to second, down to third, and all the way home."

Jake jumped in. "Are you guys gonna trash talk all day, or are we gonna go to the quarry?"

"Can't," Howie said. "Gotta put in some hours at the stink farm."

As Howie went to help his father bag the equipment, Jake followed Sira over to Mr. Rashid.

"Congratulations." Her father beamed. "In all the years your brothers tried to learn this game, they never did. When you were born, I never imagined in my widest dreams that you would be winning the World Series."

Jake stifled a laugh. Mr. Rashid's English-twisters were a lot more entertaining than Sira's funky facts.

Sira shook her head and sighed. "Dad, it's not 'in my *widest* dreams.' It's 'in my *wildest* dreams.' "

"I think 'widest dreams' is better," Jake insisted.

Mr. Rashid's brow knitted. "No, no, I must be correct. Sira is my *wildest* dream come true." He broke into a huge smile. "If she wins the World Series, we will throw all the customers out of the motel and have a big celebration!"

"Ah, Dad," Sira interjected, "we never have any customers to throw out."

"So much the easier to throw a big party!" He turned to Jake. "Your father told me to tell you that he had to go."

"Did he get a call?" Jake asked.

"No. He just said he had to go home."

A few minutes later, Jake stood over his bike and stared through the rusty backstop at the empty field. Howie had left. Sira had thrown her bike in the back of her father's station wagon. She had chores to do at the motel. Even Mrs. Bickers had retreated to her living room and cranked up her air conditioner. It wheezed and labored against the growing heat of the day.

It was almost noon. Jake had the whole blistering day ahead of him. Could be worse, he thought. He still had two weeks before he'd be sweating bullets over schoolbooks. Remembering the stretch of freedom that still lay ahead soothed his disappointment over the game. His gaze lifted beyond the outfield to the flat horizon that surrounded Patience. The sky soared endlessly above it.

When he was little, he thought the horizon was flat because it was being crushed by the weight of the sky. And there was never just *one* sky. How could there be? Everywhere you looked the sky was too big and too different to be just one thing. That was why there were clouds, he once believed. To cover the stitches where the different skies were sewn together.

Then he'd seen pictures of mountains. At first he thought the skies didn't weigh as much where there were mountains. That was what let the ground rise up to be mountains. But after Howie teased him for being so dumb, Jake figured out that skies were the same everywhere. It wasn't the sky's fault that he lived in the flattest place in the world. It was just his bad luck.

Now that he was twelve, nothing seemed as big any-more. The sky was just one thing, and it had shrunk. Now it looked more like a huge domed room, and the horizon was the baseboard wrapping around it. He smiled as he re-alized who kept finding a mouse hole in the baseboard. Wanda. It was the same mouse hole he was going to find someday.

He reached down and pulled his bike out of the dirt. As he stood up, he was startled by something in the field.

A column of dust swirled in front of third base. A dust devil. It thickened into a spinning cocoon and started to move. Jake watched it weave and stutter across the infield toward second base. Like it was running the bases back-ward. Halfway to first, it turned into the outfield and blew itself out, vanishing without a trace.

He grinned at the wonder of it. Not only was it cool to watch, it pretty much summed up his morning. Howie, Sira, the game, and third place had all come and gone like a dust devil. Even Wanda had appeared, spun through his life for a few years, then poof, done her disappearing act once again. Even his father . . .

Something inside him tightened. His father only left the game if he got a call. He never left just to go home. Something wasn't right.

8 blast from the past

The Waters & Son Plumbing van was parked in the driveway. Jake dropped his bike in the yard and took the porch steps two at a time. The screen door banged behind him.

"Dad?"

No answer. The house was eerily quiet. Too quiet.

"Dad?"

No answer.

He moved from the hall into the dining room. It hadn't been a dining room for a long time. It was the office and parts department for Waters & Son Plumbing. Jake leaned over the electric fan propped on a chair in a doorway. The oscillating fan swept its hot breath back and forth into the empty kitchen. The breakfast dishes were still on the table.

He checked the living room. The only thing that caught his eye was the rectangle of clean wood where Wanda had kept her boom box on the dusty bureau.

As he raced up the stairs, Jake knocked into one of the countless pictures on the wall. He cringed as he braced for the crash. But the glass-covered picture only swung on its wire. He breathed a sigh of relief. It was one of his father's favorites. A black-and-white print of the Roman god of toilets. His name was Crepitus.

At the top of the stairs, Jake went left down the hall. His father's bedroom was empty. He pushed open a door covered with restroom signs ranging from BONNIE and CLYDE to HERA and ZEUS. Nobody there.

He headed back down the hall toward the sun porch at the other end of the upper floor. His father liked to do acrostic puzzles there, and take naps.

Halfway down the hall, Jake stopped between two facing doors. Both doors were shut. The left door was decorated with a poster advertising THOMAS CRAPPER'S WATERFALL TOILET, guaranteeing THE ROYAL FLUSH — AS USED AT WINDSOR PALACE. The right door announced ATM, spelled out with antique flush handles. Underneath ATM, a toilet seat rigged like a doorknocker announced COMMODE CENTRAL in red paint. Usually, this door was open. His father only closed it when he was squeezed into the cramped desk behind the door.

Jake felt a surge of panic. He had no idea why his father had rushed home. Or why he wasn't answering.

He reached for the handle and slowly pushed the door open. "Dad?"

Lying in the aisle, between storage shelves crammed with the history of sanitary plumbing, was a four-foot-long box. It had been opened.

Jake stepped in and peeked around the door.

His father was behind his desk in the corner, leaning back in a chair. His long arms hung limply at his sides. His head tilted back, resting against the wall.

"Dad?"

Jim's eyes fluttered open. They stared blankly up into the forest of antique ventilation fans growing down from the ceiling.

Jake breathed a sigh of relief. "Were you asleep?"

Jim spoke in a low whisper. "I found it."

"Found what?"

His head tilted off the wall and turned toward Jake. His eyes looked like they were seeing something far away. "No one can know, Jake. You have to promise me. No one can know."

"Know what?" Jake demanded. "What are you talking about?"

"Don't you see it?"

"What?"

Jim lowered his eyes to the desk.

Jake followed his gaze. In the shadow of the desk's high back was a long object. Things suddenly tumbled into place. The long box on the floor. The UPS van he saw at the game. His father's abrupt return home.

But what was it? Jake's eyes traced a long handle made of dark twisted wood that ended in a cone of misshapen black material. "What is it?"

"What does it look like?"

Jake took a guess. "A plunger, maybe. A really old plunger."

Jim leaned forward. His eyes gleamed as he admired the

ancient thing. "That's right. But it's not just any plunger. It's the one."

"The one?"

"Yeah," Jim whispered. "The Scepter of Satan."

Jake gave him a blank stare.

Jim whispered its other name. "The Plunger of Destiny."

Jake's eyes darted to his father's face. He watched for the tiniest crack in his expression. He waited for the twitch that would tell him this was a joke. But his father's face glowed like warm stone.

Jake broke the silence with laughter. "Very funny, Dad! Great joke!"

Jim turned his head like a bird toward a sudden noise.

Jake stifled his laughter as he made another connection. "Wait a minute. Is *this* what you bought on eBay?"

"Yes."

"Is *this* why Wanda left?"

"It had something to do with it."

Jake realized Wanda was right. His father was ready for the nuthouse. "But Dad, the Plunger of Destiny, or whatever you wanna call it, it's not real."

"Who said it's not real?"

"C'mon," Jake insisted, "it's one of those things someone made up to make the story of the curse scarier."

Jim chuckled. "If someone wanted to make the history of our family scarier, I think they would've done better than a toilet plunger."

His father's flippancy made Jake dig in his heels. "Okay, even if there was a plunger, how could this be it? I mean, it's been over a hundred years. It's probably a fake."

39

Jim glanced at the plunger. "I was thinking the same thing when I bought it. The eBay description only said it had a wooden handle made from Osage orange, and a cone made from some kind of leather." He slid his fingers under the handle and lifted it reverently into the light. "But it's what they *didn't* say that makes it authentic."

Jake shook his head. "I don't get it."

Jim moved the plunger closer and slowly turned the twisted wooden handle. In the middle of the handle a small crescent of dark indentations rolled into view. "There was nothing in the description about the handle having teeth marks."

A cold fear swam up Jake's spine.

"Now, you tell me," Jim continued, "how many antique plungers are bouncing around the world with human bite marks in them?" He rotated the handle to reveal a matching crescent of dents. "Think of it. One hundred and twenty-eight years ago, an outlaw named Blackbeard was stuck on this like a dog on a stick."

Jake stared at the teeth marks. His fear snaked around his chest. "But I thought it was all a joke. If this is real, what about the curse?"

"Oh, c'mon, son. The curse, the Tooth Fairy, Santa Claus, they're all from the same factory." Jim's gleaming eyes returned to he plunger. "This isn't make-believe. This is history."

"But what if the curse is real?" Jake's fear coiled into anger. "You know what it says."

"I know exactly what it says. 'The day the Scepter of Satan returns to Patience, the final destruction will begin.'

And that's why we have to keep this a secret for now. Too many superstitious folks around here. You have to promise—"

"But what if it's true?" Jake's voice exploded in the cramped room.

His father looked at him with a mixture of concern and disbelief. "Jake, *things* are real, curses are only words."

"What if you're wrong?" Jake shouted.

He didn't wait for an answer. He bolted out the door.

9 in the beginning

Jake raced down the street on his bike.

In the time it takes a dust devil to appear and blow itself out, the whole world had changed. If the Plunger of Destiny was real, then everything about the curse could be real. If the curse was all fact, then the "final destruction" was no storyteller spicing the stew. It was coming. And Jake's vow was useless. He would never get out of Patience. He would die here just like every J. Waters before him. And it could happen at any second.

He shot past the coffin house, swung left onto Courage, and sped toward the highway.

Like most curses, this one had a full name before it became simply the curse. Its complete name was the Curse of Andars Cass.

Like most curses, it didn't beat around the bush. It got to the point. Actually, two points.

1) The town of Patience would suffer a long, slow, and miserable death.
2) The day the Scepter of Satan returned, the final destruction of Patience would begin.

Like most curses—the really serious ones—it didn't just fly off the tip of a witch's wand. It had a story behind it.

And, as with most *stories* about curses, we must now travel back in time to the birth of the curse.

In the winter of 1865–66, Jeremiah Waters was sixteen years old. Like many young men at the time, Jeremiah had heeded the advice to "go west, young man," and seek his fortune. But until he found his fortune, he had to work. So Jeremiah took a job as a mule driver for a surveying party measuring and mapping western Kansas.

Western Kansas was being measured and mapped for two reasons. In the 1860s, railroad companies were racing to lay iron roadways across the state and on to places like Denver and Santa Fe. Also, there were many pioneers trying to elbow the Indians and the buffalo out of western Kansas so they could stake their claim in the great "untamed frontier."

When Jeremiah finished driving a mule wagon for the surveying party, he found himself back in Junction City, Kansas. But now he had two important things. His wages and a vision of the future. In his vision, he saw a beautiful house rising from the prairie. It was only a sod house, but it was a start.

So he bought two barrels of whiskey, strapped them on

a mule, and headed back west along a stagecoach trail called the Butterfield Overland Dispatch. He soon reached the railroad workers who were leading the way west. They were building the railroad grade for the "steel Nile" that would soon follow. He sold whiskey to the workers for fifteen cents a shot. By the spring of 1866, Jeremiah had turned his whiskey business into a keg of silver.

But a keg of silver wasn't a fortune.

So he took his keg of silver and went farther west.

Several days later, he stopped in a place called the Smoky Hill Valley. It wasn't smoky, it wasn't particularly hilly, and nobody would call it a valley unless you wanted it to sound like a terrific place to move. Which is exactly what people in the East wanted young men without jobs to do in those days. "Go west, young man . . . please, go west."

In this "valley" that should have been named the Middle of Nowhere, Jeremiah Waters staked his claim. One hundred sixty acres. His very own quarter section of nowhere.

Actually, it wasn't his yet.

According to the Homestead Act of 1862, Jeremiah had to build a house on his claim. The house had to be eighteen feet by twenty feet, and he had to live there for five continuous years. If he did, then his 160 acres of nowhere would be more than a claim. It would be his "to have and to hold" forever and ever. Or until he decided to sell it to someone else.

Now, before anyone thinks that sitting in a shack in the middle of nowhere for five long years is a lame way of seeking a fortune, there's one thing you should know. Jeremiah knew a secret about his little piece of nowhere. When he was working on the survey party, he didn't just drive mules. He listened and learned. And he knew that the Union Pacific Railroad was planning to lay its track right across his piece of nowhere. When it did, his claim would be worth a fortune.

So, during the summer of '66, he built a sod house, eighteen by twenty feet, and planted some crops. He also spent a little of his silver on a nice chair. He set the chair in front of his sod house, sat down, and waited for his fortune to come to him.

The first thing that came was trouble.

Indian trouble.

Since the Indians weren't happy about being elbowed off their hunting grounds, they started pestering the workers building the railway and the soldiers at nearby Fort Wallace. Actually, they pestered a few of them to death. Actually, they pestered so many of them to death that work on the railroad slowed to a crawl. But Jeremiah had his chair. He was willing to sit and wait. And the Indians never bothered him, for one simple reason.

At the end of the long hot summer of '66, an Indian warrior stumbled into Jeremiah's piece of nowhere. His name was Roman Nose, and he had a very bloody nose. In fact, he'd been shot through the nose in a skirmish with the U.S. Army. But Jeremiah didn't know this. He helped patch up Roman Nose's nose and gave him shelter for a few days until he was fit to travel. Roman Nose was so thankful for Jeremiah's hospitality, he sent a message to all the Indian tribes in the area. The white boy living in the sod house in the middle of nowhere was okay. Roman Nose even gave him a name. White Boy Who Sits in Chair and Saves Noses. So, while everyone else was having Indian trouble, Jeremiah waited. He waited for the men in suits and five-dollar hats to come and buy out his land claim for barrels of silver.

He sat.

And he waited.

For two long years.

Finally, in the fall of 1868, the railroad reached within twenty-five miles of Jeremiah's sod house.

But then the real trouble began.

Money trouble.

The Union Pacific Railroad Company ran out of it. They stopped laying their steel Nile. They were so broke, no one knew if the railroad would ever make it farther west than the little town where it had stopped. Sheridan, Kansas.

Jeremiah wasn't sure what to do. So he did what comes naturally to all Waters men. When in doubt, don't move. Wait for something to react to.

He had a good sit-down.

He sat all night.

He watched the sunrise climb over the horizon.

He sat all day.

He watched the clouds building castles in the air.

Then, as the sun set behind him, his mouth popped open and these words jumped out. "Sometimes things havta git worse 'fore they git better."

Before Jeremiah could figure out what mysterious force made him utter these words, he had a vision. In his vision, he saw a beautiful town rising from the prairie.

So Jeremiah took what was left of his keg of silver, and he had his 160 acres surveyed and measured into a town. He made himself president of the town company. And he named the town after the one thing he had plenty of.

Patience.

He laid out the town grid. He named all the streets that ran north and south after the traits that had brought him to this point in life. Adventure, Courage, Labor, Thrift, Temperance, Hospitality, and Vision. He named all the streets that ran east and west after the things he would need to achieve his new vision. Faith, Resolve, Ambition, Ingenuity, Pragmatism, Endurance, and Optimism.

He put up a sign on the edge of town. PATIENCE— POPULATION 1. Then he sat in his chair at the corner of Courage Street and Resolve Street. And waited.

––––––––––

As Jake reached Highway 40, he was glad no one was outside the Tumbleweed Motel. He didn't want anyone to see him, especially Sira.

There was no traffic on the two-lane highway. He leaned right, swooped onto the blacktop, and rode west.

––––––––––

It took an entire year of waiting, but Jeremiah's prophecy—Sometimes things havta git worse 'fore they git better—finally got to the last word.

Things got better.

A lot better.

In the fall of 1869, the Union Pacific Railroad got new money and a new name. The Kansas Pacific Railroad. They started laying three miles of track a day. And they vowed not to stop until they got to Denver.

Overnight, speculators and settlers surged in front of the work crews like spilled milk across a waxed table. People poured into Patience. They bought lots from Jeremiah. Shops and houses shot up overnight. His vision rose from the prairie. Patience was a boomtown. And Jeremiah had turned his section of nowhere into a wagonload of silver.

But a wagonload of silver wasn't a fortune.

So he took his silver and bought all the claims south of town. He built a handsome wooden farmhouse. He bought a huge herd of cattle. And he worked.

For seven long years.

By 1876, Patience became known as the rose of the prairie. And Jeremiah had turned his ranch into a cattle car of silver. But a cattle car of silver wasn't a fortune.

To some people.

It was to Jeremiah. He had finally found the fortune he had come west to seek.

To celebrate, he had a good sit-down on his fine porch. He didn't have to wait long before he had another vision. He saw a wife, and children, rising up from the prairie.

So he took the train to Topeka and went courting. In two weeks, he met the woman he wanted to marry. Miss Regina Overshine. Regina agreed to become his wife, move to his cattle ranch, and raise a family.

On one condition.

Regina had recently visited the Great Philadelphia Exhibition and seen a modern convenience that was taking the big Eastern cities by storm. It was called a Dolphin Deluge Washdown Water Closet, made by Edward Johns & Company. It was a flush toilet. She had to have one. Not for her. She had to have one for her old, blind, fiddle-playing grandfather. Especially if the two of them were going to move to Jeremiah's ranch. The reason was simple. She wasn't about to walk her blind grandfather fifty yards to the outhouse every time he needed to go. Especially in a blizzard.

In 1876, nobody in Kansas had ever heard of a Dolphin Deluge Washdown Water Closet. Nobody had heard of a flush toilet. Including Jeremiah Waters. When Regina explained to him what it was, and why she needed it, Jeremiah did what a man does when his heart is set on the woman he wants to marry. He said, "Your wish is my command."

Using some of the qualities that helped him make his fortune—resolve, ingenuity, and pragmatism—Jeremiah made good on his fiancée's request. He ordered a Dolphin Deluge Washdown Water Closet, by Edward Johns & Company, all the way from London, England. He dug another well near the house. He built a windmill to pump water into a new storage tank in the attic. He installed the Dolphin Deluge with the help of the installation manual. He built a closet around the whole thing for privacy. And, last but not least, he ran a wooden waste pipe to the pit under the outhouse in the backyard.

He tested it twice. Once with the polished mahogany seat up, as the manual recommended. And once with it down. It worked perfectly.

He hopped on the next train to Topeka, married Regina, and brought her and her old, blind, fiddle-playing grandfather back to his ranch south of Patience.

10 andars cass

As Jake pedaled and ignored the burning ache in his thighs, a truck loomed out of the jiggling heat that blanketed the highway. He recognized it. A KSF truck, carrying a full load of manure.

As the truck bore down, he braced for the putrid blast that was strong enough to knock him off his bike. The smell, not the wind. He hoped it was the only thing that hit him. Cow pie shrapnel traveling at sixty miles per hour could do major damage. His day had begun with a toilet-plunger cap-slapper. He didn't need a cow-plop beanie-bopper on top of it.

The truck thundered by. Jake grimaced. The rotten blast almost ripped off his baseball hat. But that was it. He had dodged the cow-chip bullet. Maybe he was going to make it. Maybe he was going to make it to the only place that was safe.

He swerved across the center line, turned onto a gravel road, and headed south.

In the distance, a group of low hills billowed like a buckskin parachute settling on the prairie.

Back in 1876, shortly after Regina and her blind, fiddle-playing grandfather moved to Jeremiah's ranch, the real trouble began.

Toilet trouble.

But not the usual kind of toilet trouble.

It started when Regina had a party at the ranch house to introduce herself to the good people of Patience. When she showed one of the ladies the sparkling new Dolphin Deluge Washdown Water Closet, pretty soon all the ladies wanted to see it. They marveled at its beauty.

The Dolphin Deluge was made of thick porcelain with a white and blue design. The bowl looked like a large fluted seashell blossoming out of a dolphin's gaping mouth. The dolphin's body snaked into an S-curve at the base of the toilet and seemed to disappear into the floor.

At first, the ladies were frightened by the terrible roar when the chain was pulled and water thundered down from the reservoir near the ceiling. But then they marveled as the water gushed through the bowl and out the hole at the bottom.

When the men saw it they were frightened too, for a different reason. Now all their wives would want a washdown water closet. What was the point when the outhouse worked perfectly fine?

One of them grumbled, "If it ain't broke, don't a-fix it."

"What about sewer gas?" another man asked.

Sewer gas was a big deal back then. Back in the 1870s people believed that sewer gas, the kind of gas that lingers around an outhouse, was the source of most diseases. That's why the outhouse was a long walk from the house. And it's why people were in no hurry to turn the outhouse into an inhouse.

But Jeremiah had thought about this problem. "We clean the water closet with carbolic acid every day," he explained to his guests. "It's clean as a whistle."

Carbolic acid was one of the disinfectants used to prevent outbreaks of cholera, typhoid, and other deadly diseases that plagued pioneers. But you had to be careful with carbolic acid. The colorless crystals could burn your skin, and blind you if it got in your eyes.

Even though the party guests were too shy to actually use it, the Dolphin Deluge was the splash of the party.

Then came the trouble.

Andars Cass was a short young man who was long on religion. He saw everything in the world as one of two things. The work of God or the work of the devil. There was nothing in between. In his mind, the outhouse was outside for a more fundamental reason than sewer gas. The outhouse was the place where we cast out all the bad things inside us. Both the visible and the invisible. And those bad things included evil thoughts, lies, and sins. Andars called his outhouse the devil's bin.

When Andars saw the Dolphin Deluge Washdown Water Closet, he saw dark forces at work. "When evil is inside you, cast it *out!*" he bellowed. "Out of heart, out of body, out of home!"

"But Andars, the waste doesn't stay inside the house," Jeremiah insisted as he gestured toward the toilet. "It goes down the bowl and a waste pipe carries it to the pit under the outhouse."

Andars stepped closer. "Maybe so, Jeremiah Waters, but tell me this." He pointed dramatically inside the toilet. "When the evil thoughts, lies, and sins are a-bein' so big they can't fit down that tiny pipe, what will a-be then?"

This made Jeremiah stop and think. He hadn't considered blockage.

"I'll tell you what will a-be!" shouted Andars. "That there Dolphin Deluge Washdown Water Closet will a-be the devil's room!" He spit in the toilet, turned on his heels, and marched out.

Several women covered their mouths with horror, and one fainted. Some of the men nodded in agreement. Although they didn't think the devil would be taking up residence in Jeremiah's house, they did think Andars raised a practical concern. They were also relieved to see that their wives wouldn't be demanding indoor plumbing anytime soon. Let Jeremiah be the guinea pig on this one.

The party continued. Everyone had a good time dancing to the fine music provided by Regina's fiddle-playing grandfather. Jeremiah and Regina dismissed Mr. Cass as one of those people who think progress is the eighth deadly sin.

But a few months later, in March of 1877, Andars's dire prediction came true. The toilet clogged up. The good news was that Jeremiah hadn't torn down the outhouse.

The bad news was that Regina was not happy about having to walk her blind grandfather to the outhouse in the cold and the mud. Especially since she was about to have a baby. The worst news was that the Dolphin Deluge installation manual didn't contain a word about unclogging a clogged toilet.

At first, Jeremiah tackled the problem in the traditional Waters way. When in doubt, don't move. Maybe it'll fix itself.

But one morning, after an outing to the outhouse in a late-winter snowstorm, Regina stomped into the kitchen, pointed into the hall toward the water closet, and said, "I don't care if you have to go to England and get another. Fix it."

While Regina took her frustrations out on a tub of laundry, Jeremiah had a sit-down and vowed not to get up until he figured out how to fix the Dolphin Deluge. He thought about force-flushing the toilet with the entire water tank in the attic. But if that didn't work he'd have a major flood on his hands. He thought about snaking something down the hole at the bottom of the bowl. But he didn't have anything that was both flexible enough to navigate the S-shaped passage and stiff enough to unclog the toilet. As he began to think that the only solution was unbolting the toilet from the floor and going in from the other end, a loud slurping sound invaded his sit-down.

He looked across the kitchen. Regina was vigorously working over a tub of laundry with a clothes stomper.

A clothes stomper was a tool with a wooden handle and a funnel-like metal cone on the end. The metal cone was used to stomp, or agitate, clothes in a washtub to get them clean. Today, washing machines come with agitators. Back then, you had to marry one.

Jeremiah cocked his head and watched Regina with keen interest. As she jammed the stomper into the washtub, it made a predictable splashing sound, but as she pulled it out, there was a sucking sound. Then Jeremiah saw it. As the metal end of the stomper pulled up and out of the tub, a piece of wet clothing stuck to the underside of the cone, and then, with a sucking smack, fell away.

"Suction!" he bellowed, leaping from his chair.

Regina screamed and held her pregnant belly.

"Your wish is my command," he yelled, and bolted out the door.

He jumped on his horse and galloped through the snowstorm to town. He flew up Courage Street, stopped at the biggest dry goods store in town, Knight's Necessaries to Niceties. He rushed inside and almost knocked Andars Cass off a ladder. Andars was hanging a large banner that read, IN GOD WE TRUST—EVERYONE ELSE PAYS. Waldo Knight, the store's owner, was behind the counter.

"What's the hurry, Jeremiah?" Waldo asked.

"Are you a-runnin' from the devil?" Andars added.

"Andars," Waldo cautioned. "What did I tell you about preaching to the customers?"

Andars frowned. " 'Save it for Sunday.' "

"Precisely."

Andars came down from the ladder and forced a smile. "What can I help you find, Jeremiah?"

"Nothing in particular." Jeremiah stepped around him. "Just taking a look-see."

Andars followed him. "You came all the way to town in a snowstorm for a look-see?"

"Andars," Waldo called. "Leave the man alone and hang the new banner."

Andars did what he was told as Jeremiah moved down the aisles, looking at the huge variety of goods. He knew what he wanted, he just wasn't sure what it would be made of. He stopped at a mound of buffalo hides. He felt a hide's thick but pliant leather. Perfect. He stepped over to a barrel of buffalo hide scraps, selected a piece, and went to the front counter. He was glad to see that Andars had disappeared.

Waldo gave him a puzzled look. "A scrap of hide?"

"It's for Regina," Jeremiah said. "When a woman who's tying her apron strings high asks for something, I've learned not to question."

"I hope she's not going to cook it."

Jeremiah looked around and lowered his voice. "Between you and me, you know that water closet of mine?"

"Who doesn't?"

"Well, it got stuck up. But I know how to unstick it."

Waldo glanced down at the hide scrap. "Looks to me like you're gonna plug it up for good."

"Nope," Jeremiah answered. "I'm going to make a hand pump like no one's ever seen. And I'm going to unplug that thing before—"

Andars Cass stood up from behind the counter where he'd been stocking cases. His eyes blazed. He thrust a condemning finger at Jeremiah. "I told you it were the work of the devil."

"Andars," Waldo warned.

But he refused to be silenced. "As a God-fearing man I cannot hold my peace. If Jeremiah Waters sucks evil back into his home, the forces of darkness will spread far and wide!"

"Enough!" Waldo grabbed Andars and dragged him toward the door. "I've been wanting to do this. . . ." He opened the door and pitched Andars into the swirling snow. "You are no longer an employee of Knight's Necessaries to Niceties."

Andars stood on the boardwalk but didn't feel the cold. He was heated by his convictions. "I say unto thee, when one house gives shelter to Satan, *all* houses give shelter to the prince of darkness!"

Waldo slammed the door and started back to the counter. A gust of wind blew the door back open, and the storm of Andars Cass raged on. "Prepare, little town of Patience, for the devil's due!"

Waldo slammed the door again and growled as he moved back to the counter. "It's people like that that give religion a bad name."

11   the curse uncoils

Jake stood up and guided his bike down the trail through an old stone quarry. The trail zigzagged around large blocks of yellowish limestone. Some of the blocks were capped with tufts of prairie grass. Some were scarred with the tubular cuts of a rock drill. The place looked like a giant had knocked down his building-block castle.

Jake jumped off his bike and let it crash under a towering cottonwood tree anchored in a depression. The lone tree gave the place its name.

Cottonwood Quarry.

He scrambled up a steep path. The path led to the top of an outcrop of quarried limestone. He was already picturing his dive. A strong push away from the edge. A perfect swan dive into the cold black water.

It was part of his ritual. The thing he had to do when nothing made sense anymore.

After riding back to the ranch, Jeremiah used his straight-edge razor to shave the buffalo hair off the scrap of hide. Then he cut it and shaped it into a cone. He softened the edges with antelope tallow and stitched the seam on the cone so it was airtight. He cut and fashioned a sturdy branch from an Osage orange tree into a three-foot handle. He stuck the handle into the small end of the hide cone, then secured it to the handle by nailing it and binding it tight with a leather cord. He coated the lip of the funnel with more tallow to create a good seal. Then he stepped into the water closet and went to work.

He pressed his invention into the water-filled toilet bowl, making sure the cone had a good seal against the porcelain. He pushed the handle down. The leather funnel collapsed, and he pulled back. He heard a sucking sound, louder than the one he'd heard that morning from the clothes stomper. It was music to his ears. It was suction. He pushed again, and again, harder and harder, then yanked the plunger out.

For a second, the clogged water bubbled and sloshed like some sea monster had wakened from the depths. Then the water swirled down the hole. The passage was clear.

"Ha!" he shouted.

Regina poked her head into the hallway. "What happened?"

"A miracle!" He beamed at the eighth wonder of the world—seeing what is clogged become unclogged!

At the same moment that a miracle was occurring in the Waters household, a buckboard drawn by two black horses blanketed with snow made its way down Courage Street.

The driver stopped the wagon in front of the Kirkland & Flash Bank. The snow-covered man was Frederick Olabuff, the blacksmith in Patience. He had spent the day returning from Sheridan, twenty-five miles away.

While Patience was known as the rose of the prairie, Sheridan's reputation was equally colorful. In a different way. The Black Eye of Kansas, Sodom and Gomorrah, and the Cesspool of Sin were a few of the names it had picked up during the year it had been the end-of-track town on the railroad.

Frederick Olabuff walked into the bank, went straight to one of its owners, and gave Sam Kirkland the bad news. He told Sam that while he'd been playing cards in a Sheridan saloon he'd overheard a bunch of ruffians hatching a plan. The plan was to rob the Kirkland & Flash Bank. Sam immediately took the news to Waldo Knight, who was also the mayor of Patience.

That night, the citizens of Patience met in the new town hall made of limestone. After much debate, they agreed on what they should do about the pending bank robbery.

It was a four-part plan.

1) Next morning, the women and children would go to the nearby town of Wallace until the trouble was over.
2) The menfolk would *not* take up arms against the bank robbers, as was the custom in those days, because it always ended with a few dead citizens. Instead, Patience

was going to foil the gang in a unique way. All the valuables in the bank, and any other valuables people wanted to protect, would be put in a big trunk and buried outside of town.

3)   To prevent the robbers from coercing any citizens into revealing where the trunk was buried, it was decided that only one man would bury the trunk, in secret. Choosing that man was easy.

4)   Despite objections from Andars Cass, the town chose Jeremiah Waters. He was considered the most honest man in the county. He lived outside town so there was little chance the robbers would question him. He was also the least likely to skip town with the trunk because his ranch was probably worth a lot more than the valuables that would end up in it.

Before dawn the next day, the plan was put into action. The trunk was filled with small boxes and bags of valuables from the bank and the townspeople. Every box or bag was painted, carved, or stitched with the family's name.

Since Jeremiah's fortune had been completely converted to four-legged moneybags with horns, the Waters family had very little to put in the trunk. But Regina gathered the few things she considered valuable and put them in the only box she could find—her grandfather's fiddle case.

The women and children went off to Wallace.

The men closed up the trunk, sealed it with a belt of wax to ensure it would not be opened without their knowing it, and loaded it onto Jeremiah's wagon. As he drove out of town, the rest of the men gathered in the town hall and made sure no one left to spy on him. No one did. At noon, the men went back about their business and waited for the gang of robbers to ride into town.

No plan is ever perfect. Some things that you're certain will happen, don't. Some things that you never imagine will happen, do.

In the case of the Patience robbery, the first surprise was that the gang didn't ride into town on horses. They walked. Since they'd lost their horses in a poker game the night before, they had to find another means of transportation from Sheridan to Patience. So they stole a railroad sail-car.

A sail-car was a type of hand-pumped railroad car used by repair crews as they rode the rails. It had a nice tall sail on it to catch the wind and speed them on their way.

During their voyage to Patience, the outlaws nicknamed their leader Blackbeard, after the famous pirate. When they arrived, they jumped off the sail-car, cut the one telegraph line into town, and walked up Courage Street. Blackbeard and his three scruffy land-pirates entered the bank, drew their guns, and Sam Kirkland opened the vault.

Naturally, it was empty.

If you take away a bank robber's horse, it makes him mad. If you take away a bank robber's horse and make him ride a sail-car to the scene of the crime, it makes him madder. But if you take away a bank robber's horse, make him ride a sail-car to the scene of the crime, and then show him an empty vault, it makes him maddest of all.

The furious, enraged, teeth-gnashing bank robbers took

their frustrations out on Sam Kirkland. They pistol-whipped him into the street. The men in the street pleaded with the outlaws to show mercy. It wasn't Sam's fault the bank was empty.

That was when Blackbeard noticed that there was something strange about this town. Ever since they'd arrived, he had not seen a woman or child. Something smelled funny, and it wasn't the shirt he'd been wearing for a month.

Blackbeard pointed his six-shooter at Sam. "Tell me where ya hid all the loot, or Kirkland & Flash is gonna be nuthin but Flash."

The menfolk of Patience suddenly realized why most towns that get wind of a bank robbery usually take up arms against the thieves. Bank robbers tend to be bad people.

Blackbeard pulled back the hammer on his six-shooter.

A voice suddenly cut through the silence. "Ye who plumb the ways of evil should speak to the devil's plumber."

Everyone turned as Andars Cass stepped off the boardwalk into the street.

Blackbeard squinted at him. "Don't gimme no Sunday school," he growled. "Gimme whatcha know, or Sammy here's goin' to the worm bank."

"We don't know where it is," Andars said.

Several men lunged for Andars to shut him up. Blackbeard fired his gun in the air. The explosion sent the men diving for the ground. Andars never flinched.

Blackbeard walked over to him. "If yer not knowin' where it is, who is?"

Andars was as calm as a man giving someone the time of day. "Jeremiah Waters. His place is three miles south of town. Big ranch house. Two cottonwoods out front. Can't miss it."

"What's yer name?" Blackbeard demanded.

"Andars Cass."

"You made yerself a wise choice, Mr. Cass."

Andars's eyes were clear and hard. "I choose nothing but the will of the Lord."

Blackbeard and his gang rounded up all the men in town and stuffed as many as they could in the town jail. They tossed the keys down a well as they herded the others into a church and nailed the doors and windows shut. Then they stole four horses and galloped down Courage Street.

As they rode over the railroad tracks, Blackbeard put three bullets into the sail-car.

12   the pistol-grip pistol-whip

Jake's baseball shoes, socks, uniform, and cap lay in a heap on a long tabletop of stone. Stripped down to his underwear, Jake stood at the far edge of the flat rock.

He stared down at a puffy white cloud drifting across a brilliant sheet of blue. The water-filled chasm in the middle of Cottonwood Quarry offered a perfect reflection of the sky. Its high stone walls protected it from wind. Until a rock or a body broke the glassy surface, the pool was a rock-framed portrait of the sky's twin.

It was here, while looking down into the sky's mirror, that Jake had imagined what it must have been like to be one of those Greek gods he'd learned about in school. The ones that looked down through the clouds from the top of Mount Olympus and watched mortals do the stupid things mortals do.

It was here that he had made his vow to get out of Patience someday and sealed the deal with a headlong plunge into the quarry.

It was here that plummeting into his own reflection was the ritual of diving into himself and out of himself in the same second. In the history of head bonks it was known as the break-the-mirror brain-slapper.

As he stared at the sky below, he hesitated.

Big mistake.

In the moment of wavering, all the fearful thoughts he was trying to escape swooped though his mind like swarming bats. What if the curse was a hundred percent true? What if the final destruction was coming any second? Was he going to die in Patience? Shouldn't he jump on his bike and keep riding? Shouldn't he call Wanda on her cell phone so she could come back and save him? But if he ran away, wouldn't Wanda be the first place his father looked?

Jake shook the screeching thoughts out of his head. He didn't have any answers. All he knew was that his plan—Out of Patience Someday—was out the window.

Down in the glossy reflection, a cloud moved steadily to the right. Jake latched on to it and tried to focus on the one thing he had come to do. Dive.

There were several ways to go into the quarry. You could take a running leap off Tabletop Rock, or you could step down to two separate ledges that jutted out. Years ago, the ledges had been named Kennedy and Vandenberg after NASA's launching pads. Kennedy was to the left, and the one most kids favored. From there, it was a twenty-five-foot drop into deep, open water. Vandenberg, down to the right, was more scary. You could go off it okay, but down in the water, a little further to the right, a killer lurked. Two feet below the surface was a jagged block of limestone. Last Crack Rock, everyone called it. If you hit it, it was the last head bonk you had to worry about.

Jake let the cloud gliding across the shimmering water pull him to the right ledge. He stepped down to Vandenberg. The sky filled the liquid mirror so perfectly, it looked solid. He couldn't see Last Crack Rock, but he knew where it was. His eyes fixed on the spot.

Last Crack Rock.

It had never been an option. Before today. The question flashed in his mind. How much would it hurt?

Before he could answer, a sensation gripped his chest. He wasn't breathing. As he sucked in air he realized how twisted and knotted his brain had become. It was squeezing out answers like Last Crack Rock. *Go ahead, hit it and your troubles are over.* There was only one way to untangle his brain. Give himself a break-the-mirror brain-slapper.

Dive!

Jake sprang away from Vandenberg.

If the road had been dusty instead of muddy, Jeremiah Waters might have seen them coming. If he had seen them coming, the history of Patience might have been different. The destiny of every J. Waters might have been different.

But the only oddity Jeremiah noticed on that early-spring morning was Regina's blind, fiddle-playing grandfather. He was sitting on the porch, tapping out a rhythm with his foot and playing a fiddle that wasn't there. He was playing air fiddle.

Jeremiah had already regretted not sending the old

man away with Regina to Wallace. But the old man re-fused to be treated like a woman or child. Now he seemed to have lost his mind altogether. Every time Jeremiah asked him where his fiddle was, the old man would cock his good ear toward him and shout, "What's that? What am I playing?"

"No," Jeremiah would say loudly. "Where's your fiddle?"

And the old man would answer, " 'Fiddler's Drunk and the Fun's All Over.' " It was the title of his favorite fiddle tune.

Before Jeremiah went inside the house, he thought he'd try one more time. "Where's your fiddle?"

The old man kept on air-fiddling and tapping out the rhythm. "What's that? What am I playing?"

Jeremiah sighed. The best he could figure was the old man was upset with Regina for using his fiddle case to put their valuables in. Maybe the old coot thought that hiding his fiddle and denying them the pleasure of his music was a good way of punishing them for taking his case.

Jeremiah's chair creaked as he stood up and looked at the dark thunderheads rising in the west.

"Where are you going?" the old man demanded.

"Nature calls."

The old man stopped air-fiddling. "Sorry, couldn't hear you over the fiddle. What was that?"

Jeremiah threw up his hands in surrender. " 'Fiddler's Drunk and the Fun's All Over.' "

"That's it! I knew you'd get it!" Without letting go of his invisible fiddle and bow, the old man slapped his thigh with delight. " 'Fiddler's Drunk and the Fun's All Over'!"

The fun *was* all over.

A few minutes later, when Jeremiah heard the horses gallop up to the house, he was in the middle of a good sit-down on the Dolphin Deluge.

The gang reined in their horses. Blackbeard pointed his six-shooter at the blind, air-fiddling old man. "Reach fer the sky, ol' buzzard."

The old man reached but kept on air-fiddling and foot-tapping.

"Are you Jeremiah Waters?" Blackbeard demanded.

"No, just the fiddler," the old man answered in rhythm to his silent music. "Jeremiah's inside."

Blackbeard's narrow eyes slid to the front door. "Jeremiah Waters!" he yelled. "Come out with yer hands up, and the ol' fart don't git hurt."

Jeremiah knew that the town's plan to foil the robbery was only as good as the weakest link in the chain. He had a good idea who that link was. But this was no time for pointing fingers. He needed to finish his business on the Dolphin Deluge and figure out how he was going to deal with the gang of outlaws. He looked around the water closet for some kind of weapon. His eyes fell on the suction stick he'd made the day before. He had a plan.

"I'm fixing the one-holer," he shouted through the water closet's closed door. "I'll be right out."

"What?" Blackbeard shouted back.

"I'm fixing the outhouse!"

Blackbeard gave his gang a puzzled look. They were just as clueless. "What's yer outhouse doin' inside?"

"It's called progress!" Jeremiah answered.

Blackbeard had heard enough. He swung off his horse

and the others followed. Their boots thundered up the steps, across the porch, Blackbeard kicked the door open. He leaped inside with his gun at the ready. The others scooted in behind him.

They found themselves in a hallway that ran through the center of the house. A set of stairs led to the second floor. At the far end of the hall was a small room no bigger than a closet. The door was closed.

Blackbeard aimed at the door. "Come outta there nice 'n' slow or we'll turn ya into a four-holer. Savvy?"

The door slowly opened, Jeremiah stepped out with his hands in the air. In his right hand, he held the suction stick with the cone end facing up.

Blackbeard jutted his beard at the strange object. "What in tarnation is that?"

"Oh, this," Jeremiah said, pretending he'd forgotten something was in his hand. "I use it to unplug my Dolphin Deluge Washdown Water Closet."

"What's that?" the ruffian behind Blackbeard asked.

"It's a one-holer that washes itself out. Be happy to show it to you."

"Both of ya shut yer grub-holes," Blackbeard snapped. "Nobody's usin' the one-holer. We come for the loot yer hidin'."

"It's upstairs," Jeremiah lied. "I'll take you up and show you."

"You first." Blackbeard gestured him forward with his gun.

Jeremiah moved toward the corner of the stairs. "Please don't shoot. I'm about to be a father."

As Jeremiah turned at the bottom of the stair, he

suddenly whipped the suction stick down. A cascade of crystals and white dust shot from the leather cone, hitting Blackbeard in the face. His gun exploded with a shot. He dropped the gun. His hands flew to his face as he screamed in pain.

The other gang members jumped away and tried to see why Blackbeard was clutching his face and writhing on the floor.

Jeremiah grabbed for the fallen gun. He felt a sharp blow on the back of his head. He'd just received one of the standard head bonks of that time. The pistol-grip pistol-whip. He staggered against the wall. His vision blurred.

Blackbeard's agony rose into a banshee-like wail. As Jeremiah's swimming eyes searched for the loose gun, he saw one of the men pick up the suction stick and slap the handle into Blackbeard's screaming mouth. Blackbeard bit down on the wooden handle like an angry dog. His screams turned to muffled growls.

Jeremiah saw the blurry image of a gun on the floor. He reached for it. Another sharp blow turned everything black.

13 the scepter of satan

Jake pulled his arms together as his taut, straight body cut through the air. It was going to be a perfect swan dive.

The thing about diving into a flawless reflection is this. You can't see the water. It looks like you're diving into empty sky, except for the one thing flying straight at you. Yourself. The head-on collision with your twin always happens faster than you think. And because you can't see the water, it hits harder than you anticipate. No matter how many times you do it, it always comes as a shock.

Jake punctured the liquid mirror and disappeared as a small geyser of water punched upward.

He shot down into the blackness, feeling the thrilling shock of the deepening cold. Ten feet down it was so dark he couldn't see his hand. Sometimes he wondered how a body knew which way to swim in such darkness. Which way was up? But a body knew. It was one of those stubborn instincts that had a way of overriding everything else. Like the instinct of diving well clear of Last Crack Rock.

As he swam up to the play of sunlight piercing the water, he saw something white floating on the surface. It was the sign of how perfect his dive had been. His underwear. A knife-straight plunge stripped it off every time.

Jake broke the surface. His lungs grabbed air. Another stubborn instinct.

His underwear wasn't the only thing that had been stripped clean. His mind had been stripped bare too, by the jolting sensation of a mirror-breaking brain-slapper.

Now he could sort things out. Now he could figure out what to do.

In town, Waldo Knight, Sam Kirkland, and the other men boarded up in the church managed to escape. The men in the jail were still locked up. While two men fished for the keys down the well where Blackbeard had pitched them, the others got rifles and ammo from Waldo Knight's store. They mounted up and rode for the Waters place in a driving rain.

When they arrived, they found Regina's grandfather on the porch. He didn't have any wounds, but he was dead just the same. The best they could figure was heart failure. The men had seen their share of dead men, but never one who had come to rest in such a bizarre position. The old man was sitting in a chair, his arms stretched toward the sky. His hands were clenched like he was holding something. Or trying to push something to heaven. His crinkly old face was creased with a smile. But the strangest thing was his left foot. It was suspended a couple of inches off the porch.

After the facts had been gathered, and for as long as Regina Waters lived, she took great comfort in the fact that her blind, fiddle-playing grandfather had died on the upbeat.

The menfolk found Jeremiah in the hallway lying in a small pool of blood. He was alive but unconscious. A white crystalline powder was scattered on the floor. Waldo Knight smelled it and identified it. Carbolic acid.

As several men tried to revive Jeremiah, the others took a look around the house. The only damage on the ground floor was a bullet hole in the hall ceiling. The damage on the second floor was another story. The place had been torn apart, turned upside down and sideways. Some of the men wanted to go after the outlaws, but they had no idea which way to go. The rain had erased the outlaws' tracks.

When Jeremiah finally came to, everyone rushed downstairs and crowded into the living room, where he was lying on a couch. Naturally, the first question they asked was, "Did they get the trunk?"

He shook his head.

The others cheered and congratulated Jeremiah for being a hero.

"Where is it?" Sam Kirkland asked.

Jeremiah winced as he touched the throbbing knot on the back of his head. "I made a map."

"Where's the map?"

He tried to fend off the bands of pain shooting around his skull. He squeezed his eyes tight against the searing agony, trying to force a memory. His eyes opened. "I can't recall."

Some men gasped.

"Everyone stand back," Waldo Knight ordered. "Give the man some air." The men obeyed. "Jeremiah, let's start with the first thing you remember and work forward."

Between waves of pain, Jeremiah told them everything he could remember. He remembered burying the trunk in a muddy field, but he couldn't recall whose field. He remembered making a map with clear landmarks for direction. He recalled coming home and getting out of his muddy clothes. He remembered having a late breakfast, talking to Regina's grandfather on the porch, and seeing the storm clouds. And he remembered sitting in his washdown water closet. That was when the gang arrived. He remembered pouring the tin of carbolic acid into the suction stick he kept in the water closet.

"The suction stick?" someone asked.

Jeremiah explained the problem he'd had with his Dolphin Deluge, and how he'd made a suction stick to unplug it.

"Where's the devil stick now?" a familiar voice rang from the back of the crowd.

The men turned and saw Andars Cass. Andars had just arrived with the men who had been locked in the jail.

"Andars," Waldo cautioned, "if it weren't for your flappin' gums, we wouldn't be in the fix we're in now. So hobble your tongue or I'll hobble it for you."

Andars glared at him and decided to bide his time.

The crowd turned back to Jeremiah. He recounted how the gang had barged into the house and called him out. He remembered coming out of the water closet with the

76

suction stick in his hand and seeing four gunmen in the hall. He remembered hurling the acid in the leader's face. The last thing he recalled was seeing the screaming man sink his teeth into the handle of the suction stick. Then the screaming stopped, along with everything else.

"What about the map?" Sam Kirkland pressed.

Jeremiah closed his eyes and tried again. "When I got home, I remember taking it out of my pocket. But I can't recall if I was wearing my muddy clothes or the ones I have on."

"It's got to be somewhere in the house," declared Frederick Olabuff.

Waldo ordered the men to search the house. They paired up to make sure no one found the map and kept it for themselves.

Waldo Knight and Sam Kirkland checked the water closet. They waved away the stink. Apparently, in the excitement of the moment, Jeremiah forgot to pull the chain and wash away the contents in the toilet bowl. While the smell was inconvenient, they were reassured that Jeremiah had not done something really stupid like flush the map down the toilet.

They looked up at the reservoir near the ceiling. He might have hid it there. Waldo climbed up and searched. He found nothing. Since it was now safe to flush the toilet, they gladly did. The water thundered down as the Dolphin Deluge did its duty. Then the two men searched every nook and cranny in the small room. The map wasn't in the cornhusk bin. It wasn't in any of the tins or containers stored on a shelf. It wasn't in the washdown water closet.

The men turned the ground floor of the house upside down and sideways. They turned the already upside down and sideways second floor upside down and sideways again. And they scoured the attic. But no map was found.

They looked in the barns, the chicken coop, the smokehouse, and all the outbuildings. No map was found. They climbed the windmill and lowered a lantern down the well and another one down the pit under the outhouse. No map was found.

As the rain stopped and the sun began to set, the exhausted search party gathered on the porch.

Andars Cass had held his tongue long enough. The gathering on the porch looked too much like a congregation. He stepped into the muddy yard and let the spirit move him.

"Gentlemen, we are a-gathered here for one reason. When Jeremiah Waters set the throne of evil in his house, the prince of darkness was sure to follow."

The men were too tired to shut Andars up.

Andars shook a finger at the congregation. "It was jus' like I warned you. The devil's breath fouled the air and filled the Waters family with evil thoughts. With temptation and sin. And when their vile thoughts, temptations, and sins grew so monstrous they could no longer be a-washed down the sluice of Satan, all that evil did what I was a-sayin' it would. It refused to be cast out. It clogged up that pipe. And what did Jeremiah do? Did he see it as a sign? Did he turn his back on evil and cast the devil's chair from his house? No! He made himself a *suction stick* so he could reach into that pipe and draw the swill of sin right back into his home!"

"Andars," Waldo interrupted. "The only thing he did was make a tool to fix a problem."

"Tool?" Andars sputtered. "That's no tool, my friends. It's the Scepter of Satan!"

"What makes you so sure?" Waldo scoffed.

"Do you see it now? No! It's nowhere in sight. Why? 'Cause the king of evil never leaves his scepter behind. He snatched it up and mounted his fire-breathing hound from Hades." Andars thrust a clenched fist in the air. "As he rode off, in one hand he was a-holdin' his scepter." He punched the air with his other fist. "In the other, he was a-holdin' the soul of Jeremiah Waters!"

Several men gasped.

Jeremiah appeared in the front door, steadying himself against the door frame.

Andars thrust a condemning finger at him. "And I say unto thee, where the soil of Satan rises, the wrath of God floods down! Jeremiah Waters, you and your unborn son, and the unborn sons of your unborn sons, will be a-punished for this! You will watch as Patience, your rose of the prairie, withers to a broken weed! And when all that remains is the burnt stalk of its former glory, there will be a final reckoning! Judgment Day will be a-comin' to this place!"

"All right, I get the picture." Jeremiah chuckled weakly. "Since you know so much about the future, how 'bout giving me the exact date of this here Judgment Day? That way I can tell the unborn sons of my unborn sons to be elsewhere."

As the other men laughed, Andars's eyes flashed with rage. "Have your frolic! Mock me, sinners! But you and your kin will suffer your final day of retribution." He stood to his full height and answered Jeremiah. "The final destruction will begin the day the Scepter of Satan returns to Patience!"

There was something in the fury of Andars's voice that froze the blood of every man there. It was something the God-fearing people of Patience had never heard in the voice of the most fire-and-brimstone preacher.

Jeremiah broke the eerie quiet. "Since you got all the answers, Andars, I got one more question." He stepped to the front of the porch. "How'd that gang of outlaws know to come to my house?"

Andars glared defiantly back. "God works in mysterious ways."

Jeremiah looked down at the half-pint preacher in his muddy yard. He winced as a fresh pain knifed through his head. "Get him out of my sight."

And that's exactly what the men did. That night, they shaved Andars's head, tarred and feathered him, and rode him out of town on a rail.

He didn't go quietly. He cursed the town over and over, always ending with the same dire prediction. "The day the Scepter of Satan returns, the final destruction begins!"

14 family matters

Having retrieved his underwear and slipped it back on, Jake climbed the steep quarry wall using the hand-grabs and toeholds he knew by heart.

The brain-slapping plunge into the water had done more than blow away his fears. In the emptiness that followed, a glimmer of hope flickered in his mind. Just because the Plunger of Destiny had returned and triggered the final destruction didn't mean *he* had to be destroyed. Maybe he could dodge the final blow and still make good on his vow. All he had to do was keep a sharp lookout for signs of the final destruction. He'd be a detective on curse patrol, on stakeout—waiting, watching, listening for the first warning. And if he saw the end coming, he could get out of Patience before it was too late.

As his head rose above Tabletop Rock, he stopped. His father sat on the rock with his legs stretched out in front of him. He looked up from the acrostic magazine on his thighs. "How's the water?"

Jake was too stunned to answer. He couldn't believe his father had found him so easily. He climbed up on the rock, picked up a piece of limestone, and hurled it above the quarry.

It landed in the water with a plunk.

"How'd you know I'd be here?"

"Just a hunch." Jim picked up a stone. "When I was a kid"—he tossed it over the edge—"it's where I came to get away from everything."

Plunk.

Jake sank down on the rock. Just like that, his glimmer of hope was snuffed out. How could he escape the curse if he and his father were hardwired exactly the same? Right down to having the same escape-to-the-quarry gene. How was he going to dodge the final destruction when he was locked in the same J. Waters straitjacket as all the others?

———

Having washed their hands of Andars Cass, the men went back to Courage Street and the Silver Keg Saloon. They calmed their overexcited nerves with a shot of whiskey. Tarring and feathering a man was a rare event in their social calendar of church suppers and barn raisings.

Between their first and second whiskies, the women and children returned from Wallace. When Regina heard what happened, she rushed off to tend to Jeremiah and grieve the death of her grandfather. While most of the women went to church to pray that the Curse of Andars Cass was only the raving of a madman, some of them stayed and gave the men in the saloon a good talking-to.

"Did it ever occur to you," Mrs. Waldo Knight scolded as she glowered at her husband, "that Jeremiah's little bout of amnesia is a ruse?" Waldo blinked, amazed by what she was implying about a man who, the day before, had been considered the most honest man in the county.

"For all we know," Mrs. Kirkland proclaimed, shooting her husband a stern look, "he could have dug up that trunk and be halfway to Denver by now."

Sam Kirkland scratched his head. "I really doubt what's in that trunk is worth Jeremiah leaving his ranch, a thousand head of cattle, and a pregnant wife."

But the seeds of suspicion had been planted, and the men agreed to take turns keeping an eye on the Waters place to make sure Jeremiah didn't disappear with the community chest.

While Regina nursed Jeremiah back to health, everyone hoped and prayed for his memory to return so he could find the map and recover the trunk. Time healed the knot on the back of his head, but it didn't untangle the knot of memory inside.

Various cures were tried, from a hypnotist to magazines that specialized in crossword and acrostic puzzles. They believed that such word games stimulated the memory. But the only result was that Jeremiah got addicted to acrostic puzzles.

One other significant event occurred shortly after that fateful day in March 1877.

Regina took up a hammer and nailed the door to the Dolphin Deluge Washdown Water Closet shut. For several reasons. One, her grandfather didn't need it anymore.

Two, if there was any truth to Andars's claim that indoor plumbing was a trapdoor to the forces of evil, then it wasn't worth the risk. And three, since the Waters name was under a cloud of suspicion, she figured sealing up the water closet would send the right message. We're all in this together, and if a fifty-yard walk to the outhouse is good enough for our neighbors, it's good enough for us.

It was Jim's turn to throw a rock. He hefted the stone in his palm. "I know you've got plenty of reasons to be upset."

"I'm not upset," Jake answered coolly. "Why would I be upset?"

"Well, for one, Wanda left."

"Lucky her."

"Do you want to talk about it?"

"No." Jake didn't think his father wanted to hear the real reason he was upset about Wanda. That morning, he had a chance to jump in her Mustang and escape with her, but he'd blown it. Jake threw his rock. "I'll get over it."

Plunk.

"I always do."

Jim slowly turned the rock in his fingers and studied his son.

Feeling his eyes, Jake snatched another rock and threw it.

They both watched it arc over the quarry.

Plunk.

Jim tried again. "You're also probably a bit upset about dropping to fourth place in the Series."

"How do you know that?" Jake shot back. "You left the game to get your stupid Plunger."

"I called Mrs. Bickers."

Jake quickly wrapped his anger in indifference. His father leaving the game didn't matter anymore. The Plunger had delivered a new game. Survival. "So I dropped to fourth place. Big deal. We probably won't make it to Game 7."

"You really believe in the curse, don't you?"

"Well, gee, Dad, it promised Patience a long, slow, miserable death. Wouldn't you say it delivered?"

Jim finally tossed his rock over the quarry.

Plunk.

Then he began, low and quiet. "Jake, the curse is nothing but the rant of a lunatic who died a long time ago. Everything that happened to Patience since 1877 happened for a reason. There's good progress and bad progress, and, over the years, our little town got a lot more of the bad than the good."

Jim looked out at the horizon. From Tabletop Rock you could see ten miles in any direction. "There're some towns out here that certainly had a worse time of it. You can find the bones of small towns all over these parts. If the curse was true, do you really think Patience would still be standing after all these years?"

"Of course it would." Jake couldn't believe he had to point out the obvious. "Because it's just like the curse says. It's been waiting for the day the Plunger of Destiny returns to finish the job."

"To be precise," Jim said, raising a finger, "Andars Cass

said when the 'Scepter of Satan' returns, the final destruction will begin. Folks only started calling it the Plunger of Destiny after plungers became a common household item. That's the thing about curses, Jake. They're like rumors. They change with the times and whoever's telling 'em. Which makes curses and rumors equally unreliable."

He hated it when his father went off on one of his lectures. It was one of the times he wished his mother hadn't died. She wouldn't have lectured, she would have listened.

He glared at the horizon. "You just don't get it."

"Try me," Jim offered.

"It's like the superstition about walking under a ladder. Most people don't really believe it's bad luck, but they still don't go around walking under ladders 'cause it's not worth the risk. Most people don't take the chance."

"We're not most people, Jake."

Jake's face prickled with heat. "Maybe you're not, but I am. And I wanna do like most people who were born here. I wanna get out before I end up like every other J. Waters. Another loser buried on Temperance Street." He grabbed a rock, jumped up, and threw it as hard as he could across the quarry. "I'm not gonna die here!"

The rock ricocheted off the wall and fell in the water. *Plunk.*

He had sworn not to tell his father his vow. Now it had popped out. There was nothing he could do about it. He snatched his jersey off the rock and punched an arm into a sleeve.

"Wow," his father exhaled. "It sounds like you think your old man has already died here too."

Jake fought back the lump of rage squeezing his throat. He snapped the buttons in the front of his jersey. This wasn't how things were supposed to go. There was no place for anger in his new plan. And tears were totally out of the question.

Jim stood up and gazed out over the prairie. "Since you figure part of me has already moved over to Temperance Street, I figure that makes me an expert on dying. You wanna hear what I know about it?"

Jake yanked on his pants and ignored him.

"All I know is this," Jim said softly. "There's one thing worse than dying before you see what's over the horizon."

Jake scowled. "What could be worse than that?"

"Dying before you see what's under your nose."

Jake plunked down and wrestled with a sock. "Yeah, well, I've seen everything around here a million times."

"Don't be so sure."

Something in his father's voice made him glance up. His father looked down with a wry smile.

"It's time I showed you something."

15   riding with the enemy

With his bike squeezed in the back, Jake rode shotgun in his father's van. As he watched Patience drawing closer, his gut churned like a cement mixer. It felt like he was driving straight toward a car wreck seconds away from happening.

But the worst part was the Plunger of Destiny.

It was right there between them, lying on the dusty, parts-strewn console between the bucket seats.

When he asked his father what it was doing in the van, he wouldn't say. Jake resisted the urge to toss it out the window like a live grenade and kept his eyes glued to the horizon. He was on stakeout, in detective mode. His only chance was to see it coming.

The van passed the Tumbleweed Motel and turned off the highway into Gas & Goodies. The Tumbleweed and Gas & Goodies shared the same aging island of cracked cement. Jake made sure the one other customer at the gas pumps wasn't smoking. A fireball consuming Gas & Goodies was just the kind of big-bang opening salvo he expected from the curse.

"Is this what you wanna show me?" he asked. "Gas & Goodies?"

"No, I need to fill up and we need milk." Jim slid a credit card out of his wallet and handed Jake a dollar. "Get a quart while I gas up."

As Jake headed for the glass doors, he looked across the span of cement. He saw Sira emerge from one of the motel's long row of rooms. She was holding an armful of sheets. He hurried toward the doors. He wasn't in the mood to see anyone, and if Gas & Goodies was about to blow sky high, his friend just might survive if she kept her distance.

But Sira saw him, dropped the sheets into a rolling hamper, and jogged toward Gas & Goodies.

Stepping inside, Jake felt the cold hug of air-conditioning. He grabbed a quart of milk from the cooler and started for the counter.

A young woman with circles under her eyes and stringy blond hair stood at the cash register. PEARL was stitched over the pocket of her orange work jacket. Behind the counter, a baby's head bounced in and out of view. As Jake put the milk and the dollar on the counter, he noticed the baby was bouncing up and down in a jumper swing. It was Pearl's son, Sean.

"Hey, Jake," Pearl said, "heard you had a rough day at the plate."

To Jake, it felt like a week ago. "Yeah, well, stuff

happens." He figured Pearl knew about his bad game because she lived with her aunt, Mrs. Bickers, and Mrs. Bickers had probably called with a game report.

Sira came through the door as Pearl rang up the milk.

"That'll be eighty-six cents."

Sira didn't skip a beat. " '86. The blizzard of 1886 hit like God was flinging snowballs and Patience was the bull's-eye. Herds of cattle froze against the fence lines and were buried so deep by the snow that cattlemen looking for their herds rode right over them."

As Pearl slid fourteen cents out of the cash drawer, Jake held up a hand. "Please, don't count the change."

Sira gave him a finger poke. "Nice try, Tweener, but I'm not done with '86. When a rancher named Jeremiah Waters realized he was riding his horse on top of his herd of frozen and buried cattle, he turned to his young son, Jud, and asked, 'Do you think we could still sell 'em as *ground* beef?' "

As Pearl laughed, Jake stared at Sira. He had never told her that dopey tidbit of Waters family history. "How do you know that?"

"You'd be amazed what you can find in the old copies of the *Patience Rose Petal Press*. And they've got every one of 'em in the town hall basement. Where do you think I've been getting a lot of my freaky and fascinating facts?"

"I don't care where you get 'em." Jake grabbed the plastic bag with his milk and started out. At the door he suddenly turned. "Are you going there this afternoon?"

Sira was right behind him. "Probably. Wanna come?"

"No way. Just do me a favor and don't go into town today, okay?"

She practically jumped with curiosity. "Why?"

Before he could make up a reason, the door opened and Jim poked his head in. "Pearl, tell your aunt something came up and I'll be about forty-five minutes late."

"Sure," she answered, turning her attention back to Sean.

Outside, as Jim headed around the van, Sira refused to let Jake off the hook. "Why shouldn't I go into town?"

He was already sorry he'd tried to warn her. With his father right there, he had no choice but to do like the Cricket and jump. "I can't believe you just missed '45. Is that like '07, another fact that's freaky, fascinating, and nowhere to be found?" He hopped in the van, making sure to block whatever glimpse she might get of the Plunger.

Sira didn't see the ancient object on the console, but she did see through his dodge. "I didn't miss it, but there's more to life than freaky and fascinating facts, you know?"

As the van pulled away, she shouted, "I'm on to you, Tweener. You can run, but you can't hide!"

After the van was back on the highway heading east, Jim gave Jake a worried look. "I meant what I said earlier. You can't tell anyone about the Plunger."

"I didn't."

"Promise you won't."

Jake wasn't in the mood to roll over. "Why do you care if people find out about it if you think the curse is up there with the Tooth Fairy and Santa Claus?"

"It's like what you said about walking under ladders. People are superstitious. Besides, when I do tell 'em, I want it to be a surprise. Now, promise me."

If he hadn't felt like the sky was about to cave in, Jake might have laughed. Promising not to tell anyone that your dad had spent a week's worth of grocery money on a disgusting old toilet plunger was as easy as promising not to tell anyone that your dad's job was walking behind circus elephants with a shovel.

"Promise," Jake muttered as he glanced up at the sky. No storms on the horizon. That was the good news. And that they were driving away from Patience.

The van headed east on Highway 40 for another half mile, then turned south on an unmarked gravel road.

Jake shot his father a puzzled look. "Why are we going to the old ranch?"

"That's where it is," his father told him.

"What?"

"Seeing is believing."

Jake checked the outside mirror to see if Patience had gone up in a mushroom cloud yet. All he saw was the billowing cloud of dust behind them. He glanced over at the Plunger on the console. The thing jiggled and twitched with the motion of the van. Like it was alive. At one time it was. The cone-shaped Plunger had been part of a buffalo. You could still see the pinprick pattern of follicles where Jeremiah had shaved away the thick fur. Even the wooden handle showed signs of life. After all, the two crescents of teeth marks were Blackbeard's dental records. If this was some horror movie, Jake thought, the second he turned away the Plunger would spring to life and attack. Suck his brains out, or something.

He lifted his eyes back to the road ahead and kept his ears pricked for unusual noises. There was no telling what a plunger sounded like when it was about to strike.

16   the family vault

The Waters ranch had been abandoned more than fifty years. The only tenants now were wood rats and weather. The roof of the old house was caved in. Its walls tilted toward the front, giving the impression it was about to pounce. The windows were now truly storm windows—storms came and went as they pleased. The porch, where Jake's great-great-great-great-great-grandfather air-fiddled his last tune, had taken a final bow and collapsed. The windmill next to the house still stood tall, but its wheel was missing several paddles. It looked like a great crested bird going bald. Behind the house, the old outhouse was a mound of rotting boards pierced by a leafy cottonwood. The only building that had survived the weather's endless assault was the big barn.

Jim parked the van in front of the house, grabbed the Plunger, and jumped out. "Time for show-and-tell." He cut a path through the knee-high buffalo grass.

As Jake followed, his senses opened like floodgates. The brush-crunch of their feet in the grass thundered in his ears. The rasping ratchet of grasshoppers taking flight exploded around them. The bright flash of orange-yellow under the grasshoppers' wings blazed in silent warning.

Reaching the house, Jim stopped at the apron of corrugated tin that was once the porch roof. It lay in front of the house, making a rusty ramp to the front door. Jake stopped behind him. Now the only sound was the steady riffle of wind in the grass.

Jim waved the Plunger at the tin ramp. "You know, this house has always been ahead of its time. Not only did it have the first flush toilet west of the Mississippi," he said as he stepped up on the ramp, "it was the first to have wheelchair access."

Jake ignored his father's lame joke.

As Jim moved up the tin ramp to the front door, Jake stayed a step behind. Inside, the staircase still dominated the central hall. It led up to an unrestricted view of clouds by day, stars by night. On the floor, Jake was surprised to see a path of fresh pine boards zigzagging over the rotten flooring to the back of the hall.

Jim started down the zigzag walkway.

Jake hesitated. "Is this safe?"

"I've been to the cellar, checked the joists," Jim said without stopping. "The place is a fixer-upper waiting to happen." He waved the Plunger for Jake to follow.

Jake didn't move. "Dad, what are we doing here?"

"We're doing an experiment that'll hopefully put your fears to rest. C'mon."

Jake reluctantly took the path of yellow-white boards over the rotten flooring.

The yellow brick road it wasn't.

The closet-sized room at the end of the hall still had its door. It was shut and padlocked with a combination lock. Jake had never seen the lock before. Or the new boards on the floor. The few times his father had brought him to the old Waters place, he hadn't been allowed to go in the house. It was considered unsafe. "Why is there a—"

Jim turned with a hush. "Listen and learn." He handed the Plunger to Jake. "Hold this."

Jake didn't budge.

"It's a piece of history, Jake. Pieces of history don't bite."

"You haven't seen *Jurassic Park*, or *Tomb Raider*, or—"

"Science fiction. We're talking fact here." As Jim leaned closer, his eyes danced. "And family history you can bank on. Now, take it."

Jake gingerly took the Plunger, holding it like it had just come from active duty in a witches' dormitory.

Jim spun the numbered dial on the lock. "Listen up if you want to know the combination to the family vault. Right to thirty-six. Left to twelve. Right to nine."

Jake was glad Sira wasn't there. The day was tossing enough freaky facts at him without her adding to the bombardment.

The lock clacked open. Jim removed it and pulled open the door.

Under a layer of crusted dirt, surrounded by a nimbus of spiderwebs, was the Dolphin Deluge Washdown Water

Closet. The pull chain still dangled from the wooden reservoir near the ceiling. Below the mahogany seat, the great shell bowl gaped upward. The dolphin's graceful S-shaped body disappeared into the floor.

Jake teetered backward, almost stepping onto the rotten flooring, "Is that—?"

"The one and only. The Dolphin Deluge Washdown Water Closet, by Edward Johns and Company."

Jake gaped in disbelief. "It's always been here?"

"Yep. Some families have skeletons in their closets, we have a toilet. I probably should have brought it back to the house for safekeeping, but I think of it the same way Indians think of their ancestral burial grounds. It's a sacred site."

He took the Plunger from Jake. "Now it's time for a little experiment. If you really think some final destruction is coming, imagine what would happen if the Plunger of Destiny, the Scepter of Satan, returned to the original scene of the crime? The devil's pipe itself." He thrust the Plunger into the open toilet.

Jake flinched as a bolt of fear shot through him. He braced for lightning to strike, or some terrifying beast with toilet breath to explode up through the floor and swallow them.

The only thing that moved was a cloud of dust. It swirled out of the bowl and danced in the fan of sunbeams.

Jim dropped the Plunger in the toilet. The handle clattered against the seat. "There they are, the dastardly duo, back together after one hundred and twenty-eight years. The devil's bowl and the wicked old whisk. Is the sky falling? I don't think so. Why? Because the curse is nothing but a crippling vision that's been passed down from one superstitious generation to the next."

Jim grabbed the Plunger from the water closet. He thrust it in front of him as he took the zigzag of boards back to the front door. "If you're gonna have a vision . . ."

Jake hurried after him.

"Then I say do what every J. Waters has done since Jeremiah staked his first claim." Jim stopped at the open door and jabbed the Plunger outside. "Have a vision of the future!"

Jake peered past him to see what he was pointing at across the overgrown yard. "The barn?"

"Not just any barn. Soon to be the ATM. The American Toilet Museum!"

Jake shook his head in dismay. "Dad, even if you're right and the curse is bogus, where are you gonna get the money to open a museum?"

"As rain follows the plow"—Jim thrust the Plunger at the sky—"money follows the Plunger."

"And if it doesn't?"

His father lowered the Plunger and took in the old ranch. His eyes suddenly lost their sparkle. They were flat, expressionless. Lean eyes. The old-timers have a name for them. Prairie eyes.

Prairie eyes see two things at once. They see the ground at your feet, which delivers the fruits of labor. And they see the distant horizon, which delivers the destructive acts of God. Prairie eyes are quiet, neutral, ready for whatever the ground or the horizon delivers.

Jim shrugged. "Then nothing changes and we go on with our lives." Turning to Jake, his face creased with a smile. "But a life without dreams, Tweener, isn't worth a toot in a tornado."

As his father strode down the ramp back to the van, Jake wanted to scream, *Du-uh! Why do you think I wanna get out of here?* But he didn't. His father wouldn't understand. His father was a half-bubble off plumb.

"Hey!" Jim shouted when he reached the van. He raised the Plunger as a wood rat leaped out of the passenger side window and disappeared in the high grass. He started to bring the Plunger down but checked his swing. Killing a rat wasn't worth damaging one of the American Toilet Museum's most prized relics.

As Jake joined him they peered in the van. The rat had chewed through the plastic bag and the bottom of the milk carton. A pool of milk filled the passenger seat.

Jim grabbed a rag from under the seat and began soaking up milk. But there would be no stopping the sour-milk time bomb now ticking away in the hundred-degree heat.

To Jake, this was no accident. It was a sign. And he knew what it meant. The final destruction didn't have to come as a big-bang thing. It might begin like a famous poet once put it. It might come in on little cat feet. Or, in this case, little rat feet. It could all start with an act as small and insignificant as spilled milk.

On the ride back to town, with the Plunger of Destiny jiggling in the milk-stained seat and Jake sitting on the console, he made his second vow of the summer. To be the Sherlock Holmes of the High Plains. To be on the lookout for the smallest clue. The first tiny scratch in death by a thousand cuts. And if he saw the first paper cut of the apocalypse, maybe he would have time to save more than himself. Maybe he could save his friends, his father, and everyone in Patience.

17   courage street

As the van passed Endurance Street, Jake turned to his father. "Where are we going?"

"To Mrs. Bickers's. Got a little job there."

"Can't you drop me?"

"Nope. Now that you know all the family secrets, it's time you learned a thing or two about the family trade."

Driving up Courage Street, Jake decided not to tell him that when he left he wasn't planning on packing the family monkey wrench. He scoured the wide brick street for tiny telltale signs of doom.

The Patience Service Station was still out of gas and offering thirty-two pounds of pressure from its hoseless air pump.

Nothing new there.

The old limestone town hall had its red and white OPEN sign hanging in the glass door, with a small qualification taped to the bottom of the sign: "The last Friday of every month."

Business as usual.

Moving along the street, Jake scanned the sweep of shops lining each side. Under the running sidewalk overhangs, forged into battered belts of tin by decades of snow and hail, the shop windows were dusty, dark, and empty.

Nothing had changed. The curse had closed High Plains Hardware, the Hair Station, and Lockhart's Meat Locker long before the Plunger of Destiny had returned.

The rose of the prairie had lost its bloom some time ago, but it wasn't pushing up daisies quite yet. At the north end of Courage, the van approached a cluster of small businesses still clinging to life.

The Smoky Hill Cafe was a tiny eatery with six tables inside and a couple of picnic tables out front. It wasn't Lillian Huffaker's cooking that kept the cafe in business. It was the fact that the kitchen was Mrs. Huffaker's only kitchen. She figured as long as she had to feed herself, she might as well feed the occasional customer.

Her best customer, Red Olabuff, owned the business across the street, Mr. Tired Tires Tire Company. He had so many discarded tires that they were stacked in tall pyramids around his multibayed garage. Mr. Olabuff called it his research and development facility. It was where he brainstormed his "million and one uses for old tires." He had invented a process of turning old tires into building materials, but his store, and his Mr. Tired Tires website, had yet to sell any Tired Tires Tool Sheds or Tired Tires Doghouses.

Mr. Olabuff held two positions of honor in the community. He was chief of the volunteer fire department and postmaster. Being postmaster was convenient because the Patience Post Office was right next door, hidden behind a pyramid of tires.

The tiny brick post office was the most important building in town. For good reason. When a town loses its post office, it loses its zip code. When a town loses its zip code, it disappears off the map. Literally. No zip code, they take you off the map.

The van moved past the post office and several houses before it reached the last street in town and turned left on Faith Street. Across the street, Mange Field was empty in the sweltering heat of the early afternoon. It had the forlorn look of the last kid chosen for a pickup game.

Nothing new there, Jake noted. This was how Mange Field always looked.

A moment later, Jim stepped onto Mrs. Bickers's porch. Jake followed, lugging his father's heavy toolbox with both hands. A note was pinned to the screen door.

Jim read it. "Went to Wal-Mart in Goodland. Be back before supper."

Jake set the toolbox down. "Great. Can we go home and get lunch now?" His churning anxiety was now sharing stomach time with hunger pangs. Being on curse patrol and never knowing what was around the next corner was a major calorie burner. If he was going to stay on Sherlock duty, he needed a sandwich.

"Okay," Jim said, heading down the steps, "in just a minute." He strode around the side of the house. "C'mon, bring the box."

Jake hefted the toolbox and followed. The sandwich he

103

had been making in his head disappeared and was replaced by the image of a plumber's apprentice lugging a heavy toolbox across the deck of the *Titanic*. He set the box beside his father, now kneeling next to an outside spigot.

Jim opened the faucet and let water run onto the burnt grass. He opened the toolbox and pulled out a small plastic bag containing a sample cup. He ripped open the bag, filled the cup with water, then grabbed a small strip of test paper from the toolbox and dipped it in the cup. The paper turned light lavender. "Don't you want to know what I'm doing?" he asked.

"You're making lavender paper."

"Very funny, wise guy. I'm testing for nitrates. They're a type of impurity, and with well water you need to test for 'em every six months." He held up the lavender test strip. "This is a reading of about nine. That's okay, but a little high. So we run a backup." He pulled a more elaborate test kit out of the toolbox, opened it and filled a small test tube with water, then sealed it and tucked it into a mailer bag. "Any questions?"

"Yeah." Jake closed up the toolbox. "Why do you carry around a thirty-pound toolbox for two plastic test kits that weigh next to nothing?"

Jim laughed. "Because the number of times you go back to your van for a tool equals the number a times a customer thinks, 'Does this guy know what he's doing?'"

Jake grunted as he reached for the toolbox, but Jim beat him to it and lifted it off the grass. "C'mon. After I drop this mailer at the post office, I'll make you a lunch fit for the prince who wanted to be a plumber. Did I ever tell you about the prince who wanted to be a plumber?"

Jake rolled his eyes. "About a million times."

"Okay, you're spared," Jim chortled as he headed back to the van.

The van pulled up in front of the post office. Jim jumped out with the mailer bag and disappeared around the back of the van. Jake eyeballed the tire pyramids in front of Mr. Tired Tires Tire Company. They didn't look like they'd shifted in some imperceptible pre-earthquake tremor.

The van's back door opened. Jim grabbed a towel and tossed it up front. "Cover it. Don't let anyone see it. And you better sit in the driver's seat so it doesn't look weird."

Jake gladly covered the Plunger with the towel.

Having seen Jim Waters head into the post office, Red Olabuff walked over from Mr. Tired Tires. He was a big man who easily filled out his double-extra-large overalls. He wore a light blue U.S. Postal Service shirt underneath. He had a ruddy face which he claimed "had a few miles on it, but never needed a retread."

Jake slid over into the driver's seat. He looked up and continued his search for curse-creep. The American flag stirred lazily at the top of the flagpole in front of the post office. Rising from the top of the pole was the town's last gift from the state. A tornado siren.

A thought raced through his mind. There was another option he hadn't considered. Blowing the whistle. All he had to do was run into the post office, hit the tornado siren button, and when everyone ran to the town hall to take shelter in the basement, he could hold up the Plunger and scream, "The Plunger of Destiny has returned! Run for your lives!"

But then he thought of another possibility. What if his father was actually right? What if the curse was nothing but an empty superstition? What if he ended up looking like Chicken Little waving a toilet plunger?

"Hello, Tweener."

Jake jumped. A foot away, two blue eyes danced under the ragged brim of a Colorado Rockies hat. It was Mr. Lockhart.

The kids in town called him Oil Can because he was always squirting tobacco juice. There was usually a little oil spill on the craggy beach of his chin. Today was no exception. In the last century, Mr. Lockhart had owned Lockhart's Meat Locker. In this century, the only butcher left in town was time, and time had trimmed most of the fat off Mr. Lockhart. Under his wrinkled brown-paper skin, he was all bone and gristle.

Jake recovered from the shock. "Hey, Mr. Lockhart, where'd you come from?"

Mr. Lockhart jabbed a gnarled thumb across the street. His voice sounded like a rock tumbler full of flint. "Just had lunch at the cafe. Saw your pop's van, thought you might be with 'im."

The mention of lunch made Jake's stomach growl. "Did you wanna see me?"

The old man's eyes narrowed. "You durn straight."

Jake swallowed. Did Mr. Lockhart know something?

18 a strange twist

Jake watched Oil Can's lips pucker like raisins. He squirted a stream of juice onto the street, adding a fresh spill to his chin. He was a regular *Exxon Valdez*.

"Just wanted to say hang in there, Tweener," he said with a juice-stained grin. "Just 'cause today you dropped balls like a gumball machine and swung the bat like a crippled flying mantis don't mean tomorrow won't be a brighter day."

Jake breathed a sigh of relief. Oil Can had been at the game that morning. He always sat in one of the empty dugouts. That way he could spit north, south, east, or west, and no one complained.

"Can I ask you something, Mr. Lockhart?"

"Let's have it."

"What if tomorrow's not a brighter day? What if things get worse before they get better?"

Oil Can's blue eyes locked on him.

Jake plunged on. "What if tomorrow you woke up and the cafe was gone? The post office, everything? What if Patience was wiped clean off the map?"

Oil Can spit a long stream, and sleeve-mopped his chin. "Lemme tell you sumthin, Jake Waters. It's not boards 'n' brick that make a town. It's blood 'n' sinew. And where there's blood 'n' sinew there's hope." He tipped his hat back. "Now it's my turn to pop you a question." His beak of a nose sucked in air as his eyes slid past Jake. "Whatcha hidin' under that there towel? Dead animal?"

Jake grabbed the towel-covered Plunger and quickly moved it behind the seats. "No, sir, that's sour milk you're smelling. We spilled a bunch. Pretty bad, huh?"

"Gonna get worse," Oil Can chuckled, then spit a geyser. He pushed his newly slimed chin in the van and inhaled deeply. "But as bad smells go it's a change from the Seventh-Inning Stench." He pulled back and offered some parting advice. "Always look on the bright side, Tweener. Nobody hitches their wagon to a scowl."

As he turned and started to shuffle home, Jake threw him one more question. "Mr. Lockhart, do you believe in the curse?"

Oil Can turned back, fixing Jake with hard eyes. "Why you askin' me that?"

Jake had to think fast. "I'm taking a poll. It's for my over-the-summer school project."

Oil Can grunted. "Do I believe in the curse?"

"Yes, sir."

Oil Can scratched the stubble under his chin, and his eyes twinkled. "Well, Tuesdays, Thursdays, and Saturdays

I do. Mondays, Wednesdays, and Fridays I'm more hopeful." He chuckled as he started away.

Jake wanted to grab the Plunger of Destiny, wave it out the window, and ask Mr. Lockhart if that was his final answer. But he'd promised his father to keep it a secret.

Jim came out of the post office with a handful of mail. Jake immediately noticed the strange look on his face. His mouth was twisted in an odd smirk. Jake slid over to the console as Jim got in and put the mail on the dashboard. One letter had been opened.

Jake wondered if the strange expression on his father's face was it. The tiny change he'd been looking for. "What's up?"

"Nothing." Jim started the van.

"C'mon, what happened?"

"*Ad Astra per Aspera.*" Jim smiled and backed up.

As they drove back down the street, a green pickup drove toward them. It was Mr. Knight's F-250, with a plastic fertilizer bag on the roof advertising Knight's Soil & Fertilizer.

Mr. Knight's pickup had more nicknames than anyone or anything in town. Dung Buggy, Ploppy Jalopy, Manuremobile, and Gaguar, to name a few. As thankful as everyone was that KSF was keeping Patience from disappearing off the map, Marvin Knight's success was the target of some resentment. But calling his truck dirty names wasn't the only way the townspeople put it to him. They had also elected him mayor.

As the truck came closer, Mr. Knight reached out and waved down the van. Jim pulled up next to the pickup. It was one of the benefits of living in Fly Speck, USA. A little chat over the yellow line wasn't illegal. Even if it was, there was no sheriff to give you a ticket.

Mr. Knight gave them a friendly nod. "Are you comin' tonight, Jim?"

"Wouldn't miss it for the world," he answered.

Mr. Knight shook his head with mock pity. "You still got your head in that toilet museum idea, don't you?"

"Well, Marvin, I'd rather be up to my eyeballs in history than up to my nose in a forty-acre cow pie."

Mr. Knight grinned and came right back. "You know the KSF motto: Don't smell it, sell it. But when it comes to saving Patience, I think we can do better than an outhouse with a velvet rope around it."

"Oh, I've got better than that," Jim boasted. "Just arrived today."

Jake's jaw dropped. He couldn't believe his father was about to blow the secret when he'd made such a huge deal about making him promise not to tell anyone.

"What's that?"

Jim pulled the gearshift into drive. "You'll see tonight."

"Lookin' forward to it," Mr. Knight said as he gave Jake a glance. "Hope you do better at the plate tomorrow."

Jake tossed off a "Thanks, Coach," and the vehicles parted. "Dad, are you nuts? If you show 'em the Plunger there'll be a riot."

"Better than that," Jim said with a satisfied smile.

Jake saw the same look in his father's eyes that he'd seen that morning in Wanda's. The look of someone who'd wrestled their demons and won. "What?"

"This is it, Tweener. This is what I've been waiting for."

"What?"

Jim lifted the opened letter off the dash. "This is from the state historical society. I applied for a grant to put together a proposal on the museum. They're interested, but before they give me the grant they want to see my collection."

Jake was dumbstruck. "People want to come here and see all that stuff?"

"Yep. I got a week to get it in shape."

"A week?" Jake threw up his hands. "The town'll probably be gone in a week!"

Jim turned onto Endurance Street, and grinned at Jake. "For your information, Mr. Doom 'n' Gloom, the curse can be interpreted two ways. It says, 'The day the Scepter of Satan returns to Patience, the final destruction will begin.' Maybe the 'final destruction' is actually the destruction of the *curse*. Maybe Patience is on the verge of a renaissance."

Jake slid over into the passenger seat. Whether he smelled of sour milk didn't matter anymore. Not when his father had totally left the orbit of Planet Reality. There was no arguing with him. There was no convincing him that his good news about his ridiculous toilet museum was probably nothing more than the calm before the storm.

Jake sat upright as a lightning bolt shock-flashed in his head. That was it. The letter.

The telltale sign he'd been looking for.

The first cut of a thousand cuts was so subtle, it was a gentle pat. It was the classic setup. Just like when one of his teachers started with one good thing about an essay, then followed up with the three dozen ways it sucked. Hypnotize him with a compliment, then bring down the hammer!

"You all right?" Jim asked as the van turned into their driveway.

"Ye-ah," Jake said, his voice breaking. He cleared his throat. "Just starved." If the curse was going to be this clever and cunning, he had to keep his body and brain well fed, ready for action 24/7.

When Jake hopped out of the van, another flash of lightning seared through his brain. What if the final destruction came at night? When he was asleep?

As Jim came around the front of the van, Jake stood frozen in the driveway. "Dad, I can't stay here."

"For lunch?"

"No, tonight. I can't sleep here."

Jim stopped, took off his hat, scratched his head. "I was wondering when that superstition synapse was gonna fire."

"Better superstitious than sorry," Jake shot back.

Jim studied him with bemused resignation. "Tell you what, Tweener. After lunch, we'll take your pup tent and your camping gear out to the quarry."

Jake was stunned that his father had such a good idea. "You'll let me camp by myself?"

"You're old enough. It's that, or stay here and get devoured by the final destruction."

19 town meeting

The sunset blazed across a sky so massive it made an Imax movie look like a peephole.

A dozen citizens made their way toward the town hall.

Jim was already inside, sitting in the back row of folding chairs, his head buried in an acrostic magazine.

Earlier that afternoon, he had helped Jake set up his pup tent on Tabletop Rock at the quarry. Jake named the spot Camp Stakeout because it had a clear view of Patience. When he tried to get Howie to join him for their "big last camping trip of the summer," Howie accused him of plotting with Sira to sabotage his shot at winning the World Series. There was no way he was going to risk a bad night's sleep before Game 6. After the Series, yeah, he'd go camping for the rest of the summer. As much as Jake wanted to tell Howie that the rest of the summer was in serious jeopardy, he didn't. For two reasons. The promise he'd made his father, and because Howie held a secret about as long as a dog holds on to a tossed slice of lemon.

Jake wished he was watching the sunset out at Camp Stakeout, but he had one more thing to do before he left town for the night. As people filed into the town hall, he set a tape recorder on the piano next to the microphone stand. He was finally beginning his over-the-summer school project. Of course, the odds of finishing it weren't great, but he figured if he somehow survived the final destruction he'd still have to start eighth grade over in Sharon Springs. He didn't think his social studies teacher was going to buy the excuse that the curse ate his homework.

Unlike Sira's project, Jake's project was designed to require the minimum amount of research and paperwork. He was pretending to be a reporter for the long-dead *Patience Rose Petal Press*, and he was going to file a story on that night's meeting. All he had to do was listen to the tape, write up what was said, and hand it in.

Next to the piano, Mr. Rashid suddenly appeared in the narrow stairwell coming up from the basement. "Hello, Jake. Since when did you take an interest in town affairs?"

"School project," Jake answered as he positioned the recorder.

"That's what Sira's doing downstairs. Reading old newspapers."

"Now?" Sira's bizarre study habits always amazed Jake. When it came to "butt travel" she was a regular marathoner.

"She still needs to find ten more freaky and fascinating facts," Mr. Rashid explained. "She's pulling her hair out." As he went to find a seat he added, "And her eyes, and her nose, and her ears."

Jake's smile vanished when he saw Mr. Lockhart staring him down from the front row.

Oil Can spit into the empty tuna can he used as a spittoon, then looked back up with accusing eyes. "I thought your school project was a poll on the curse."

"It was," Jake said as he groped for the right words. "But no one would give me a straight answer, so I changed it." Then he quickly sat down on the bench behind the piano.

As well as providing cover from Oil Can, it was a good spot for someone pretending to be a reporter. He'd be out of sight during the meeting, and he could turn the tape over if he needed to. He hoped it wouldn't be necessary.

A few minutes after seven, Red Olabuff stepped up to the microphone. He faced the two dozen people scattered among the chairs. Jake turned on the recorder.

"Welcome, everybody," Mr. Olabuff began. "Glad you could tear yourselves away from your busy schedules." He got a rueful chuckle from the audience. "As you know, we're here to talk about the future of Patience. But no one can talk about it better than our mayor, and the man who's footin' the bill for this friendly little competition. Marvin Knight."

Mr. Knight stepped to the mike to generous applause and took off his KSF baseball cap. Above his horseshoe of dark hair, he was bald as a headlight.

"Thank you. Like my mama used to say to my daddy when he handed her his paycheck, 'Well, bless yer heart 'n' half yer gizzard.' "

Even though they'd heard the line dozens of times, the crowd threw him a laugh. The only one who didn't was Jim Waters. He still had his head in his acrostic.

Mr. Knight got down to business. "Tonight we're here to kick off the Patience Revival Project. When I opened KSF a few years back, I made a promise. The first year the company got in the black—"

"The company's been in the *black* every year," Mr. Lockhart interrupted. "Up to its knees."

Mr. Knight laughed along with the others. "That's right, Tom. And if it weren't for humor, KSF wouldn't be where it is today. There's a reason my garden fertilizer is a big seller with the city slickers down in Kansas City and up in Denver. Because with brand names like Dung Shui and Pie-Agri, we're not only helping 'em raise fine flowers, we're raising their spirits. You know my motto: If you can't laugh at yourself, you might as well go jump in a settling pond.

"Now seriously, folks," he continued, "this is the first year KSF has made a profit, and I intend to celebrate that by investing in our future. That's what the Patience Revival Project is all about. I mean, if little ol' Lucas can be a tourist mecca with a cement version of the Garden of Eden, why can't we come up with something as good? So, now it's time to open up the mike to ideas. And if we all hear one we like, then the Patience Revival Project is gonna get behind it one hundred and ten percent. Who wants to start?"

No one moved.

Jim fought off the urge to get up. He couldn't wait to announce his news about the American Toilet Museum. But he didn't want to blow everyone out of the water before they had a chance to speak. He was saving the best for last.

Someone did go first. Then a steady stream of people stepped up to the microphone.

The next hour went something like this:

- Mr. Lockhart proposed that if Oakley had the biggest prairie dog in the world, and Cawker City had the world's biggest ball of twine, why couldn't Patience have the biggest ball of duct tape?
- Not original enough, the others said.
- Lillian Huffaker proposed turning Patience into the Marble Capital of the World. She offered her collection of cat's eyes, clays, clearies, steelies, and boulders to start it off.
- Not big enough, the audience pointed out.
- Zain Rashid felt they weren't thinking American enough. He wanted to build a huge maze, but not in a cornfield like most mazes. The Amazing Maze of Metal would be made from old farm equipment, and people could get lost in it while driving their four-wheelers and ATVs.
- Red Olabuff protested that Zain had stolen the maze idea from his Mr. Tired Tires website, which offered to build mazes and putt-putt golf courses from old tires.
- For the sake of community spirit, Mr. Knight suggested all maze proposals be dropped.
- Mrs. Bickers campaigned for a Kansas version of the ball dropping in Times Square. She envisioned a huge crowd ringing cowbells and counting down to the New Year as a prairie dog was slowly lowered from the old grain elevator.

- Someone pointed out that the only crowd it would attract would be animal rights activists.
- Everyone expected Mr. Olabuff to propose something like turning Patience into the Tired Tire Capital of the World, but he surprised them by suggesting a fire festival. It would celebrate the way prairie fires restored the soil and rid the prairie of trees. Everything would be fire themed, from the Firewater Saloon to the ten-alarm chili. He planned to dress up as Vulcan, the Roman god of fire, and lead the festival.

In the middle of Mr. Olabuff's proposal, Jake's tape recorder clicked off. He turned the tape and resumed recording as Mr. Olabuff summed up his idea.

"It would be like those strawberry festivals where people come and pick their own. Except at the High Plains Fire Festival you could start your own grass fire. Do you have any idea how many people would go for that?"

As people debated the fire festival's pros and cons, Jake decided he needed a reporter break. He checked to see that the tape recorder was running and slipped downstairs.

20   hark! enter death!

The town hall basement wasn't as creepy as the coffin house, but it still scored high on the menace meter. There were plenty of cobwebs and dark corners, and there was no telling what could be hiding behind the three massive stone pillars that divided the room.

Jake had been in the town hall basement once before, when he helped his father collect several old toilets that had been replaced with newer models. His father had a collection of local toilets he planned to display in their own section at the ATM. He planned to call it County Seats.

From the bottom of the stairs, Jake called toward the cocoon of light in the far corner. "Hey, Cricket, you there?"

"Yeah," came her answer.

He hurried past the shadowy pillars and found Sira standing at a long table between floor-to-ceiling shelves.

She was leaning over an old yellow newspaper and wore white gloves.

"What's with the gloves?"

"History, Jake. It's very delicate." She waved a glove over the newspaper. "This one's over seventy years old." She pointed at the surrounding shelves. They looked like they were built for maps, or really big pizzas. "You're looking at ninety years of the *Rose Petal Press,* and you won't believe what I just found."

"What?"

She glanced down at the open paper and read the date at the top of the page. "July 15, 1934."

He braced for the two facts about '15 and '34 that were sure to follow. They didn't.

"Ring a bell?" she asked.

"No."

She carefully lifted the paper and turned it back to the front page. Jake's eyes widened as he saw the headline.

PATIENCE FOUNDER
JEREMIAH WATERS DIES

"Listen to this." She read from a column. " 'On Monday last, Jeremiah Waters fell down the stairs of his ranch house and struck his head. After three days of delirium resulting from his fall, he passed away. Family members who were gathered at Mr. Waters's bedside said he died peacefully. When asked if he had any last words, Jud Waters, his only son, reported that before he slipped away, the elderly Mr. Waters opened his eyes. "They shone with a clarity I had not seen in days," said Jud. "His pale cheeks flushed with a last bloom of life. His voice burst from his throat with a strength that gave us hope he might live another decade. But the words he spoke were akin to the riddles he had been speaking for days. His last words were this: *I fall leaving unknowable secrets. Hark! Enter death!* Then he closed his eyes," Jud said, "and less than a minute passed before his breathing stopped and he marched on to meet his maker." ' "

She looked at Jake. "You ever heard that before?"

He stared down at the yellow paper as the tiny words blurred out of focus. "No."

"Has your father?"

"I don't know."

She grabbed his arm and he jumped. "Jake, this could be a clue."

"A clue to what?"

"To the map. Or to where he buried the trunk."

"You know about the trunk?"

She threw up her hands in protest. "Hel-lo! I've been reading the *Rose Petal Press* from October 26, 1870, to July 15, 1934. I know everything!"

"Then you know about the Plunger of Destiny."

"They don't mention it in the newspaper stories, but of course I know about it. It's part of the legend."

Jake hesitated. "Uh, it's not a legend."

Sira stared at him. "What do you mean?"

He sagged into a chair. Being on detective duty most of the day had wiped him out. He didn't want to break his promise to his father, but he wasn't sure he could handle another day under the dangling sword of doom. Not alone, anyway.

She sat in the chair next to him. "You don't look so good, Tweener. Are you okay?"

He looked into her large brown eyes. "Can you keep a secret?"

"Have I blabbed to anyone about your vow to get out of town?"

"No," he admitted. He took a deep breath and searched for the right words. He only found four. "The Plunger of Destiny."

"Yeah"—she nodded encouragingly—"I told you I know all about it. It's—"

"Real," he blurted.

Cricket didn't flinch. "How do you know?"

"My dad brought it back."

She stared with widening eyes. "Here? To Patience?"

"Here."

Her eyes gleamed. "That's so freaky!"

"It's not freaky!" he exploded. "It's terrible!"

She pulled back, lifting her white gloves. "Okay-okay, don't blow a gasket. Go back to the beginning. How'd it get here?"

After Jake told her about his father finding the Plunger on eBay and buying it for his museum, he asked her if she believed in the curse, including the final destruction. She told him that her grandparents believed in curses and her parents only pretended to believe in them to make her grandparents happy. But she, the first all-American Rashid, did not believe in curses. "I believe in history, the Bill of

Rights, and the right of women to play Major League Baseball," she ended triumphantly.

It was more of an answer than he wanted to hear.

"What about you?" she asked. "Do you believe the curse is a hundred percent for real?"

Before he could answer, Cricket leaped. "Wait a minute, of course you do! That's why you told me not to come into town today. You were worried about me dying in the final blowout." She touched his arm with a gloved hand. "Jake, that was really sweet."

As heat surged into his cheeks, he heard his father's voice in the room above. He quickly stood up, knocking his chair over backward. "I gotta go hear my dad." He headed for the stairs. Reaching enough shadow to cover his blush, he turned back and pointed at the old newspaper. "If you wanna hear some news that's fresher than 1934, you might wanna come."

" '34," she proclaimed as she stripped off her white gloves. "The founder of Patience dies and leaves a clue to buried treasure."

21   dirty words

Jake and Sira stood at the top of the stairs and listened as Jim Waters proposed how Patience could fill a slot in every travel brochure rack in the state. The ATM. The American Toilet Museum.

It was late. The small crowd was restless and grumpy. Brainstorming how to compete with a concrete Eden and the world's biggest ball of twine wasn't easy. But that wasn't what was making them irritable. They already knew about Jim's dream of a toilet museum. About his house stuffed with bathroom junk. A lot of it had once belonged to them. They'd been letting Jim haul away their discarded toilets, tubs, and sinks for years.

"I know, I know," Jim said over the rising murmur of crankiness. "But if we're going to create something that sets us apart, we have to look to what makes Patience unique. We have to think homegrown. An amazing metal maze, a prairie dog drop, and a fire festival are all good ideas, but they're not homegrown. Now, an American toilet museum is part of our history."

The murmur grew louder.

"Why in tarnation would we want a toilet museum?" asked Oil Can. He spit into his tuna can. "Thanks to KSF, we're already known as the stinkiest town in the west."

"That's right," Mrs. Bickers chimed in. "We've been called Cow Pie Junction, Doodoo City, and Crapola, Kansas."

"We're already the laughingstock of the state," shouted Mr. Olabuff. "If we open a toilet museum we'll be the butt of every butt joke in the country!"

Over the laughter, someone yelled, "Take a seat, Jim."

"On the porcelain throne!" someone added.

As much as Jake felt for his father, he was glad about one thing. He was getting it all on tape. Maybe if he played it for him enough times, his father would finally give up on his toilet museum and stop dragging the family name through you-know-what.

Jim didn't budge. He knew his idea was a hard sell. All the great ones were. It was time to play one of his trump cards. He leaned into the mike. "Let me ask you a question." His low voice quieted the crowd. "How many of you know what happened to the original Dolphin Deluge Washdown Water Closet?"

The room went silent. The toilet that had triggered the Curse of Andars Cass didn't get talked about much anymore. Some believed it was bad luck to bring it up. Some preferred to leave it buried in the drifting dunes of memory.

Jim broke the tense silence. "Well, I'm here to tell you,

the Dolphin Deluge is still here. And it's a gold mine waiting to happen."

Sira elbowed Jake in the ribs and whispered, "Really?"

"Shhh," he hissed back. He was still on detective duty, and this was a crucial moment. He scanned the faces locked on his father. They stared with prairie eyes. But Jake wasn't sure what they were seeing. Fertile ground, or the wrath of God coming over the horizon?

Mr. Knight stood up and cleared his throat. "Jim, with all due respect to your family, and all the Waters men and women who have done so much for this town, I'd like to say one thing. The Knight family may have been here a year or two less than your people, but my family has never forgotten the history of our godforsaken little town. And the fact is, the day that *toilet* came to Patience was the day all the trouble began." His voice rose as the cork on his emotions loosened. "A gold mine, you call it? That thing was nothin' but a Trojan horse of trouble. The fact is, if it weren't for that infernal toilet this town never would have been cursed! This town never would've begun the long slide—no, the long *flush* it's been suffering for one hundred and twenty-eight years! So don't think for a minute that KSF, the one thing that's keeping this town alive, is gonna give a plug nickel toward puttin' the original Waters family crapper on a pedestal!"

The crowd burst into enthusiastic applause.

Jim watched with a hard smile.

Jake knew exactly what he was thinking. Sometimes things have to get worse before they get better.

"It's your money, Marvin," Jim said calmly, then turned

to the others. "I know you think I'm halfway to the nut-house, but I want you to know, just so there's no surprises around here." He pulled a letter from his back pocket and held it up. "This is from the state historical society. And they're thinking about giving me a grant to start my museum."

There was no applause, no congratulations, not even a boo or a hiss as the great-great-grandson of Jeremiah Waters strode up the aisle, picked up his acrostic magazine, and walked out.

Jake noticed the strangest thing. As his father left, no one looked at him. They glanced away. After the door rattled shut, the silence was menacing. It was a silence only heard in small towns. The silence reserved for a man who has gone against the tribe.

The moment he heard that silence, Jake knew what it was. The silence of yet another way the end might come. Besides a big bang, or death by a thousand cuts, the final destruction of Patience could also come from within. An inside job.

He felt someone shaking him. "Jake."

If Sira said something after that, he didn't hear it. He snatched the tape recorder off the piano and ran the gauntlet of prairie eyes.

22 a walk home

The night sky squeezed the last color out of the sunset. Jake jumped on his bike and rode after the figure retreating down the street. His insides tumbled with emotions, but the one that pressed the hardest was the ache of sympathy for his father. He'd been shunned. He was alone. Jake knew about feeling alone.

He jumped off his bike and walked beside his father.

Jim slowed his pace. "You know why they call 'em small towns?"

"Why?" Jake obliged.

" 'Cause they're filled with small-minded people." Jim took off his hat and ran a hand through his hair. "You know what else?"

"What?"

"You're not the first J. Waters that wanted out."

Jake tripped on an edge of brick. "I'm not?"

"Nope. I know what it feels like to wanna turn your back on this place. To start anew somewhere else."

"You?"

Jim glanced down at Jake. "Is that so surprising?"

"Well, yeah."

His father looked ahead into the gathering darkness. "After I met your mother and we got married, that's what I did. I got away from here. Got as far as Wichita. But then she got sick. You were just a baby, and we had to come back. We needed to come live with your grandmother. So we came back . . . and here we stayed, in this brain-shrinking backwater. That's what this town should do. Change its name to Brain Reduction, Kansas."

They walked another half block, listening to the dry ripple of the wind in the cottonwoods.

Jake finally screwed up the courage to ask a question he'd always wanted to. "Mom died when I was three. We could have left after that. Why didn't we?"

Jim waved off a mosquito with his hat. "I always told myself it was because it was my turn to take care of Grandma. But the real reason is because I'm not as smart and cunning as the fox. For the most part, we're all dumb as fleas."

"Fleas?"

"I've never told you about the fox and the fleas?"

Jake thought he'd heard all his father's stories. A hundred times. He shook his head.

Jim tugged his hat back on. "There was a fox infested with fleas. The fleas were driving him crazy. So he took up a stick in his mouth and did something foxes hate to do. He walked into a lake. The deeper he got, the more the fleas jumped up his flanks and onto his back. He kept going deeper until only his head was above the water. The fleas hopped on his head. Then the fox did what every instinct told him not to. He submerged his head under the water until only the stick was above the surface. The fleas all jumped on the stick, and the fox let go of the stick. The fox was rid of his fleas, and the fleas drifted away to their fate."

"The end?" Jake asked.

"The end."

"Which J. Waters made that story up?"

"None of 'em. Foxes have really been known to do that. If we were as smart as the fox, we could do the same with the *fleas* in our lives. All the pestering fears and troubles that gnaw at us. But when our lives are infested with troubles, do we use our brains? Do we take a risk to get rid of 'em? Do we go under? No, we follow our base instincts. We cling to our raft of fears."

Jake was startled to hear the bitterness in his father's voice. He'd never heard it before.

As Jim went on, his voice softened. "When your mother died, I wasn't smart like the fox. When my chance came to hold my breath and go under, I didn't have the strength. When the chance came for us to get out, I didn't have the courage. If anything, I was more like a flea. I hopped on the stick, and here we've floated ever since."

"Left to our fate," Jake added.

"Yes and no." Jim's eyes brightened as he raised a finger. "That was then and this is now. Now I'm the fox. *We're* the fox. We're going underwater, Jake. And when we come back up, it's going to be a whole new world."

As his pace quickened, Jake had to hustle to keep up.

"The museum is going to happen. Look what we've got. The first flush toilet west of the Mississippi. The first toilet plunger ever invented. The state historical society. And that's only the beginning. We've got the curse. But we're going to call it the *Legend* of the Plunger of Destiny. Who knows how far it will go? The museum could grow into a theme park." Jim swept his hands toward the stars. "I see a water park with plumbing-themed rides. I see haunted outhouses. I see reenactments of the day Blackbeard attacked the ranch. I see an Imax movie!"

As they neared the corner of Courage and Endurance, Jake was glad his father was back to his old self.

But so was Jake. His eyes were fixed on the coffin house jutting from the ground. Usually, when he came home at night, he went around the block to avoid it. Now he had to go right past it. In the growing darkness, the house looked like a great toad, half-burrowed in the earth, waiting to snare anything that happened by. Just waiting for the curse to prod it into action.

As they drew closer, Jake waged his own battle against the instincts churning inside him, stirring up eddies of fear.

An approaching headlight reflected in one of the coffin house's low windows. All Jake saw was the flicker of a glittering eye.

He snapped into action, leaped on his bike, and pedaled.

"Turn on your light," Jim shouted after him.

Jake flipped on the flashlight in the clip on his handle-bars and rode toward the highway. Toward the full moon that soared above Camp Stakeout.

He leaned his bike against the cottonwood tree at the quarry, turned off the flashlight, and left it in the clip. The moon was so bright he didn't need it.

As he climbed the steep path to Tabletop Rock, he made sure to be extra noisy. Snakes. But the only thing he saw that surprised him was his moon shadow.

He crawled into the pup tent and stretched out on top of his sleeping bag. It was too hot to get in. Especially since he was sleeping in his shorts, T-shirt, and shoes. Just in case something happened in the middle of the night.

He pulled the tape recorder from his pocket, rewound it for a couple of seconds, and played back the eerie silence at the end of the town meeting. Maybe, he thought, the recording had picked up something. Some kind of ghostly echo that would reveal a clue to the how and when of the final destruction. But there was only the hiss of a cheap recorder.

After he heard the clunk of it being grabbed off the piano, and his footsteps running out, he stopped the tape. Then he pressed the record button. Like the detectives he'd seen on TV, he made notes on his find-ings for the day. "Big bang, thousand cuts, or inside job. Don't know which, but am on the lookout for all three."

He hit the stop button. He could have elaborated but chose not to. What if someone listened to the tape and found out about the Plunger? He set the recorder within reach, at the ready in case something happened.

The chorus of night noise flooded around him. Crickets, cicadas, the throaty trill of frogs, and the rustling titter of the cottonwood in the dry part of the quarry. But the night sounds couldn't drown out the herky-jerky thoughts still thumping in his head like Super Balls in a box.

He wondered if Wanda was psychic. Or if she had her own foxlike instincts? Like animals that know something's wrong and start moving to high ground before the floodwaters come.

He kicked himself for telling Sira about the Plunger of Destiny. If she told someone and the town found out, he wondered if everything would come full circle. Would they tar and feather his father and ride him out of town on a rail? Would Jake be riding behind him on a minirail?

He tried to twist his brain around Jeremiah's bizarre last words. "I fall leaving unknowable secrets. Hark! Enter Death!" Did they really talk like that back then? Or did death make you say the darndest things?

And he wished he could hit the rewind button. Go back twenty-four hours. When his only worry was how he was going to do in Game 5.

The cascade of thoughts finally began to settle. The wind in the cottonwood and its dry rendition of falling rain began to cool his troubled mind.

Some Plains Indians believe the wind sings a thousand songs in a thousand voices. The song of buffalo grass. The song of swirling leaves. On the day the Plunger of Destiny returned to Patience, it was the song of the cottonwood that finally lulled Jake Waters to sleep.

23   day two on curse patrol

After a breakfast of two granola bars and water, Jake headed back to town for Game 6. The day before, he'd brought his uniform and glove to the quarry in case he overslept and had to go straight to the game. But the game was the least of his worries. He was on high alert. On the lookout, hear-out, sniff-out, touch-out, and taste-out for the curse's next move.

The first attention-grabber came as he rode past the Tumbleweed Motel. Sira swooped out from behind the motel on her bike and shot toward him. Her Louisville Slugger lay across her handlebars. She caught up with him as he made the turnoff into town.

"What are you doing out here?" she asked.

He wasn't in the mood to explain. "Warming up."

She laughed. "Nice try, Tweener. I stopped by your house last night after the meeting. Your dad told me you went camping. Where'd you go?"

He gave up. He had never been a good liar. "The quarry."

"Well, that answers my question from last night."

"What question?" Cricket was already jumping and it wasn't even eight-thirty.

"You really do believe in the curse."

"So what if I do? If you had my family history, you'd believe it too."

Their bikes rattled over the railroad tracks.

She gave him a sympathetic smile. "True, but I've got news for you, Tween. Even if the curse is real, the final destruction isn't coming until *after* Game 7."

"What makes you so sure?"

She steered with one hand and thrust her bat in the air. " 'Cause I've got the Bat of Destiny. And the Bat of Destiny says I'm gonna win the World Series!"

During Game 6, Jake waited for something awful to happen. A beanball, a who's-got-it confusion-cracker, or one of the KSF trucks careening out of control and plowing into the bleachers during the Seventh-Inning Stench.

But nothing bad happened.

In fact, good things happened right and left. All his mother's jock genes kicked in and Jake had his best game of the Series. For the first time in her life, Rosie hit a ball over the infield and got a double. Howie hit the longest home run anyone could remember. And when Jim Waters showed up at the beginning of the game, no one hung garlic bulbs around their neck or pulled out wooden stakes.

People looked him in the eye and spoke to him as if the incident at the meeting had never happened. The only time it came up was when Jake came to bat with the bases loaded. Oil Can yelled, "Come on, Tweener, knock one into the Dolphin Deluge!" Everyone thought it was a big joke.

After Howie hit a line drive to the shortstop for the last out of the game, Jake trotted in from left field. The crowd applauded the Workup Wildcats for a terrific game.

"If anyone wants to know," Mrs. Knight shouted, "the record for the most points scored in a World Series game has just been broken. The new record is 105 points."

Sira ran up next to Jake. "Oh-five. In 1905, the first forward pass in the history of football was thrown in Kansas in a game between Washburn University and Fairmont College."

For once, Jake was glad to hear one of Sira's freaky facts. It meant she wasn't upset by slipping from first to third place. And it wasn't because her Louisville Slugger had gone cold. It was because Jake and Howie were blasting the ball all over the field.

"The new leader at the end of Game 6," Mrs. Knight announced, "is Howie 'Kapowie' Knight, with 87 points."

Sira scrunched her face, trying to recall the fact that went with 87.

"In second place, with his best day ever, Jake 'Tweener' Waters, with 84 points."

Sira gave Jake a high five. " '84. In 1884, the first bull-fight in America was held in Dodge City, Kansas."

"And not far behind," Mrs. Knight continued, "in third place, Sira 'the Cricket' Rashid, with 76 points."

Mrs. Bickers shouted from her porch, "Thatta way, Cricket. Let 'em get out front, then spank 'em on the way by!"

As the crowd laughed, Sira grinned and whispered to Jake. " '76. In 1976, Kansas celebrated the bicentennial by making a full-sized Liberty Bell out of Turkey Red wheat."

While Mrs. Knight worked through the other scores and Sira rattled off facts, Jake stopped listening. A smell had grabbed his attention. It was a slight whiff of the Seventh-Inning Stench, even though the last KSF truck had passed by a half hour before. The smell was coming from the direction of KSF. Whenever the stink blew into Patience, it meant the wind had shifted and was coming from the northwest.

Jake checked the horizon beyond the outfield. The sky was clear, just like it had been all morning. Then he checked the sky to the south. Only a few puffy clouds.

After Mrs. Knight finished the standings and the crowd broke up, Howie punched Jake in the arm. "Way to go, killer. Just don't do the same tomorrow, okay? This is *my* Series." He pounded his chest like a gorilla. "King Kapowie!"

Sira slid over to Howie as she remembered something. "87. Nice score, Howie. Did you know that in 1887, women in Kansas got the right to vote in town elections, and Argonia, Kansas, elected the first woman mayor in America?"

Howie threw up his hands. "Great. Another number from Sira's Book of Slumber. The only number I care about is Game 7, which is, guess what, my lucky number."

Sira's brow knitted. "Mine too, if I could find a freaky or fascinating fact that happened in oh-seven."

Howie put a hand on Sira's forehead like she had a fever. "Yep, the egghead is overheating again." He turned to Jake. "What do you think, Doc, should we take her to the quarry and throw her in?"

"Yeah." Jake nodded. "Let's do it."

The three of them led the way as the other five Workup Wildcats followed on their bikes. There was no better way to celebrate their record-scoring game than with a cold plunge into the quarry.

Howie leaped off his bike first. He scrambled up the rocky path ahead of the rest. "Last one in's a pig's pucky-booboo!"

As Jake started up the path, dodging the loose rocks tumbling down behind Howie, a strange thing happened. Everything slowed down, like the world had clicked into slow motion. A fist twisted in Jake's gut as he realized what it was. It was the slow-mo before an accident.

"Howie, wait!"

But Howie was already on Tabletop Rock throwing his shirt off.

"Don't jump!" Jake yelled.

"Nice try, loser!" Howie scrambled out of his pants.

Jake reached Tabletop just as Howie did a running leap right over Vandenberg rock and yelled, "Howie-bunga!"

Jake heard the splash as he ran to the edge. A white mushroom cap of water spread over Last Crack Rock. The fist in his gut shot up like an uppercut, knocking the air out of him. He couldn't breathe.

Howie's head suddenly punctured the surface. "C'mon in! The water hasn't been peed in since you woke up this morning!"

The other kids laughed and tore off uniforms. Jake sucked in air.

Sira stopped next to him and began stripping down to her spandex and sports bra. "What's the matter? Is there some monster down there you're not telling us about?"

As Jake began pulling off his uniform, he kicked himself for being so paranoid. Yesterday, nothing major had gone down, and today, only good things had happened. He was beginning to wonder if believing in the curse was making him as loopy as his dad. Maybe it was another Waters gene he needed to switch off. The half-bubble-off-plumb gene.

As other kids jumped into the water, Sira stepped down to Kennedy and turned back with a mocking smile. "See you down there, pig's pucky-booboo."

For the next hour Jake forgot about the curse. He was too busy playing a game of water polo that started up after one of the kids found a hedge apple floating in the water.

Sira was the first one to leave the game and climb back up to Tabletop. Reaching the top, she called down to the others. "Hey, guys, better get up here."

"What?" Howie shouted back up.

"Don't ask, just get."

Jake was the first to scramble up the rock wall. There was something in her voice that snapped him back to detective mode.

When he reached Tabletop, she was standing with her back to him and staring at the horizon. He jumped up beside her as the chill on his wet skin turned to goose bumps.

A line of towering thunderheads was rolling in from the northwest. His father called them the "black buffaloes who eat blue skies for lunch." And these black buffaloes looked like they wanted a piece of Patience for dessert.

"Do you think we can make it back to town?" she asked.

"No way." Jake studied the gray tongues hanging down from the thunderheads. "And I'm not sure it's rain."

That's the thing about the black buffaloes who eat blue skies for lunch. The ones that eat too much sky too fast get wicked cases of indigestion. And whether you're a cloud or a carnivore, binge eating usually ends the same way. Upchucking. Add some lightning and thunder and you've got a herd of hurling black buffaloes.

A flash of lightning licked down from one of the storm clouds and jabbed into a field west of town. A ripping clap of thunder greeted Howie as he joined them.

"Whoa! Where did those come from?"

"Don't know." Jake felt the cold air surging in front of the storm. "But it's gonna be here in about two minutes." He grabbed a big rock and pushed it inside his pup tent so the storm wouldn't blow it into the quarry.

As the younger kids reached Tabletop, they froze at the sight of the huge storm rolling over Patience.

Jake tried to sound calm. "Grab your clothes, get down to the pit, and find a block to hide under."

Rosie started to pull on her uniform. "No," he ordered. "Get dressed after you're under cover."

Howie hustled the younger kids down the rocky path. "Go-go-go! Get under a rock, not the tree. It's a lightning magnet. Go-go-go!"

Jake and Sira stole one last look at the thunderheads. The black herd had swallowed Patience. Gray-black tongues stretched down from the roiling beasts as they spilled their guts.

"You think this is it?" she asked.

He shot her a look. "You mean the curse?"

"Yeah."

"I thought you didn't believe in curses."

She started to answer, but they both flinched as a trident of lightning plunged into the distant highway. The ear-splitting explosion that followed was the only starter gun they needed. They raced down the path, half-bouncing, half-sliding as they went. They dashed for an overhang of cut limestone where Howie and two other kids had taken cover. Jake and Sira had to squeeze against them to fit underneath.

The sky darkened and the storm slid over them like a giant stadium closing its roof. Then came the sound of a million snare drums. As lightning and thunder flashed and reverberated against the limestone walls, the sky buffaloes blew their lunch. Not the kind of upchuck that slimes. The kind that slams.

Hail.

Stones the size of Ping-Pong balls shattered on the limestone blocks while others pounded the ground.

Under the overhang, Jake's and Sira's noses were inches from the cascade of ice. Clutching their uniforms against the chill, they were too scared to get dressed. If they lost their balance and fell forward, it was the kind of hail that could dent your skull. In the history of head bonks, it was known as the hail-nailer idiot-maker.

While hailstorms can destroy crops, turn auto dealerships into junkyards, and knock out heavyweight champions, there's one good thing about them. They don't last long. Rain clouds can take days to get everything out. Hailstorms like to get it over with.

When it ended, the limestone pit was transformed. The ground was covered in three inches of hailstones and ice chips. It looked like God had dropped his Slushee.

Jake plowed through the hail in his bare feet. The broken ice made it feel like he was walking through thorns. He tried to pull one of his baseball shoes on, but he slipped and fell. The others laughed as they tugged on their shoes under the overhang. Jake didn't think it was funny. Still on his back, and getting an icy massage, he pulled on his pants and shoes.

His baseball shoes made walking easier. He found the other three kids under another overhang. No one was hurt.

He wondered if everyone in town had been so lucky.

24 half a town

As they made their way to their bikes, the sun blasted from behind a cloud. It transformed the hail into a sea of sparkling diamonds. Under the cottonwood, they found their bikes half-buried in an icy trail mix of hail, leaves, and broken twigs.

Jake figured if the hail had stripped the cottonwood half clean, his pup tent was probably a goner. Death by a thousand rips. There was no time to check. He was more worried about Patience. Death by a thousand dings.

Picking up an ice-cold bike and straddling a frigid seat on a hot summer day was a new sensation for all of them. At first they rode unsteadily through the hail, but by the time they reached the gravel road Howie had discovered a new game. If you rode over a hailstone just right, it shot off to the side and could hit another biker.

As the kids dodged and weaved through the stones, shooting ice marbles at each other, Jake plowed ahead. He wasn't in a playful mood. And if this was the end, it looked like something he remembered from Sunday school. The world was going to end in fire and ice. There was no shortage of ice, and no telling what the lightning might have started in town.

While Sira tried to catch up to him, Jake checked out the fields of wheat and corn flanking the road. The wheat was flattened and sticking up in jagged cowlicks. The corn was shredded and tattered like someone had harvested it with a machine gun.

Reaching the highway, the riding got easier. Most of the shattered hail on the asphalt was now a slushy gravel of melting ice. Fingers of steam curled up from the road, creating a misty ribbon of white leading back to town.

Sira kept her front tire in the trail Jake cut through the slush. "Shouldn't we wait for the others?"

"Howie's with 'em," he answered. "They're okay." He squinted through the thickening mist rising off the road. "Listen for cars, and watch out for fallen power lines."

When they reached the turnoff into town and the motel, they saw Sira's parents surveying the damage. The red neon lights that had spelled out TUMBLEWEED MOTEL were gone. The hail had punched in the windshield of the Rashids' station wagon. It was now the car with a thousand dimples. But no one was smiling.

Mrs. Rashid spotted Jake and Sira. "Nisira!" she shouted, and slid over the ice with outstretched arms.

Sira grimaced. She wanted to go into town with Jake and see the damage. She didn't want to be stuck at home doing a thank-Vishnu-we're-safe hug.

"Mom, I can't stop!" she yelled as she coasted through a blanket of chipped ice. "It's solid ice!"

As they approached the railroad tracks, the layer of hail became so thick they had to get off their bikes. They dropped them on the roadside and shuffled through ankle-deep hail. The sight before them looked like a dream.

The bottom half of Patience was swallowed in fog, while the second stories of houses and buildings rose above it, floating like boathouses on "Lake Patience." The tops of telephone poles jutted up like buoys, and trunkless trees looked like leafless, shattered bushes. Below that, everything was Christmas card white. Never mind that it was August and the heat was edging back to ninety.

They entered the fog and approached the intersection at Endurance Street. Jake didn't know what was creepier: that the coffin house on the corner was now an ominous outline in the swirling mist, or that the thick layer of hail made it look like it had crouched deeper into the ground.

As they moved into town, more shapes loomed out of the fog. A few battered cars and trucks. Broken branches and limbs stuck up from the hail. The metal awnings over the sidewalks had a fresh set of dings in their sagging skins.

"My feet are freezing," Sira said. "I wish I had my boots." Her voice seemed to boom in the eerie stillness.

"Me too," Jake said. "Follow me." He moved to the sidewalk on the left side of the street. Under the metal awning there was only a thin layer of ice shards. As they walked past empty stores, their feet warmed up.

"Where is everybody?" she asked.

"I don't know."

"Maybe they all got their heads bashed in."

"Nah," he said with a frown. "They might be stupid for living here, but they've got the sense to get out of a hailstorm."

"Whatever, I think I'm going to get a freaky and fascinating fact out of this."

"Yeah," he agreed. "Too bad it's not oh-seven."

"Really." Sira looked out at the hail-covered street. "I just figured out what it looks like."

"What?"

"Like the whole place got put into mothballs."

"It's worse than that," he said as small mountains of black tires loomed out of the mist. "You know how they always pull a white sheet over a dead body?"

"Yeah."

"I think the curse just pulled a white sheet over Patience."

Sira laughed nervously. "Here's the creepy part. We're on the wrong side of the sheet."

They paused at the end of the awning. If they wanted to keep going they had to wade through the hail again. He plowed into the ice. Sira followed.

The outline of the Smoky Hill Cafe pushed out of the mist, along with the faint sound of voices.

"Do you hear that?" Sira whispered.

Before he could answer, the sound of muffled laughter sent him into a shuffling jog. He pulled open the cafe door.

Inside, Oil Can Lockhart, Mrs. Huffaker, and Mr. Olabuff were gathered around an old-fashioned ice cream maker. Oil Can steadily turned the crank on the ice cream maker as he glanced up at Jake and Sira. "They can smell it a mile away."

"Brings 'em in like bees to the buttercup," Mrs. Huffaker added.

Mr. Olabuff pounced on the kids' puzzled expressions. "Thunderstone ice cream!" He pulled a golf ball–sized hailstone out of a bucket and tossed it to Jake.

Jake caught it and grinned with relief. If the chief of the volunteer fire department was making thunderstone ice cream, then the fire and ice ending was a false alarm. But best of all, they were going to celebrate the near miss with Mrs. Huffaker's famous ice cream.

As he and Sira waited for the ice cream, the other Workup Wildcats arrived at the cafe, along with half of Patience. Since there were no power lines down, no fires to put out, and no bodies in the street, whatever damage assessment needed to be done could wait until everyone participated in the cafe's greatest tradition. Thunderstone peach ice cream.

Jake, Sira, and Howie took their ice cream bowls outside to a picnic table, brushed off the melting hail, and sat.

Jake's first taste of creamy peach perfection hit his mouth like a pebble in clear water. The ripples of pleasure spread in all directions. Lips, tongue, throat, right into his brain.

The cafe's screen door creaked open. Oil Can stepped out, holding a bowl of ice cream. "You know why thunderstone ice cream tastes so good?"

With their mouths full, the threesome could only manage, "Mmm-mmm."

Oil Can gestured to the sea of hail covering the street. "Because not everybody gets to live like this."

"Like what?" Sira asked.

"Where the sky's so close, you can eat it." Oil Can jammed a spoonful of ice cream into his mouth.

Jake took another bite and let the glorious sensation of thunderstone peach ice cream surge through him. It felt like a prayer being answered. The prayer went like this. *Dear God, if the end is coming, can it please be after dessert?*

25 crime and punishment

By midafternoon, the temperature was back to a hundred. Most of the hail had melted except for scattered piles where it had been shoveled. Steam rose from the piles like smoking mounds of ash. The only other hail that hadn't melted was the stashes of thunderstones that Mrs. Huffaker told kids to pack in their freezers. That is, if they wanted future servings of thunderstone ice cream.

While Jake and Howie stuffed a large stash in the Rashids' basement freezer at the motel, Sira got a lecture from her father about not stopping when she rode by on her bike. She probably would have been grounded, but she did show up with a container of thunderstone ice cream. Apology accepted, Sira left her parents in the kitchen marveling over bowls of peach-filled bliss.

In front of the motel, Jake and Howie stood next to the Waters & Son Plumbing van. Howie was inspecting the outside of the van.

"I'm telling you," Jake told him, "you won't find any new dings. He went to Goodland on a parts run and missed the whole thing."

Unconvinced, Howie disappeared around the other side of the van, continuing his inspection.

As Sira came out of the office she saw Jim walking over from Gas & Goodies with a soda and a bag of chips. "Hey, Mr. Waters."

"I saw your bikes," he said. "Anybody hurt?"

"Nope, but it was unbelievable!" she exclaimed. "We really thought this was it."

Jim gave her a puzzled look.

Jake started to speak but Sira cut in. "You know, the curse."

Jim shot Jake an accusing look. Jake raised a finger to shush Sira but she went on. "And the return of the—"

"Ahhhhhh!" Jake screamed as he flailed his arms. "Did you see the size of that bee?"

Sira gave him a bug-eyed look. "What bee?"

He gestured with his head. "It went behind the van."

Howie came around the back of the van. His interest in finding hail dings had vanished. "The curse, and the return of what?"

Sira froze.

"The return of the heat wave," Jim interjected.

"Yeah, the return of the heat wave," Jake echoed. "Cricket was telling me earlier about the heat wave of 1936. We thought we might be able to break the record."

"Right," Sira jumped in, joining the cover-up. "Did you know, Howie, in 1936 it was over a hundred degrees in

Kansas thirty-six days in a row. We've had five in a row. Thirty-two more to go and we set a new record!"

Howie's eyes dropped shut. "Sira's Book of Slumber strikes again."

Jake and Sira relaxed. He was buying it.

Jim opened his soda. "Listen, you three, I need help moving all the museum stuff out to the barn at the ranch. Gotta get the place ready for the history folks. Do I have any volunteers?"

Howie scooted toward his bike.

"Oh, come on, Kapowie," Jake teased. "It'll make you stronger for Game 7."

"No thanks." Howie jumped on his bike. "When it comes to moving the nasty and the gnarly, my dad keeps me plenty busy."

As Howie rode away, Jim took a swig of soda and turned to Jake. "Gee, I wonder how I'm going to punish you for sharing our little secret." He turned to Sira. "And you for almost spilling it to the world."

Jim, Jake, and Sira spent the next half hour hauling boxes down from the two upper rooms at the Waters house. The boxes overflowed with toilet history. Chamber pots, antique plumbing supply catalogs, a collection of toilet paper dispensers that ran the gamut from tins and rollers to the old standby during the outhouse era, the Sears & Roebuck catalog.

After a dozen trips up and down the stairs in the one-hundred-plus heat, they were drenched in sweat. Jim encouraged them to drink plenty of water. They were less than twenty-four hours away from Game 7 of the World Series. "Remember," he cautioned, "there's no dehydration in baseball."

As Jim and Sira maneuvered a six-foot framed print of Edward, Prince of Wales, down the stairs, Sira read the quote at the bottom of the print. " 'If I could not be a Prince, I would rather be a plumber.' He really said that?"

Jim raised an eyebrow. "You've never heard the story of the prince who wanted to be a plumber?"

"Never."

Jim happily obliged. "In 1871, when Edward, the Prince of Wales, and two of his friends visited one of his country houses, they all came down with typhoid. His friends died, but Prince Edward survived. A plumber traced the typhoid to the pipes of a newly installed water closet in the country house, and he fixed the problem. Edward was so impressed, he wished he could be a plumber." Reaching the bottom of the stairs, Jim backed out the front door.

"So why didn't he become a plumber?" Sira asked.

He took the print and propped it against the porch wall. "The prince's family made him stay in the family business and become King Edward the Seventh." He shook his head woefully. "Life is filled with such missed opportunities."

Sira giggled, then a loud noise pulled their attention upstairs.

"Jake, don't break anything!" Jim moved back inside.

She followed on his heels. "Mr. Waters, can I ask you a question?"

"Shoot."

"Where's the Plunger of Destiny?"

He stopped at the bottom of the stairs. "It's in a safe place. Why do you ask?"

"I'd love to see it."

He palmed the sweat off his forehead.

She pressed. "Next to you, I probably know more about the curse than anyone else."

"I doubt that."

"You'd be surprised. I know the Plunger of Destiny was originally called the Scepter of Satan."

He smiled, impressed.

She didn't let up. "I love history, and it's the one thing this town has a ton of."

Jim started up the stairs. "True. Too bad so much of it's a downer."

Sira jumped past him. "A 'downer' is slang from the hippie era, but you could use it in your museum's publicity material. I can see it now." She sprang to the top of the stairs and spread her hands across an imaginary banner. "The American Toilet Museum. What a Downer."

He laughed. "I like the way you think. When I open the museum, would you like a job?"

"I'm there."

Jake came out of the back room straining under the weight of an ancient-looking urinal.

"Sira just came up with a great slogan for the museum," Jim said. " 'The American Toilet Museum. What a Downer.' "

Jake grimaced as he hefted the urinal. "She loves history, she's half-crazy, and she wants to work in a toilet museum. If we weren't different colors, I might think we were switched at birth."

Sira laughed, and Jake almost tripped. Jim's hands shot under the urinal. "Careful!" He took it from Jake. "This is a Jennings corner-model urinal, circa 1900. It came from King Edward the Seventh's private railway station."

Sira jumped with excitement. "You mean the same guy who wanted to be a plumber?"

"That's right," Jim boasted as he carefully navigated the stairs. "This isn't some run-of-the-mill urinal. The crowned heads of Europe peed in this thing."

Sira grinned at Jake. "Isn't history cool?"

He dripped sweat and sarcasm. "Yeah, especially when it comes with a curse attached to it."

A few minutes later, Jake and Sira wrestled a zinc bathtub down the stairs. The phone rang in the kitchen. Jim went to answer it.

When he came out on the porch, Jim told them that he'd go ahead and run the first vanload of stuff to the ranch. In the meantime, they were to keep bringing stuff down.

After he drove away, Jake appointed himself foreman and called a water break. As they poured glasses of ice water in the kitchen, he noticed something scrawled on the notepad by the phone: "Nitrate 16." He grabbed his glass and followed Sira out to the porch.

They sat on the porch swing and rocked it to create a breeze. It was better than nothing in the sweltering heat. Jake bit down on an ice cube, reducing it to gravel in his mouth. "I say we just sit here till he gets back."

"But he said to keep moving stuff down."

"Yeah, but he also said 'there's no dehydration in base-ball.' " He chewed the ice to slush and swallowed. "Do you know what nitrate is?"

She thought for a second. "Nope. What is it?"

"All I know is that it's some kind of impurity."

"Do you have a dictionary?"

Jake had to smile. Leave it to Cricket to make the big jumps. Like from not knowing something to thinking of the dictionary. She was amazing that way.

Jim Waters stopped at Gas & Goodies and went inside. He found two gallon containers of bottled water and carried them to the front counter. As usual, Pearl was at the cash register, but the jumper swing behind the counter was un-occupied. Sean was taking a nap in a portacrib behind her.

Jim set the gallon containers on the counter. "Pearl, you're still at your aunt's place, right?"

"Yeah."

He dropped several bills on the counter. "How soon be-fore you get off work?"

"In about an hour. Why all the questions?"

"I want you to take this water home with you."

Pearl tilted her head. A straggle of blond hair fell across her wry look. "I've had a few old guys offer to buy me a drink, but never one who wanted to buy me two gallons of sky juice."

Jim ignored the jab at his age and took his change. "You probably don't know this, but I'm also the town's water supply operator. One of my duties is to submit water samples for testing on all the wells. The lab just gave me the results on your aunt's well."

Pearl's interest perked up. "Is it poisoned?"

"No, not poisoned. But no one should be drinking the water. Especially your baby. So take the water home and tell your aunt I'll be over tomorrow to see what we can do to fix the problem. If you want, I'll put the water in your car."

Sean woke up with a gurgly sound, and Pearl turned to pick him up. "Yeah, that would be great. It's around the side."

26 to the stink farm

Jake looked over Sira's shoulder as she scanned the open dictionary on the desk in his room.

"Here it is," she said. " 'Nitrate.' "

"What's it say?"

"Well, it's some kind of chemical, 'nitric acid,' and it says, 'fertilizer consisting of sodium nitrate or potassium nitrate.' "

"Fertilizer?" Jake's face scrunched in puzzlement. "If nitrate's part of fertilizer, what's it doing in Mrs. Bickers's well water?"

Sira gave him a baffled look. He explained about the water test on Mrs. Bickers's well, and how his father had followed up with a second test.

"Maybe she overfertilized her yard," Sira offered. "And it got down into her well water."

"Can nitrates do that?"

She shrugged. "I don't know, but we know someone

who probably knows more about fertilizer and nitrates than we do."

Jake smiled, getting the connection. "Howie. C'mon, let's go pay him a visit."

"Now? But we're supposed to—"

Jake was already out the door. Sira followed, dropping her objection. Moving old bathroom stuff was just another hot and sweaty job without Mr. Waters's tales of toilets and princes who would be plumbers.

Jake and Sira rode their bikes along Faith Street, and out of town toward KSF. Since they'd already gotten their daily whiff of KSF during the Seventh-Inning Stench that morning, they weren't thrilled about getting a double dose. But Jake had seen enough detective shows to know that some of the best clues are often found in the nastiest places. He also knew that most detectives had a plan. The plan he devised with Sira was simple. Split up when they got to KSF and see what they could each find out about nitrates and fertilizer.

As they approached the big KSF gate, they were enveloped by the swirling aroma of rotting manure. There was nothing subtle about the odor that surrounded KSF in a cocoon of stench. It was like they'd punctured the surface of a gas giant like Jupiter or Saturn. And once you were inside the KSF gas giant, the only relief came when your smell receptors became so overwhelmed, they went into nasal hibernation.

With noses crinkled, they rode through the open

ranch-style gate. The big arched sign over the top announced KNIGHT'S SOIL & FERTILIZER—A RESIDUALS MANAGEMENT COMPANY. The second part was Mr. Knight's attempt to dignify the bottom-line nature of KSF. It was about as effective as an empty can of air freshener.

Jake and Sira followed the entrance road, which cut through a vast stretch of settling ponds. Each pond was a third the size of a football field and filled with cow manure at various stages of drying. These ponds were one of the first links in what Mr. Knight called the manure-handling chain.

The various links in the manure-handling chain went like this:

- KSF trucks loaded with bovine waste stopped at the slump scale and got weighed.
- The heaviest trucks, the ones containing too much liquid, dumped their slop into a settling pond, where the water evaporated until it became manageable manure—known at KSF as man-man.
- The lighter trucks, the ones filled with drier man-man, were sent to the tipping dock, where the material was dumped.
- Bulldozers pushed the man-man into long windrows, where composting heated it up and killed some of the nasty things that thrive in manure.
- Loaders fed this compost, or "green gold," into the digester, a giant tube the size of an airliner cabin that worked like a slow sausage grinder.
- Three days in the digester cooked all the other

nasties out of the green gold and turned it into "black gold."

- The black gold got moved to the blending barn, where it was mixed with other materials to make Dung Shui, Pie-Agri, and the other products of KSF.
- The finished products got moved to the bagging barn, where they were sealed in plastic bags decorated with Brandy Bovine, the company mascot and spokes-cow on the KSF website.

Jake and Sira rode around the empty slump scale. Jake hadn't been out to KSF all summer. There was only one reason a kid would want to visit KSF on a regular basis. To watch the heavy equipment. Bulldozers, front loaders, and scoop loaders moved over the sprawling facility like giant metal ants. If you were into big machines, KSF was the place to be.

Besides winning the World Series, big machines were exactly what Howie was into the summer before eighth grade. It was why he'd agreed to work part-time for his dad—so he could learn how to drive bulldozers and scoop loaders. But before he could operate the big machines, Mr. Knight made sure he started small. Really small. As in buttons.

Howie's first job at KSF had been working the buttons in the slump scale office and informing the drivers where to dump their loads: in a settling pond or at the tipping dock. By starting Howie there, Mr. Knight had more than safety in mind. If Howie was going to take over KSF someday, Mr. Knight wanted his son "to learn the business from the manure up."

Jake led the way toward the tipping dock. That was where Howie worked now. He was still pushing buttons, but what the buttons did was much more exciting.

A truck cab shot a black geyser of diesel smoke in the air as it drove away from the tipping dock. Jake and Sira rode around it and spotted Howie in the control booth at the side of the dock. The dock held what the truck had been hauling: a long container about the size of a semi-trailer. It was open at the top and brimming with green-black manure.

As they got off their bikes, Howie hit a button and the tipping dock went into action. Two huge hydraulic lifters started slowly pushing one end of the container into the air. The jolt of motion caused a dark blanket of flies to balloon off the manure. The buzzing blanket settled back down on a fly's version of an all-you-can-suck buffet.

"Hey, Howie," Jake shouted above the whine of the hydraulics.

Howie stepped out of the control booth. The lifters would take several minutes to raise the container high enough to release its contents. "What are you guys doing here?"

"We've got a question."

"Yeah, where's the bathroom?" Sira jumped in. "I really gotta go."

Howie spread his arms wide. "Hey, you've come to the right place."

"No, seriously, Howie," she said, shifting from one foot to another. "Where is it?"

Howie pointed to a large metal barn. "Closest one's in the bagging barn."

Sira took off at a jog. Howie eyed the progress on the dock. The lifting end of the container was only a few feet up. "I thought you were helping your dad move toilet stuff."

"We're on break."

"So you came out here to see me move manure?"

"No, I got a question."

"Shoot."

"What do you know about nitrates?"

Howie laughed. "What do I know about nitrates?"

Jake didn't know what was so funny. "Yeah."

"For one, we're surrounded by 'em."

"I don't get it."

Howie bugged out his eyes as if everybody should know. "Nitrates are the main ingredient in cow manure."

"Can nitrates float through the air?" Jake asked. "You know, be carried by the wind."

"Oh, yeah." Howie nodded seriously. "They do it all the time."

Jake felt a surge of excitement. "Really? They can?"

"Yep, but the only flying nitrates I know about are bird poop and bat guano." Howie looked up and faked getting an eyeful of bird poop. "Splat! Oh, man, I've been slimed by nitrates!"

As Howie laughed, Jake resisted the urge to join him. "Are you saying the nitrates in cow manure don't fly around?"

"Only if they're from flying cows." Howie checked the container again. It was a third of the way up. "Since when did you care about nitrates?"

Jake had anticipated the question. Howie knew him well enough to know that nitrates, flying or otherwise, weren't on his gotta-know list. "Since I started my over-the-summer project."

"I thought you were doing a report on that bozo meeting last night."

"I was, but it turned into too much work. I've decided to do a thing on nitrates."

Howie checked the rising container again. "Well, that's all I know about 'em. Cow nitrates get dumped here, and it's mostly what goes out in the bags. Nitrates in, nitrates out. If you wanna know more, you should go talk to my pop. He's in the office."

"Good idea. Maybe I'll talk to him after the game tomorrow."

Howie grabbed Jake's arm and hustled him toward the low end of the tilting container. The high end was jutting toward the sky at a forty-five-degree angle. "You gotta see this."

"What?"

"It's like the biggest dump in the world. It's really cool. You can put it in your nitrate report." He retreated into the control booth and pointed toward the bottom end of the tipping dock. "Watch!"

Jake turned just as the hinged door at the end of the container swung open and tons of manure spilled out. A cloud of flies exploded upward as the multi-ton cow pie hit the ground like a mushy meteor hitting the earth. As it slid and grew in all directions, the worst thing was the smell. It burned Jake's nostrils and blasted his smell receptors out of hibernation. With stinging eyes, he turned away.

Howie pounded the control booth counter with his fists and bellowed with laughter. "Gotcha!"

"Very funny." Jake was glad to see Sira coming across the yard from the bagging barn.

As Jake headed for his bike, Howie staggered out of the booth, trying to control his laughter. "If that blast of gas doesn't scramble your brain for Game 7, I don't know what will."

Jake got on his bike. "Yeah, but if one blast can scramble my brain, what does inhaling it all day do?"

Howie ignored him and called to Sira. "Did you find the can?"

"Yeah, thanks," she said as she reached her bike.

"No, thank *you*!" Howie exclaimed. "For leaving us a few of your personal nitrates. We can never get enough around here. Nitrates rule!"

Jake shook his head and pushed off. "See you tomorrow, crazy Kapowie."

"Bring your A-game, both of you. 'Cause this is waa-waa-waaaaarrrrr!"

Jake waited until they got out of earshot. "So, what'd you find?"

"I checked out a bunch of fertilizer bags. They've all got 'nitrate' written all over them."

"Yeah, Howie said as much. Fertilizer is packed with nitrates."

"Why is this so important?" she asked.

"I don't know. I only know that just because we had a hailstorm that turned into peach ice cream doesn't mean the nitrates in Mrs. Bickers's well are gonna turn into chocolate."

Sira laughed. "Jake, maybe you're thinking about this too much. I mean, maybe you should start thinking about tomorrow's game."

Jake gazed ahead at the ragged stubble of Patience's skyline. "Maybe this *is* tomorrow's game."

———

That evening, Jake had dinner with his father before heading out to Camp Stakeout. He asked him about the note by the phone, "Nitrate 16." But his father was strangely evasive. All he said was that it was nothing to worry about. Jake wasn't sure if his father was mad at him for taking off to KSF, or if he just wanted to get back to moving stuff downstairs. There was still lots to do before the historical society showed up and gave the museum what his father called the big scratch 'n' sniff test.

———

At the quarry, Jake's earlier suspicions were confirmed. The hail had shredded his tent into camouflage netting. It didn't matter. The moon was up, and it was a beautiful night to sleep under the stars.

Jake dreamed he was at the opening-day party for the American Toilet Museum. It was a huge success, and it looked like the museum was going to elevate Patience from no-profile to low-profile. But then everything was ruined. A flock of flying cows bombarded the museum with nitrates.

27 game 7

The next morning, the beginning of the final game in the World Series of Workup was almost as weird as Jake's dream.

Mr. Knight was late.

Mr. Knight was never late.

Batting practice and warm-ups still started at eight-thirty because Mrs. Knight arrived with the equipment bag and Howie pitched. At least, until Jim Waters walked over from Mrs. Bickers's house and took the mound.

At ten minutes till nine, Mrs. Knight assured the fans and players, "Don't worry, he'll be here. Something must have come up at the farm."

"Like what?" Oil Can shouted from his chicken-wire dugout. "A bad batch of Dung Shui?"

Mrs. Knight ignored the laughter and opened her laptop. It wasn't easy being the First Lady of Fertilizer.

At five minutes till nine, Mr. Knight drove up in his

pickup, jumped out, and headed for the mound. He was greeted with applause and friendly ribbing.

"Just wanted to see if you could get along without me," he jauntily informed the crowd.

"Everything all right?" Jim asked as he offered him the baseball.

With his back to the crowd, Mr. Knight snatched the ball out of Jim's hand. "May the best player win."

His hostile tone startled Jim. He decided to let it go. "May the best player win," he echoed, and walked off the mound. He turned back. "By the way, Marv, we need to talk."

Mr. Knight forced a smile. "I couldn't agree more."

As Jim walked to the bleachers, he wondered if Howie had said something about the encounter in the motel parking lot. He wondered if their cover-up had not been a cover-up after all. He wondered how much Marvin knew.

His worries were interrupted by Mr. Rashid. "Jim, I saved you a seat," he called from the end of the bleachers.

Most of Patience had come out for the final game. The small set of bleachers was full. The spillover sat in lawn chairs scattered along the baselines. Mrs. Rashid had even come to see if her daughter would become the first girl to win the World Series of Workup. Mrs. Bickers was on her porch, armed with her cowbell, gong, and binoculars. The only thing different was a bottle of drinking water resting on the rail. A gift from Jim Waters.

After Mrs. Knight read the standings and the batting order, Mr. Knight shouted, "Play ball!" The crowd applauded as the players took the field.

The field had already sucked up the melted hail from the day before. The moisture had greened up the outfield, and the patches of henbit dotting the infield bristled with tiny purple flowers. Except for Mr. Knight being late and a little on edge, it was a terrific beginning. Everyone was up for the game. Even Mange Field.

In Game 7, the shortest route between out #1 and out #54 went something like this.

- Outs #1–18 (also known as the 1st to 3rd innings):
- Howie, Jake, and Sira spray hits all over the field
- Their scores climb into the high 90s.
- Outs #19–36 (aka the 4th to 6th innings):
- Howie Kapowie lives up to his nickname and hits three homers in a row (aka the bat trick)
- The Cricket answers with a flurry of short hits and stays right with him
- Jake's bat goes cold, especially after a grounder bounces off a patch of henbit and hits him in the side of the head (aka the bad-hop dome-dinger).
- Outs #37–53 (aka, the 7th through 8 and 2/3 innings):
- The game rises into the battle everyone expected—Howie Kapowie vs. the Cricket of Karachi
- It's Kapowie, with his reckless swing turning him into a pretzel or blasting home runs to the horizon
- It's the Seventh-Inning Stench
- It's Cricket, with her relentless ground balls, line drives, and bold dashes between the bases

- It's the crowd going nuts as they trade the lead back and forth
- It's Mrs. Bickers losing her voice screaming for Sira but still making plenty of noise with her cowbell, gong, and empty water bottle pounding on the railing.
- It's out #53.
- It's Cricket in the lead, 121 to 118, and if Howie doesn't score 3 points to tie or 4 points to win before he hits into out #54 . . .

It's over.

Just as a bullet train must slow down before reaching its station, this account will hit the brakes before pulling into Out #54.

Howie stepped up into the batter's box and landscaped the dirt.

On the mound, Coach Knight did the same in front of the rubber. Not because he wanted to throw three perfect fastballs past Howie. He wanted to throw a perfect pitch right down the middle. Everyone knew this. It was his son up there. He wanted him to win. The old-timers have another saying. "City slickers call it conflict of interest. We call it small-town glue."

Coach Knight wound up and let go.

Howie swung hard, and missed.

In center field, Jake watched Howie untangle himself.

Coach Knight took some speed off his next pitch.

But Howie swung too soon. Strike two. He slammed his bat in the dirt.

"C'mon, Howie," Mrs. Knight yelled. "Split the difference."

Coach Knight wound up and threw a beautiful pitch. Perfect speed. Middle of the plate.

Howie's swing uncurled. He hit the ball on the barrel. CRACK!

The ball sailed high and long.

Jake picked it up against the hot blue sky, turned, ran back. At first he thought it was never coming down— home run, five points, Howie takes the lead. Then he intentionally strikes out for out #54. Game over. Howie gets his championship.

But the ball began to drop.

And drop.

Jake stole a quick glance to find the fence. He was right there. He stopped and looked back up. The only ball he found was the blazing sun.

He threw up his glove, squinting against the searing light. He saw a blur of darkness. Something hit his glove as he tripped and fell on his back. He felt something thump against his chest. He raised his head. He saw the ball rolling toward his chin.

If he'd had time to think, he might have let the ball roll off his chest. But it happened so fast, instinct took over. His jock gene fired. He grabbed the ball with his bare hand and thrust it in the air.

It was a catch.

Howie was out. Out #54.

Game over.

As Jake stood up, Mrs. Bickers banged her gong and

rang her cowbell. The other players crowded around Sira at third base and raised her on their shoulders. Mr. and Mrs. Rashid jumped up and down in the bleachers. It was their widest dream come true.

Walking in from the outfield, Jake watched the celebration. Sira's victory gave him a surge of joy. Then he saw Howie, still holding his bat, coming toward him. Jake's insides flooded with dread.

They met at second base. Howie's face was red, twisted with anger. "I can't believe you did that!"

"It was a total freak accident," Jake explained.

Howie got in his face. "No, being your friend was a total freak accident! It'll never happen again!"

Jake recoiled.

Howie slung his bat in the dirt and ran off the field.

Jake couldn't move. He felt like his best friend had hurled a handful of fire ants in his face. The hateful sting of Howie's words brought water to his eyes.

Howie ran past Mrs. Bickers's porch. She stopped ringing her bell and rasped, "Hang in there, Kapowie. There's always next year."

The balloon of hurt swelling inside Jake suddenly popped. *There's always next year* hit him like a rude slap. Since Mr. Knight's first pitch, Jake had lost himself in the soaring pleasure and catapulting drama of the game. But *There's always next year* brought him crashing back to earth. And to the truth of what had just happened.

The curse had been biding its time, lying low, waiting for the right moment to strike. Waiting to work its black magic in the outfield. Waiting to assist in a miracle catch.

First the town had turned on his father. Now his best friend had turned on him.

Next year? There wasn't going to be a next year.

As he walked across the infield, he shoved this terrible knowledge to the back of his mind and joined the jubilant celebration. Sira's victory meant more to her than a thousand freaky and fascinating facts. There was no way he was going to ruin it for her.

Mr. and Mrs. Knight were good sports as they presented Sira with the World Series of Workup trophy. Sira thanked everybody for the honor, including Mrs. Bickers for making Mange Field as loud as Yankee Stadium, and Howie for being such an inspiring opponent. But she saved her biggest thanks for last.

"And I want to thank Jake, because there's no way I'd be holding this trophy if it weren't for his awesome catch!"

The crowd cheered as Jake tried to be invisible.

"And one more thing," she shouted. "Thank you, Mrs. Knight, for giving me 121 points. '21. In 1921, in Wichita, the first White Castle in the world opened!"

The players groaned. It was one thing they weren't going to miss now that the season was over. Numbers from Sira's Book of Slumber.

As the small crowd dispersed, Mr. Knight pulled Jim and Jake aside. "I apologize for Howie being such a sore loser," he told them. "And I want him to apologize too. The sooner the better. So how 'bout coming over to the house? We'll get him to dust off his manners and make this right."

Jake tried to tell Mr. Knight it wasn't that big of a deal and Howie would get over it. But Mr. Knight insisted the season couldn't end on such a sour note. The Seventh-Inning Stench was bearable, an off-season stench was not.

28   small-town glue

Usually, Jake liked going to the Knights' house. It was the only house in town with central air-conditioning. In the Waters house the only pockets of relief from the heat were in front of a fan or the open refrigerator. In Howie's house you didn't have to go to the cool, the cool came to you wherever you went. But now, as Mr. Knight led Jake and his father into the living room, there was something else pressing from all sides. Tension.

Mrs. Knight silently waited for them with tall glasses of iced tea and lemonade. Jake thought it was odd they had fresh tea and lemonade all made up, ready to go. Like they were expecting them. Maybe they were the victory drinks for the victory that didn't happen. Like the champagne in the losers' locker room.

He and his father sat on the couch while Mr. Knight went upstairs to get Howie out of his room. After Mrs. Knight made sure they were comfortable, she disappeared. For some reason, this was shaping up to be a guy thing.

Mr. Knight led his son downstairs. Howie had already changed out of his KSF uniform.

The year before, when Howie lost the Series to Tommy "the Crushman" Conners, Jake and Howie had held a ceremony and burned Howie's uniform. Jake wanted to suggest that they skip the apology and go burn this year's uniform. Jake's too, for making the catch. That way they could go back to being best friends for what little time they had left.

Jake watched Howie clump down in a chair and glare at the floor. He didn't look like he was in the mood for a ritual burning. Unless it was Jake at the stake.

Jake stared at the ceiling and opted to go with the traditional J. Waters strategy: When in doubt, don't move. Especially if you've got a cool glass of lemonade to finish.

Mr. Knight swiveled his overstuffed chair away from the big-screen TV and sat down. "Thanks for coming over."

"Thanks for having us," Jim said.

Mr. Knight took off his KSF hat and scratched his dome. He flashed them a tight smile. "You know, ever since Jeremiah Waters founded this town and my great-great-grandfather Waldo opened his store, there's been one thing that's never changed. It's the thing that's kept this town from blowing away like a tumbleweed. It's being neighbors and doing what neighbors do. Enjoy the good times together, help each other out during the bad. We don't wanna be rich and famous. We just wanna be good neighbors."

Jake furrowed his brow and tried to will Howie to say

I'm sorry. The sooner he did, the sooner Mr. Knight could put the lid back on his brain and the sooner he and Howie could go work this out on their own.

"That's why I opened KSF," Mr. Knight continued. "To help my neighbors. I'm not out to make a killin'. I just wanna keep this town alive."

"Dad," Howie interrupted. "Can I just apologize?"

Mr. Knight lifted a silencing hand. "Let me finish, son. I haven't finished *my* apology." His eyes shifted to Jim. "Last night, during the meeting, the way I treated you and your idea of the American Toilet Museum was very un-neighborly. I wasn't helping you out, I was putting you down. That's not the kind of neighbors our families have been over the years. I'm sorry for what I said. And to fix it up, I've decided that the Patience Revival Project is going to support your museum one thousand percent."

Jake glanced at his father. Jim's gaze was locked on Mr. Knight. Jake couldn't tell if he was too stunned to speak, or if he was staring at him with prairie eyes.

"Well?" Mr. Knight turned his hat in his hand. "What do you think of them road apples?"

Jim took a sip of iced tea. "From not wanting to give me a plug nickel to 'one thousand percent'—what changed your mind, Marvin?"

"You said it last night, Jim, but I wasn't listening. 'Homegrown.' That's what makes this town great. And that's what's gonna make the American Toilet Museum a winner."

"Why do I get the feeling there's a catch?"

"There's no catch." Mr. Knight flashed his big smile. "I

just expect you be neighborly too, and help me out if I need it."

Jim set his iced tea on the coffee table. "I think I know what you mean, but give me an example."

Mr. Knight glanced at the ceiling. "Okay, for the sake of argument, let's say the nitrate level spiked up in one of the wells in town." He looked straight at Jim. He wasn't smiling anymore. "I'd expect you to tell me about it first. That way, I could fix the problem before the State Department of Health and Environment called up and accused KSF of polluting the water table."

A connection flashed in Jake's mind. Nitrates didn't travel through the air, they traveled in underground water.

"Wait a minute," Jim said, sounding puzzled. "DHE called?"

"As if you didn't know," Mr. Knight snapped.

"Hold on." Jim raised a hand. "All I did was send a routine water sample to a private lab."

"Well, how about unsending it?"

Jim blinked. "Excuse me?"

"How 'bout calling the lab and telling 'em it was a corrupted sample?"

"Why would I do that?"

"So I can fix the problem with the Bickers's well myself. If you're such a big fan of homegrown solutions, that would be the homegrown solution here."

Jake slid Howie a look. Howie stared at him with probing eyes. Jake knew exactly what he was thinking. Was this what Jake's trip to KSF was about? And all his questions about nitrates? Jake gave him an unknowing shrug and tried to look on the bright side. At least he was back on his ex–best friend's radar.

Jim cleared his throat. "And what happens if I *don't* say it was a corrupted sample?"

"Then DHE and the EPA show up tomorrow and do their own test on the well."

Jim raised his hands in disbelief. "Marv, you can't fix the problem in a day."

"I know that. That's why I need a neighbor's help."

"Why are you so worried about DHE and the EPA?"

"Why?" Mr. Knight slammed his glass down on a side table and iced tea splashed onto the carpet. "Because the last time the EPA came out here, they found a dead deer in one of my settling ponds. Then they slapped me with an order to fence in the ponds because they saw 'em as some kind of La Brea tar pit sucking all sorts of animals into extinction. I almost went belly-up meeting their ridiculous demands. And now, if they find a little nitrate spike in one well, they'll have what they've wanted all along. An excuse to shut me down."

"Marvin, of all the feedlots and gas companies polluting the water table out here, the EPA is gonna go after a little fertilizer farm? Aren't you being a little paranoid?"

Mr. Knight rose out of his chair. "God, you're naïve!" He took a step toward Jim. "Do you have any idea who the local director of the EPA is? Do you know who's coming tomorrow?"

Jim remained calm, refusing to be baited. "No, but I'm sure you're going to tell me."

"Her name's Sandra Cass!" Mr. Knight shouted. "Ring a bell?"

Jim shook his head. "Not really."

"She's a direct descendant of Andars Cass! She knows if she shuts down KSF it'll destroy us. It'll bring the final destruction her great-great-grandfather predicted. And it'll transform Andars Cass from religious nut to *prophet*!"

Jake gaped at Mr. Knight. He didn't want to believe what he was hearing. He didn't want to believe that the curse could be so cunning and devious.

Jim burst out laughing. "You actually believe that's what this is about? What some lunatic said in the nineteenth century?"

"I don't know, but that's what she wants. To shut me down!" Mr. Knight spit back. "And bury this town!"

Jim stood up. "Marvin, all I know is the facts. We've got a well with a nitrate level of sixteen parts per million. Anything above ten parts per million can cause cyanosis and is dangerous to small children. High nitrate levels in groundwater are usually caused by fertilizer runoff. We've got a fertilizer farm a mile from the polluted well. It would be a smart thing to test other wells close to the farm, and the EPA is coming tomorrow to help us do that." He raised his lecturing finger at Mr. Knight. "And you think the 'neighborly' thing to do is to falsify a test so the EPA backs off? Then let the homegrown problem provide the homegrown solution? Sorry, Marv, I've got a different idea of what makes a good neighbor." He turned to Jake. "Let's go."

Jake scrambled to his feet. He wasn't exactly sure what

all this nitrate stuff meant, but he knew it was powerful enough to set neighbor against neighbor.

Mr. Knight raised his hands in defeat and let out a friendly chuckle. "You know, Jim, you're absolutely right. We've gotta work this so it's right." He extended a hand for a shake. "Thanks for setting me straight. I'm gonna make it right. You have my word."

Jim studied him for a second, then shook his hand. "Good." He started out of the room, Jake followed.

Then Jim turned, remembering something. "Oh, Howie. I'm sorry you lost the championship."

Even though Jake's gut told him the odds of him and Howie ever being best friends again had only gotten worse, he couldn't stop himself from throwing out a peace offering. "See you around, Kapowie."

Howie glared at him and scowled. "Like I got a choice."

29   the calm before the storm

On the way home, Jake sat on a towel covering the milk stain on the seat. The seat was dry, but that didn't stop a cloud of sour milk odor from enveloping him. He could have avoided the nasal abuse by riding his bike home, but given the new evidence pointing to the final destruction, he had some questions for his father.

"What's sigh-a-noses?"

"It's cyanosis," Jim corrected. "It's the illness you get when your body takes in too many nitrates."

"What happens?"

"First off, your skin turns blue."

"Blue?"

"That's right. Nitrates interfere with how much oxygen you have in your blood. If you get too many nitrates in your system, it's like your blood starts holding its breath."

"Did Andars Cass say anything about us all turning blue?"

"I doubt it. Nobody knew about cyanosis back then. Even today, the end-of-the-world nuts care more about the date than the colors of the apocalypse."

Jim turned the van onto Endurance Street. "A little extra nitrate in the drinking water isn't a big deal as long as it's taken care of. But Jake, if Mr. Knight thinks some descendant of Andars Cass is out to get him and his little fertilizer farm, then it's even more important that the Plunger of Destiny stay under wraps. I'm not even going to show it to the historical society. If it got out that it was here, Marv would probably organize a posse and swing me from a tree."

Jake nodded. "One more question?"

"Shoot."

"Can you catch any diseases from sour milk gas?"

Jim gave him a serious look. "Yeah. Putritus."

"Really?"

"But there's an easy cure."

"What?"

Jim smiled. "Sweat it out."

And that was what Jake did the rest of the afternoon. Sweat. He helped his father remove more of the collection from the upper rooms. Sira would have joined them, but she was busy at the motel, helping her parents get ready for the party to celebrate her World Series victory.

As he worked, Jake realized that clearing out the rooms was like the time he took apart a lawn mower engine. It had looked like a small job at first, but when he dismantled it and spread out all the parts, he was amazed how much there was to a two-stroke engine.

Curses were like that too, he thought as he carried a stack of old bathroom scales downstairs. At first he had thought the curse was going to play out straight as an axle. *The day the Plunger of Destiny returns to Patience, the final destruction will begin.* But in the unraveling of those words, it was amazing how twisted and complex the end could be.

Later that night, just about everyone showed up for Sira's victory party. There were two long tables of food. One was American food, the other Pakistani. The punch bowl was the centerpiece of the American table. The World Series of Workup trophy was the center of the Pakistani table. A baseball trophy rising from a landscape of tandoori chicken, lamb curry, beef kabobs, saffron rice, yogurt, and chapati bread was probably a first in the history of the game.

Mrs. Knight came but didn't stay long. She claimed that her husband and Howie weren't feeling well but they sent their congratulations to Sira. No one questioned the story. For good reason. Half the partygoers worked at KSF.

Jake didn't care about who did or didn't show up. He had other worries. When he wasn't being slapped on the back for his "catch of the century," he was studying everyone with Sherlock eyes. He was looking for anyone with the slightest tinge of blue.

But as the night wore on, he only noticed one color change. The more people ate, drank punch, and danced under the tiki lights, the rosier they got.

Later, as he lay on Tabletop Rock and listened to the

song of the cottonwood, he worried about that bloom on people's cheeks. After all, wasn't it the same flush of life that had colored Jeremiah's cheeks before he uttered his last words, and died? Could Sira's party be the town's last blush of life?

30   a surprise visitor

With the baseball season over, Jake rode into town the next morning for a full day of helping his father. The historical society people were coming in a few days, and only half of the collection had been moved to the old barn out at the ranch. And they still had to arrange it in a way that would convince the visitors that, as Jim put it, "The bathroom is more than a temple of convenience, it's a temple of history."

Fortunately, Sira rode up on her bike and asked to help. Unfortunately, her idea of helping was asking five questions for every box she carried downstairs.

"Mr. Waters, I don't get the poem at the bottom of this bowl," she said, looking into the open box she was carrying.

"What's it say?" Jim asked as he set down a model of a two-story outhouse designed for use when the snow was so deep you had to use the second story.

She showed him the box. Inside, at the bottom of a glazed bowl, was a large eye. She read the poem surrounding the eye. " 'Keep me clean and use me well, and what I see I will not tell.' What's that supposed to mean?"

"It's a chamber pot," he explained. "It's like if they put an eye at the bottom of a toilet. 'Keep me clean and use me well, and what I see I will not tell.' "

As the meaning dawned, her eyes lit up. "Wow, that's freaky."

"And tame compared to what they put in chamber pots during the Civil War." He started back inside.

She followed. "What'd they do?"

"They put images of Abe Lincoln and Jefferson Davis in the bottom of them."

"So if you were a Yankee you could—"

"Rain down on Jeff Davis's head," he chortled as Sira screwed up her face in a combination of disgust and delight.

Jake passed them on the stairs. He carried a bushel basket of antique toilet brushes.

"Jake," Sira bubbled, "did you know—"

"I know, I know." He kept moving. "I know it all. If I could flush my brain, I would."

Jim laughed as he wrapped his arms around a bulky toilet at the top of the stairs. It was designed to look like an American Eagle.

Sira grabbed a box of antique bathtub toys and followed him down. "Okay, Mr. Waters, now it's my turn to try and stump you."

"Shoot."

"Do you know what Jeremiah Waters's dying words were?" Just because the baseball season was over didn't mean Cricket stopped jumping.

Jim carefully moved down the stairs with the heavy toilet. "I think it was either 'Hark! Enter Death' or 'This toilet is killing me.' "

She ignored his joke. "You know, before he said, 'Hark! Enter Death,' he said, 'I fall leaving unknowable secrets.' "

"Don't say *fall*." Jim reached the bottom of the stairs and struggled out on the porch.

She put down her box. "As dying words go, don't you think they're kind of weird?"

He grunted as he set the toilet on a table.

Jake came back up on the porch after putting the bushel basket in the van. "Every time you guys take a history break, I'm taking a water break," he announced, and headed back inside.

Jim studied Sira. "You've been doing your homework, haven't you?"

"I like homework. Especially when it leads to buried treasure."

"You and everybody else with a shovel."

She gave him a quizzical look. "What do you mean?"

"Jeremiah Waters wasn't only loopy the day he died. He'd been loopy for a couple of years. He did all sorts of strange things, including drawing treasure maps, hiding them, and then pretending to discover them. Or he'd plant them and let others find them. Every time a map was found, the townsfolk would dig a hole in some field. For his last two years, Jeremiah became the man who cried 'treasure.' So by the time he got around to uttering his last words, there were quite a few people who were happy Death finally shut him up. Of course, Jeremiah had the last laugh. After he died, two more maps were discovered, and two more empty holes were dug."

Sira yanked a notebook from her pocket and flipped it open. "But the newspaper account said, '. . . the elderly Mr. Waters opened his eyes. *They shone with a clarity I had not seen in days,* said Jud. *His pale cheeks flushed with a last bloom of life. His voice burst from his throat with a strength that gave us hope he might live another decade.*'" She looked up at Jim. "The last two years of his life don't fit with his last words. Something happened."

"I don't follow." Jim wiped his face with a bandana.

Sira took a breath. "Making fake maps is the act of a man who's loopy and *thinks* he knows what he's doing. But the last thing he said, 'I fall leaving unknowable secrets,' are the words of a man who *admits* he doesn't know. I think something changed in the last moments of his life. Maybe he remembered something."

Jim took off his cap. "Interesting theory, but I have a different one."

"What?"

"You know how criminals deny their crimes all their life, but when they get to their deathbed, sometimes they fess up?"

"Yeah."

"Well, Jeremiah had been crying 'treasure' for two years, and maybe he felt bad about it. 'I fall leaving unknowable secrets' was his deathbed confession. His admission that he simply couldn't remember where the map or the trunk was."

As Sira pondered his theory, a voice interrupted from the yard. "Is Jake here?"

They turned and saw Howie standing next to his bike.

"Jake," Jim called into the house, "someone to see you."

Jake came out on the porch with a glass of ice water. He was surprised to see Howie.

Howie kicked the burnt grass with his sneaker. "You know the scariest thing about seeing my dad be a total jerk?"

Jake shrugged. "What?"

"It's like seeing a preview of a movie. But it's not a movie, it's who you're gonna be when you grow up."

"You know, Howie," Jim said, "there's an expression that describes what you're feeling. 'The apple doesn't fall far from the tree.'"

"Yeah, that's about right," Howie replied. "But this apple isn't hanging out under that tree."

Then Howie apologized for the way he'd treated Jake after the game, and to Sira for being such a sore loser.

"It was a dumb-luck catch," Jake told him.

"It was a dumb-luck win," Sira added.

In the awkward silence that followed, Jake relished the moment. Maybe that was the one thing the curse couldn't destroy. Friendship.

Jim broke the silence. "So why don't you three musketeers celebrate the reunion out at the quarry?"

Jake jumped at the suggestion. "Great idea."

"Actually, Mr. Knight," Howie said, "I don't mind pitching in and helping you move all this stuff."

"Terrific!" Jim grabbed a plunger and thrust it in the air before Jake could object. "That makes us the *four* musketeers. All for one and one for all!" He charged back into the house.

Jake rolled his eyes at the good news–bad news. Good news: Howie was his best friend again. Bad news: Howie suddenly liked sweating up and down stairs more than swimming in the quarry.

31 the manure hits the fan

When the next van load was ready to go, Jake, Sira, and Howie opted to stay at the house and finish emptying the rooms. It was better than taking a ride in the "stink box." Within a half hour, the trio got everything down to the porch. Jake and Howie wanted to celebrate with a pitcher of fresh lemonade. As they headed to the kitchen, Sira went upstairs to use the bathroom. It was the first time Jake and Howie had been alone.

"So, were you spying for your dad when you came out to KSF yesterday?" Howie asked.

Jake took down a big plastic pitcher from a cupboard. "No, I was spying for myself. I heard him say something about nitrates, and I wanted to check it out."

"Well, it doesn't matter anymore." Howie shrugged. "My dad's making it right."

"Good." Jake filled the pitcher at the sink.

Upstairs, Sira splashed her face with cold water. As she

toweled her face dry, she noticed something in the mirror. She turned and checked out the print hanging on the wall. It depicted a sprawling Roman bath where both men and women were bathing. They were all naked. At the bottom of the picture, a note card had been taped to the glass. She leaned closer and read the printed note.

Rules for coed bathing in a Roman bath, circa AD 100.
1. Don't stare.
2. Behave as if you're fully dressed.
3. Break the rules and you're out.

As she gave it an appreciative smile, she realized that the note had been put there by Mr. Waters and that this was probably something he wanted for the museum. She opened the bathroom door so she'd have both hands free to hold the print. Lifting it away from the wall, she was surprised to see a rectangular seam in the wallboard. It looked like the outside edge of a hidden medicine cabinet.

She stared at it as the sound of the boys in the kitchen drifted upstairs. Her curiosity got the best of her. She put down the print, worked her fingernails into the seam, and pulled the cabinet door open.

As her eyes fell on what was inside, she gasped.

In the kitchen, Jake and Howie stood in front of the open fridge. Jake searched for lemons as Howie pulled up the bottom of his sweaty T-shirt and used it to scoop cold air.

Jake found one lemon that was mustard yellow. He

curled his lip in disgust. "We can always make iced tea. You wanna see if Cricket wants tea?"

Howie didn't want to leave the cloud of cool air. "What are you gonna do?"

"Would you rather stay here and make tea?"

"Nah, I'll go." Howie dropped his shirt and turned back into the heat.

Sira's mouth hung open as she stared at the object in her hands.

The Plunger of Destiny.

She heard Howie coming down the hall. She jammed the Plunger back inside the secret cabinet and fumbled with the cabinet door, trying to close it. When she turned to pick up the print, she found Howie standing in the doorway.

"What's the big secret?" he asked with a sly smile.

"Nuthin. I found another print that has to go down."

His eyes darted to the hidden cabinet. "I mean what's in the wall?"

"Nuthin."

"Yeah, right."

As Howie moved into the bathroom, she tried to block him with the print. "Jake!"

Jake heard the panic in her voice, followed by the crash of breaking glass. He flew out of the kitchen.

By the time he got upstairs, it was too late. Sira stood in the hall, in a spill of glass reaching out of the bathroom. She looked terrified. He ran to the doorway.

Inside the bathroom, Howie held the Plunger of Destiny. "What is this?"

"Nuthin," Jake said, trying to sound like sticking old plungers in the walls was a regular thing in the Waters house.

"If it's nuthin, why was it hidden?" Howie turned the dark, twisted handle in his hands.

As Jake hunted for an answer, the dark crescents of Blackbeard's bite marks rotated into Howie's view. "What's this?" He squinted at the marks; then his eyes popped wide. "Ahhh!" He dropped the Plunger like it was a rattlesnake. He lunged past Sira and Jake. "No wonder everything's screwed up!" He flew down the stairs.

"He knows what it is!" Sira yelled. "You gotta go after him!"

Jake dashed for the stairs. "Call my dad and tell him what happened."

By the time Jake got to his bike, Howie was almost at the end of the street. If Jake was going to catch him, he'd have to fly. And take shortcuts.

Jake jumped the curb and cut through the yard behind the coffin house. Getting so close to the house that wanted to eat him alive in his dreams was bad enough, but the real nightmare would start if Howie blew the whistle on the Plunger of Destiny.

As Jake hit Courage Street, Howie was only forty yards ahead. "Howie, wait! We gotta talk!"

Howie sped on and shot past his own street.

Jake groaned. Howie wasn't going home. He was going straight to KSF. There was only one way to catch him. Another shortcut.

As Howie veered left onto Faith Street and raced

toward Mange Field, Jake cut left onto Resolve Street. He shot up an overgrown driveway and through an empty lot. He jumped the ditch, into Mrs. Bickers's backyard. He put his head down and pedaled hard across the burnt-out grass. If he totally busted it, he could cut Howie off at the end of Mange Field.

Jake looked up. At first, what he saw didn't compute. There was a large dark patch on the yellow grass. It looked wet. It didn't make sense. And just like when he'd grabbed the ball off his chest at the end of Game 7, he didn't have time to think. He swerved to avoid the dark patch. Bad choice. His tilting bike hit the patch and went down. As he slid, water and muddy grass sprayed everywhere.

When he stopped sliding he heard the sound. He looked over and saw water gushing from the outdoor faucet at the back of Mrs. Bickers's house. There was no time to turn it off.

He jumped up, yanked his bike out of the mud, and took off. As he passed the front of the house, he saw Mrs. Bickers watering plants on her porch.

"Mrs. Bickers," he yelled, "you left your water on in back!"

She gave him an unconcerned wave.

Howie raced past the end of Mange Field.

For the next mile Jake did his best impression of Lance Armstrong. He ignored the screaming pain in his thighs as he pedaled furiously.

Up ahead, Howie skidded through the open KSF gate and punched an electronic keypad on the other side. The electric gate began to close.

Jake put it into hyperspeed. He didn't make it. He fishtailed to a stop as the gate clanged shut. Gasping for breath, his lungs filled with the sour stench of rotting manure. He kicked the gate in frustration. There was a security keypad on his side of the gate too, but he didn't know the code.

Stretching from each side of the gate was a high fence. The fence the EPA had ordered Mr. Knight to put up to save animals from drowning in the settling ponds.

As flies glommed on to the gate, Jake peered through it. Howie was riding toward the main building. Mr. Knight's truck was parked out front. There was no stopping it now. Howie was going to do the Chicken Little. *The Plunger has returned! The Plunger has returned!*

Riding back toward town, Jake made his third vow of the summer. He vowed never to underestimate the curse again. And never to be surprised by the strange, twisted, serpentine route the curse seemed to be taking as it slithered toward the final destruction.

He didn't reach the end of Faith Street before his vow was tested. The next twist was parked in front of Mrs. Bickers's house.

A water truck. It was pumping water into the wellhead in her front yard.

As he rode by, he realized why the outside faucet had been left on. And how Mr. Knight was "making it right."

32 taking sides

Jake used the pay phone in front of the post office to call his father's cell. He got through. Sira had already told him about Howie seeing the Plunger, and he was headed back to town. When Jake told him about Mrs. Bickers's open faucet and the water truck filling her well, there was a long silence.

"Dad, are you still there?"

"Yeah. Where are you?"

"In front of the post office."

"Stay there. I'll pick you up in a couple minutes."

When Jake hung up, Mr. Olabuff appeared from around the side of the post office. He was dragging a garden hose.

Jake's heart jumped into his throat. What if Mr. Olabuff overheard him talking about the Plunger? He had to try to find out.

Mr. Olabuff turned the nozzle on the hose and started watering the planters in front of the post office. They were tractor tires filled with flowers.

"Hey, Mr. Olabuff." Jake waved.

"Hey, Tweener. I saw you and Howie fly by earlier. Who won the race?"

"Howie. But it's two out of three."

Mr. Olabuff chuckled as the phone rang inside the post office. He put the hose down and went to answer it.

Jake was pretty sure Mr. Olabuff didn't know. But then Jake wasn't sure how people would react when they found out the Plunger of Destiny was back. If Howie's reaction was typical, Jake and his father might as well go to a witch trial wearing pointy hats.

The van pulled up, and Jim called to Jake. "Hop in."

"What about my bike?"

"Leave it."

He got in and looked for Sira. "Where's Cricket?"

"I told her to go home. She doesn't need to be a part of this."

When they arrived at Mrs. Bickers's house, the water truck's pump motor was droning loudly as it filled the well. Jim parked the van and got out. Jake followed.

Mrs. Bickers sat on the porch, nursing an iced tea. "Hello, Jimmy. Would you like some tea? I made it with bottled water."

"No thanks," he answered. "What's going on?"

She answered with a question. "Is there a law against getting your well filled when it's almost empty?"

"How did it get almost empty?"

"Forgot to turn the water off. I think I'm gettin' the Alzheimer's."

Jim leaned against the porch rail. "Mrs. Bickers, getting a fresh load of water isn't going to solve the nitrate problem."

"It will until Marvin has a chance to fix it."

"So the water's a gift from Marvin?"

She set her jaw. "What you don't get, Jimmy, is that we can solve our own problems. We don't need a bunch of tree-kissin' feds telling us what to do. 'Specially since every time they show up to fix somethin', they break three other things in the fixin'."

Because of the noisy pump, they didn't hear the pickup until it screeched to a stop in front of the house. Mr. Knight and Howie jumped out and moved across the yard.

Jim turned back to Mrs. Bickers. "You know, Mrs. Bickers, on second thought, an iced tea would be nice."

She didn't budge. "We're fresh out."

"Any problems, Mrs. B.?" Mr. Knight called.

"No. Jimmy was just leavin'."

Not moving, Jim waved a hand at the water truck as the driver shut down the pump. "So this is your idea of setting things right?"

"For today, it'll do," Mr. Knight answered. "It'll buy me the time I need to solve the problem."

"What if every well on the street has high nitrates? Are you going to buy them loads of fresh water too?"

"If I have to."

"And everyone else in town?"

"If that's what it takes."

Jim let out a derisive laugh. "Marvin, even if I was willing to do it your way, do you really believe everyone would go along with this? Do you think they'd risk their health because it was the 'neighborly' thing to do? Just how long do you think you can keep this a secret from DHE and the EPA?"

Mr. Knight exploded. "Don't lecture me about secrets! How long have you been hiding the Plunger of Destiny?"

Jake shot an accusing look at Howie. He glowered back.

The sound of breaking glass pulled everyone around. A puddle of ice cubes, broken glass, and tea spread next to Mrs. Bickers's chair. She stared at Jim with fierce eyes.

Mr. Knight moved to the porch rail. "That's right, Mrs. B. The Plunger's back, and all of a sudden there's nitrates poppin' up in your well. It almost makes me a believer."

Mrs. Bickers kept her eyes locked on Jim. "If that don't beat all. A Waters man drove the first nail into the town's coffin, and now a Waters man drives in the last. Jimmy, you don't have the sense to push a wheelbarrow."

Jim shook his head disparagingly. "With all due respect, Mrs. Bickers, we all have the right to stick our heads in the freaky beliefs of our own choosing. And here's mine. Toilet plungers don't kill people, but bad water does."

He walked off the porch and Jake followed.

As Jake moved past Howie, Howie shot a hand up to his forehead and flashed Jake the "L" gesture for loser.

Takes one to know one popped into Jake's head, but he refrained from saying it. He knew it was just the curse pulling Howie's strings and tossing him back under the family tree.

As Jim and Jake climbed into the van, Mr. Knight flipped open his cell phone.

33 from bad to worse

When they drove down Courage Street, Mr. Olabuff lumbered out of the post office. The front of his overalls and his postal shirt were covered with dark stains. "Jim!" he yelled, waving them down.

Jim pulled the van across the street. Mr. Olabuff didn't look hurt, but he was very wet.

"A pipe burst!" he hollered, wiping water off his face. "It's gonna soak the mail if I don't get it shut down."

Jim grabbed a monkey wrench off the console.

Jake followed them into the post office. He thought a broken water pipe was small potatoes for the curse at this late stage of the game. But then he reminded himself how pointless it was to predict the curse's next twist on the road to ruin.

Mr. Olabuff led them into the post office's back room. The room was divided by a wall-to-wall, floor-to-ceiling metal screen with a door in it. Through the partition and behind a stack of boxes, the water sprayed up against the back wall.

Mr. Olabuff stepped through the door in the partition. "I got the break hitting the wall, but I can't find the shut-off."

Jim stepped past him and pushed through mail carts and boxes toward the spray of water. Jake was surprised by a hand on his back and the shove that followed. He tripped over a box, then caught his balance and turned. Mr. Olabuff was retreating through the door in the partition.

Jim moved a box and stared down at the "break." It was the end of a garden hose, clamped to the back of a chair, shooting the spray of water up the wall.

The door in the metal barrier clanged shut.

Jake threw himself against it, trying to force it open. But he was no match for Mr. Olabuff pressing against the door on the other side as he fumbled with a padlock.

Jim rushed back through the boxes. "Hey!"

Mr. Olabuff got the lock on the door and clicked it shut. Breathing hard, he stepped away from his prisoners.

Jim threw out his hands. "Red, what in Sam Hill are you doing?"

"Something I'm entitled to do as fire chief. Citizen's arrest."

Jim was stunned. "For what?"

"Reckless endangerment of the town."

"You gotta be kidding!"

"Wish I was. Now, would you please turn off the hose? I don't want the mail to get wet."

"You turn it off!" Jim yanked his cell phone from his pocket. "I'm calling the sheriff in Sharon Springs."

Jake watched as Mr. Olabuff's face blanched. He looked like what Jake thought a dead man might look like. He looked like the face of the curse. Then things went into slow motion.

The beeps from the dialing cell phone echoed off the walls as Mr. Olabuff's hand wrestled with a pocket in his overalls, then disappeared inside. When he pulled it back out, Jake wasn't sure what was sticking out of Mr. Olabuff's meaty hand. It looked like an extra finger. It swam into focus. The barrel of a snub-nosed revolver.

"Gimme the phone," Mr. Olabuff whispered flatly.

Jake stared at the black eye of the barrel fixed on his father. It shook slightly in Mr. Olabuff's trembling hand. It felt like the gun was vacuuming everything normal out of the room. Jake's eyes darted between Mr. Olabuff and his father. They stared at each other with prairie eyes. Quiet, neutral, terrified of what might happen next.

His father's voice was quiet, shaded with sadness. "Red, who did you just become?"

The big man looked thrown by the question. Then the blood returned to his face. "I'm doin' you a favor."

Everyone flinched as a voice jumped out of the cell phone. "Verizon wireless four-one-one connect. For English, please stay on the line."

Jim flipped the phone shut, dropped it on the floor, and kicked it under the cage door.

34 the big-aha mind-blower

Jake listened to Mr. Olabuff shut the front door of the post office and lock it. Then came the low staccato of his father laughing. It quickly ramped up, getting louder. Jake stared in disbelief as his father staggered around, laughing and batting boxes out of his way.

Jake moved to the back wall and turned off the hose. The hissing spray went silent along with the laughter. Jim slumped down on a box.

"Dad, what's going on?"

"Besides everyone losing their mind, it's pretty simple," Jim said wearily. "They want me out of the way when the EPA shows up today to check Mrs. Bickers's well. They can have their wish and then some. We're getting outta here."

Jake looked around. The back door Mr. Olabuff had squeezed the hose under was locked. The only other exit was a small window high on a side wall. "How?"

"I don't mean out of here," Jim explained. "I mean out

of Patience. I don't know if it's the curse, or if everyone's been smelling the stink farm so long it's rotted their brains, but this cow plop of a town should have been allowed to dry up and blow away decades ago. It's not fit for people anymore, it's only fit for dung beetles. And that's what we'll become if we stay. Dung beetles."

Jake was shocked. Not by the words but by who was saying them. "What about your museum?"

"The dream of a dung beetle," Jim shot back, "feeding on the dregs of the past. The American Toilet Museum. Nobody wants to look at old toilets. The only good toilet is one that works. And that's where the museum's going. Down the toilet."

"Dad, we just spent three days moving everything out to the ranch. The history people are coming. I mean, maybe this is like you always say, 'Things have to get worse before they get better.' "

Jim gave him a hard look. "Okay, you tell me. I've just been locked up and threatened with a gun by a man I've known all my life. There's a lot of ways it could get worse, but right now, Jake, I'm having a hard time seeing how it's ever gonna get better. You tell me how things could possibly get better."

Jake stared at his father's face. It was twisted and warped in a strange way. Jake felt like asking him the same question he'd asked Mr. Olabuff. *Dad, who did you just become?*

Jim looked away.

Jake felt a wave of panic. His father wasn't just looking away. He was disappearing before his eyes, like a dandelion puff in a gust of wind. "What happened to *Ad Astra per Aspera?*" Jake demanded. "To the stars through difficulty, and all that?"

Jim's voice rankled with bitterness. "You know where I got that?"

"No."

"I stole it off the state emblem. And that's exactly what every J. Waters has done to survive. Scavenge off whatever we can find. When we lost our cattle, we became farmers. When we lost our land, we became plumbers. When we lost construction jobs, we became bathroom doctors who made house calls. And when people moved away and abandoned their bathrooms, I raided them for artifacts. And now, what's my vision of the future? Some cockamamie toilet museum. Scavenging the past. You're right, Jake. It's time to break the Waters mold. It's time to get outta here."

Jake sat on a box as he struggled in a riptide of confusion. A few days before, hearing those words, he would have jumped for joy. But now the words he'd longed for sounded wrong.

And he couldn't escape his father's bitter torrent of words. They crashed into him like a great wave that knocks you down, then drags you into the undertow of hopelessness.

His chest ached. He felt his face tighten against tears he couldn't stop. But before the first sob overtook him, a memory flashed in the swallowing blackness. He was walking beside his father when Jim said, *I wasn't as smart as the fox.*

Then Jake heard his own voice answer. *Be the fox. The fox who was smart enough to go under.*

And that's exactly what he did. He stopped struggling against the tears and turmoil and all the "fleas" gnawing at him. He let the vortex of his fears pull him to the depths of despair.

As he sank through the darkness, his body relaxed. His mind went silent. He felt the same calm he felt in the cold depths of the quarry right after a break-the-mirror brain-slapper.

In the stillness, a strange thought loomed out of nowhere, like one of those eerie fish that live in the deepest trenches of the ocean. *What if,* Jake thought, *what if Jeremiah Waters, in his last dying breath, was really trying to say something?*

The answer exploded in his head.

He leaped to his feet. "Dad! What if Jeremiah remembered something at the last second? What if his last words, 'I fall leaving unknowable secrets. Hark! Enter Death!' mean something?"

Jim looked up with dull eyes. "Sira said the same thing. Believe me, they were the words of a man driven mad by a mystery of his own making."

"But what if they weren't?" Jake shouted. "What if his last words were his *last map to the treasure?*"

Jim's mouth twisted into a scornful smile. "The only map I'm interested in is the one that gets me out of Patience." He pointed up at the small window. "And it starts up there. I bet you can fit through it." He stood up and moved to the back of the room. He ripped the hose off the metal chair and used the chair to smash the small window high in the side wall.

Jake didn't move. "You didn't answer my question."

"You're only twelve, Jake. Save your what-ifs for the future, not the past. Now, crawl out the window, go to the house, and fetch me the bolt cutter."

Jake hesitated as his father set the chair down for him to climb up to the window.

"C'mon," Jim said impatiently. "It's time to go while we still have the chance."

Jake knew there was no talking to him. Not now. He hopped up on the chair, got a boost up, and picked the last bits of glass out of the window frame. Then he squeezed through the opening and dropped to the ground.

Before taking off, Jake jumped up and pulled himself back up to the window. "Where are we going?"

"Don't know." Jim pulled an acrostic magazine from his back pocket and sat down. "Maybe Las Vegas."

Jake dropped and scooted along the side of the building toward the street. His bike was still lying in front of the post office by the pay phone. His plan was simple. Grab his bike and take the back way home. Riding down Courage Street was too much of risk. If Mr. Olabuff saw him, there was no telling what he might do.

Jake checked the street. It was clear. He dashed out, grabbed his bike, and quickly wheeled it back along the side of the post office.

As he passed under the broken window, it hit him like a train in a tunnel. In the history of head bonks, it was known as the big-aha mind-blower.

35   a mystery solved

Jake leaned his bike against the wall under the window and scrambled up on the seat. Standing on it, he could see inside.

"Dad, it's an acrostic!"

Jim held up his magazine. "Yes indeed."

"No, what Jeremiah said. Write it out. 'I fall leaving unknowable secrets. Hark! Enter Death.' "

Jim wrote down the first letter of each word.

I F L U S H E D

He stared at it, then whispered the words. "I flushed."

"If he flushed," Jake blurted, "that's where he hid the map. He flushed it down the toilet!"

Until this moment, what had happened *after* Jeremiah Waters had been knocked out by one of the outlaws and *before* Waldo Knight and the first group of men arrived from town had always been a mystery. But Jake and Jim Waters had just made a crucial discovery.

As Jeremiah lay still on the floor, two of the outlaws picked Blackbeard up and hauled him out to the porch. Between the suction stick still clamped in his teeth and his painful snarls, Blackbeard looked more like a rabid dog than a bank robber. The outlaws sat him down in the chair next to Regina's grandfather. With the old man air-fiddling "Fiddler's Drunk and the Fun's All Over" and Blackbeard growling his song of pain on the toilet flute, they made a strange pair of blind musicians.

Meanwhile, the third outlaw, the one who had been curious about Jeremiah's indoor outhouse, picked up Blackbeard's gun in case Jeremiah came to. But before he went upstairs to help the others turn the second floor upside down and sideways in search of the map, his curiosity got the best of him. He checked out the indoor outhouse. When he saw that it was some kind of fancy one-holer with water in it, Mother Nature let him know that now was as good a time as any.

After a good sit-down, the outlaw stood up and admired his work.

As to the mystery of why he chose not to flush, Jim and Jake came up with two possible answers. The outlaw wanted to leave his work for others to admire. Or, he had never seen a flush toilet before and had no idea that he was supposed to pull the chain. But why he didn't flush wasn't important. Only the fact that he didn't.

And this was what Waldo Knight and Sam Kirkland discovered when they performed their inspection of the water closet later. Their mistake, which anyone could have made, was assuming that it was Jeremiah Waters who had forgotten to flush.

Jim paced in his post office cell and threw Jake another question. "When Jeremiah was dying, why didn't he just come out and say, 'I flushed'?"

Jake was on such a roll he felt like he had an answer to everything. "He'd become an acrostic nut, he was still half-crazy, and he was dying. Maybe it was the best his brain could do at the time."

"Maybe." Jim nodded. "When memories come flooding back, they can come out in weird ways. Like in a dream or a riddle."

"Or maybe he was talking in code for a reason," Jake added. "Maybe there was someone in the room he wanted to keep it from. It doesn't matter. The important thing is he gave us a clue. And he was saying 'I flushed' because he suddenly remembered that's where he hid the map!"

Jim stopped pacing. "But if that's true, why didn't it end up in the waste pit under the outhouse?"

"I don't know, but they looked there and never found it," Jake almost shouted. "And then Regina nailed up the door to the toilet. The map could still be stuck in the pipe or in the toilet."

Jim grinned up at Jake. "You know, you just might be right. So get going," he added, shooing him off. "We've got a map to find and a treasure to dig up before we get outta here."

"We're still going?"

"Of course we are, Tweener. You can't go to Las Vegas without money."

Jake wasn't sure what he meant. "Dad, are you saying we're gonna take it all?"

"Why not? If they're gonna lock us up and treat us like criminals, we might as well live up to their expectations. Now go."

As Jake jumped down and got on his bike, a bad feeling sloshed around inside him. His father, and every J. Waters before him, had always said that if the trunk was found, the contents would be returned to the proper families. It had always been considered the community chest. Now his father wanted to do exactly what everyone had suspected Jeremiah of doing. Stealing the trunk for himself.

But that was the point, Jake told himself. To break the J. Waters mold, right? So why shouldn't they take the trunk for themselves? Then they really could get out and start someplace else. Maybe they'd even be millionaires.

He cut through a yard and turned down the street toward Endurance. A white sedan drove up the street toward him. It didn't look familiar. As it drew closer, the driver's bare arm reached out and motioned to him.

Jake stopped next to the car. A small woman with wraparound sunglasses and short black hair was behind the wheel. A man in a dark suit sat on the passenger side. But it was the round sign on the door that caught Jake's eye. A green and blue flower inside a circle of words: UNITED STATES ENVIRONMENTAL PROTECTION AGENCY.

"Could you direct me to Faith Street?" the woman

asked as she cast a disapproving glance at the dried mud on Jake's legs and shorts.

He hesitated. If he wanted, he could save her the trip. He could tell her about the fresh water in Mrs. Bickers's well. But things were changing so fast, he wasn't sure what to do. He stalled for time and hit her with a pop-up. "Sure, ma'am. Do you mind if I ask your name?"

She gave him a curious look. "Sandra Cass. What's yours?"

Jake couldn't believe he was staring at the great-great-granddaughter of Andars Cass. She was a living piece of the curse. The question was, how far had this apple fallen from the tree?

"Hello," she said, impatiently waving a hand in front of him. "Do you have a name?"

"Jake Waters." As soon as he said it, he wished he could suck the words back. Her mouth bent into what he thought was a smile. She lowered her sunglasses. Her small dark eyes bored through him.

"Well, well, well, you must be Jim Waters's son."

"You know my dad?"

"Not personally, but I know all about your family, and why you've never left Jerkwater, Kansas. You could say our families go way back." One of her narrow eyebrows arched up like an inchworm. "I have my reasons for keeping an eye on this place."

He swallowed. "Why?"

"History, Jake. That's what fascinates me most. And all the things that went down here in 1877." Her shining eyes disappeared behind her sunglasses. "So tell me, Jake Waters, which way to Faith?"

Jake couldn't give her directions fast enough. She was creepy times ten. He turned and pointed up the street. "Just keep going to the last street and take a left. That's Faith."

"Pleased to meet you, Jake." She flashed him a leering smile as the window rose up, sealing her inside the AC.

He watched the sedan drive away. He wasn't sure how much she knew, he only knew that Mr. Knight was right. She had it in for Patience. Who knows, maybe EPA stood for the Exterminate Patience Agency.

Before he turned and pushed off, something pulled his eyes up to the rooftops. Beyond them, a thick band of gray clouds crawled up the wall of the sky.

36 complications

When Jake rode into his front yard, another surprise waited on the porch.

Sira jumped up from the swing. Her face was pinched with concern. "I'm so sorry, Jake. I tried to hide it from him. Did I totally rip the lid off Pandora's box?"

Jake didn't stop as he moved into the house. "Pretty much. But it doesn't matter anymore."

She followed him into the dining room filled with plumbing supplies. "Why? What happened?"

He grabbed a bolt cutter off the wall.

"What's that for?" she demanded.

"Mr. Olabuff locked my father in the post office."

"You're kidding."

"I wish I was. He even pulled a gun on us."

Sira's eyes widened. "All because of the Plunger?"

"It's more complicated than that." He slid past her and headed for the door.

"What do you mean?"

"There's no time to explain."

"Did they hurt him?"

"Not yet."

Sira headed for the kitchen. "I'm calling nine-one-one."

Jake ran back through the door.

She picked up the wall phone and dialed.

He grabbed the phone and slammed it back in the cradle. "No!"

She jumped back, confused. "Are you crazy?"

"I know what I'm doing."

"Oh yeah? What are you doing?"

He kicked himself for telling her about his dad. Now if he left her alone she'd call the police. Things were complicated enough without the sheriff showing up. Mr. Knight was right about one thing. This had to stay neighbors dealing with neighbors. He needed time to think.

"What's going on?" she demanded. "C'mon, Jake, you're not telling me something."

"I said it's complicated."

"Do I look stupid?"

"No, but it's got nothing to do with you. It's got to do with stuff that's been going on for a long time. It's got to do with my family and the Knights and the curse."

Sira's eyes flashed with anger. "Maybe my family hasn't been here as long as yours. Maybe we're not the white-bread pioneers that founded this place, but that doesn't mean it isn't our home too. And if the curse is going to rip this place up, do you think it's going to go, 'Oh, the

Rashids, they've only been here a few years, let's give 'em a break'? I don't know what planet you've been living on, Jake, but innocent bystanders get killed all the time. So don't tell me this is between the Waters and the Knights! It's about all of us!"

She kept shouting but Jake had stopped listening. He was distracted by a vision playing in his head. He saw Sira's warm brown skin turning dark blue and sickly. He saw Pearl standing behind the counter at Gas & Goodies. She was as blue as the inside of a blueberry donut. Baby Sean bounced up from behind the counter in his jumper swing. He was the color of Windex.

Then a question echoed in Jake's mind. *Who had he just become?* The answer came in a flash. Mr. Knight, Howie, Mr. Olabuff, his father, and now even he, were all carriers of the curse. It had leached up from the earth. It was in the water. It was in their veins. And now it was in their hearts.

Jake held up a silencing hand. "Okay, Cricket, I get the point."

A rumble of thunder sounded in the distance. It pulled him to the front of the house.

Coming out on the porch, they both saw the massive storm front in the distance.

Jake took it in with prairie eyes. Quiet, neutral, without a doubt. The final destruction was not only coming up from the soil, it was coming over the horizon. Big bang, a thousand cuts, inside job. The perfect storm.

There was only one thing to do.

Change of plan.

He turned to Sira. "I think I know where the map is."

Her eyes popped wide. "The map?"

Jake leaped down the porch stairs. "Yeah, I'll explain on the way."

Sira followed as he wedged the bolt cutter into his bike rack. "Are we going to bust out your dad?"

"Not yet. He wouldn't be happy knowing I told you about the map. First we try to find the map, then we bust out my dad." Jake jumped on his bike and grabbed another look at the threatening sky. "But we gotta hurry."

As they took off and rode down Endurance Street, a figure darted from behind the trailer home across the street. Howie.

He ran across the yard and up onto the Waterses' porch. He checked to see if Jake or Sira had looked back and seen him. He watched as they swerved their bikes left on Courage and rode toward the highway. They hadn't.

Howie opened the screen door and disappeared inside.

37 the water test

The man in the dark suit stood in Mrs. Bickers's kitchen. While he dipped a test strip into a plastic cup, Sandra Cass leaned against the counter with her arms crossed. She half listened as Mr. Knight explained why he was there.

"As mayor of Patience, naturally I'm concerned about my constituents and the safety of their drinking water."

Ms. Cass slid him a dubious look. "I'm sure your concern has nothing to do with you also being the owner and operator of a fertilizer plant."

Mr. Knight suddenly remembered that even though he'd put on a jacket and tie for the occasion, he'd forgotten to remove his KSF baseball cap. He took it off and slid a hand over his dome. "Hypothetically speaking, Ms. Cass, even if there was a small spike in nitrate levels, it could be caused by any number of factors. It could be—"

"I'm aware of those factors," she said. "Why don't we

just wait for the results?" She turned to the man in the dark suit as he examined the test strip. "Henry, what have you got?"

"Not much." Henry eyed the pale lavender color that had appeared on the strip. "About six parts per million."

Mr. Knight smiled. "I'm no expert, but don't the levels have to be above ten parts per million before there's a problem?"

Distant thunder rumbled, and Ms. Cass glanced out the kitchen window. It framed a dark sky. She started to look away, but something caught her eye.

She turned to Mrs. Bickers, who had kept quiet despite a scowl on her face that hinted at her true feelings about people from the government. She would rather let lepers in her house.

"Been doing a little reseeding?" Ms. Cass asked.

Mrs. Bickers's face clouded with confusion before she made the connection. "Yep," she boomed. "If you don't stay on top of the henbit it'll crawl right through the door."

Ms. Cass turned to Henry. "Take a sample for a lab test." Then she walked out the back door. Mr. Knight scurried after her, followed by Mrs. Bickers.

Ms. Cass walked to a patch of yard covered with a layer of straw. She toed away some of the straw. The grass underneath had greened up from a recent soaking, but it wasn't new grass. She stepped on the grass. It squished, bringing water to the surface and a frown to her face. "Did you say reseeding, or soaking? As in several hundred gallons."

Mrs. Bickers couldn't contain her contempt any longer. "You're here to test my water, not to tell me how to keep my lawn green."

As Ms. Cass started back toward the house, Mr. Knight tried to keep it diplomatic. "Is there a problem?"

"No, no problem." Ms. Cass moved past them through the door. "But being the mayor who's concerned about the safety of your drinking water, I'm sure you won't mind if we test another well." She kept moving, issuing orders. "Henry, bring the test kit and let's take a walk."

Mr. Knight hurried after her. "Do you really think that's necessary?"

"Absolutely," snapped Ms. Cass.

As the two of them came out on the front porch, followed by Henry and Mrs. Bickers, they were greeted by a flash of lightning and the thudding boom of thunder. Their eyes darted to the horizon.

The storm filling the northwest sky looked like a giant layer cake. A dark mass pressed down on a band of gray, and under that was a narrow strip of clear, sunny sky. Lightning bristled and pulsed in the upper layer. This cake was still baking.

"Dad!" a voice yelled.

Howie raced up the sidewalk on his bike. He was holding something across the handlebars. He jumped off and let the bike crash in the grass as he held up his prize. "Dad, I got the Plunger of Destiny!"

Everyone on the porch froze.

Except Ms. Cass. She strode across the yard to Howie. "Well, well, if it isn't the dreaded Scepter of Satan," she gloated as she took it from him and examined it. "Yes, it's certainly the one I've heard about."

She carried it back to Mr. Knight and pushed it toward him. He hesitated. "Don't tell me you believe in curses, Mr. Knight."

"Of course I don't," he growled, and grabbed it from her.

"Neither do I," she added as she looked over her shoulder at the ominous storm on the horizon. "But on days like this, even the most scientific mind must consider the possibility of forces beyond our understanding." She turned back to him with a malicious smile. "Have a nice day, Mr. Mayor."

As she headed for her car, a confused Henry followed. "We're leaving?"

"Yes," she informed him. "We'll come back another day." She opened the car door and threw one more dart at Mr. Knight. "Provided this place *has* another day."

As the EPA car took off, Howie broke the tense silence. "Wow, now I can say I've met the Wicked Witch of the EPA."

"You didn't exactly help," Mr. Knight barked.

Howie threw up his hands. "What did I do?"

Before his father could answer, the storm cell lay down a picket fence of lightning in the sliver of clear sky on the horizon. The growl of thunder rolled toward them.

Mr. Knight turned to Mrs. Bickers. "Better get inside. Looks like we might get another delivery of thunderstones."

Her eyes never moved from the Plunger. "Or worse."

"No need to fear, Mrs. B.," he said dismissively as he moved to his truck, casually waving the Plunger. "It's nothing but an old stick and some buffalo hide." To emphasize the point, he flipped it indifferently into the truck bed.

The clatter that followed was echoed by a rip of thunder.

38 the map trap

Jake and Sira rode through the high grass in front of the old Waters place, scattering grasshoppers as they went. They dumped their bikes and scooted up the tin ramp to the house. Jake bounded along the zigzag of boards in the hallway.

Sira stayed right behind him. "What if the map's not in the toilet?"

"Then it's somewhere in the pipe between here and the outhouse." Reaching the closet, he grabbed the padlock and spun the dial to the first number.

"What if, when Jeremiah flushed it, it went all the way to the pit under the outhouse? It would have rotted away by now."

"Yeah," he agreed, spinning the dial left. "But they checked the pit and didn't find anything."

He spun the dial back to the right. The lock popped open. He swung the door wide.

The Dolphin Deluge Washdown Water Closet was still encased in a frame of cobwebs and covered with dust. Thunder rumbled and growled behind them.

"Wow." Sira took in the blue and white shell bowl, tapering into the dolphin's gaping mouth. "It's beautiful."

Jake motioned for her to step inside the closet. "Then go ahead, be my guest."

"What?"

"If you think it's so beautiful, you stick your hand down the hole and see if the map's stuck in there."

She shot him a grin. "I would but this could be a major historical moment. If anyone should find the map, it should be a Waters, don't you think?"

"I thought you'd say something like that." He pried up a thin stick of wood from a splintered floorboard and used it to clear the spiderwebs around the toilet. He knelt next to the bowl.

Thunder cracked behind them, turning Sira around. The storm front was getting closer.

"C'mon, Jake," she urged. "It won't bite."

He poked the stick into the dusty toilet and rattled it in the hole. "It's not the dolphin I'm worried about. It's black widows."

He stuck his hand down the hole and reached up with his fingers into the curve of the Dolphin's snakelike body.

Sira watched breathlessly as his wrist wiggled in the hole.

"Nothing." He pulled out his hand and studied the bottom of the toilet where the waste pipe entered the floor.

She stared at his dirty hand. "I hope that's just dust."

He wiped his hand on his shorts. "Me too. As in low-nitrate dust." He eyed the base of the toilet. "Look at this."

She knelt down on the other side of the bowl.

He pointed at the dolphin's body. It was shaped like an S lying on its back. "I can only get my hand in the first half of the S. We've got to check the whole thing."

"How are we gonna do that?"

"We have to break it."

"No way!" she protested. "This is the most important thing in the American Toilet Museum. It would be like going to Philadelphia and breaking the Liberty Bell. Your father would kill you!"

Jake wasn't so sure about that anymore. If anything, his father was going to kill him for telling Sira about the map.

He studied the bolts where the toilet was fastened to the floor. They were crusted with rust. He got up, stepped out of the closet, and picked up the last pine board in the zigzag path. "We gotta break it."

"No!"

For a second, he thought she was going to throw herself over the toilet. Like one of those animal rights activists who lie down in front of bulldozers to protect an endangered habitat. But this would be a first. A toilet rights activist.

Sira pointed at the wood around the toilet. "Look, the wood's all rotten. We can probably rip it right off the floor."

He dropped the board and slid around the other side of the toilet. "Okay, we'll give it a try. If it doesn't work, we break it."

He lifted the mahogany seat, and they grabbed the rim of the bowl. He pushed, she pulled. It moved slightly. As they rocked it back and forth, the rotten floor rose and fell.

"It's working," she said.

"Harder!"

As they rocked, the sound of creaking and crumbling wood grew louder. The rim of the bowl tipped further and further each time. He gave a huge push, and the sound of breaking wood was drowned out by a clap of thunder.

The wood under the toilet suddenly gave way, crumbling in a cloud of dust and flying splinters. They tried to hold on to the toilet, but it was too heavy. It plunged through a tattered hole in the floor.

They cringed, bracing for the sickening sound that would follow. The toilet landed in the cellar with a dull thud. They swapped a quick look, jumped up, and ran outside.

A stiffening wind buffeted the tall grass. They found the entrance to the storm cellar at the side of the house. The storm doors had caved in years ago. Hesitating, they stared down into the shaft of light penetrating the darkness. A sudden gust of cold wind gave them goose bumps.

"Do we have a choice?" Sira asked.

Jake glanced up at the looming storm. It looked like the sky was lifting a huge dark blanket over Patience. And it was about to cover the sun. "No, and we're about to lose light."

He lowered himself onto the jumble of rotten wood that had once been cellar doors. "Watch out for nails."

As they slid their shoes across the dirt floor, the sound

of skittering animals darted out of the shadows. "And wood rats," he added.

There was just enough light to make out the shape of the toilet on the cellar floor. They moved toward it and found it resting on a pile of rotten sacking. It was lying on its side. Sira breathed a sigh of relief. It was still in one piece.

Jake bent down and reached into the bottom end of the toilet, the tail end of the dolphin. He wasn't worried about spiders anymore. After a ride in a plunging "elevator," spiders were probably no different than people. If you survived the fall, you got out as fast as you could.

His fingers felt the cool porcelain on the inside of the S-trap. Even after so many years, it was still smooth. Then his fingers brushed across a rough surface. It wasn't as cool as the porcelain, and it had a curved edge. He prodded the edge. Something fell into his hand.

His heart pounded as he withdrew it.

In the dim light, they stared at the object in his palm. It was some kind of old container, about the size of a fat wallet.

The cellar went dark. The storm had swallowed the sun.

They grabbed each other's hand and groped their way back to the rectangle of dim light in the cellar entrance. As soon as they stepped up on the pile of rotten wood, they took a closer look at the container. It was rusty and made of tin. It looked like it might have once held small cigars or some kind of medicine.

Jake carefully worked the top off. A folded piece of cloth or hide jutted up from inside the tin.

They exchanged a look.

He touched it. "It feels like leather."

"Open it. But be careful, it might fall apart."

He slowly pulled it out and handed the tin to Sira.

A sharp clap of thunder almost made him drop it.

He gently unfolded it.

It was the size of a handkerchief and made of hide. There was an "N" with an arrow pointing up. A line ran across the bottom of the leather square. Above the line was a cluster of dots with the letter "P." Above the "P," two perpendicular lines of dots framed the top left-hand corner. One line ended with the number "37," the other with "31."

Sira gasped. "It's the map!"

"I hope so."

"What else could it be?"

"Jeremiah's last joke."

The shrill pulse of a tornado siren rode in on the wind.

He folded it up and slipped it back into the tin. They scrambled out of the storm cellar and looked toward town.

Against the seething black wall of the sky, the wheat fields looked neon green. In the distance, a gold car passing along the highway glittered like a rolling coin. At the edge of town, the grain elevator stuck up like a luminescent white tooth.

A blast of wind almost knocked them backward into the cellar. They grabbed each other and braced against the wind.

"There's no place to take cover out here," she shouted over the hissing grass and rattling seedpods.

Jake looked around. The roofless house and the rickety barn looked as reliable as a tent in a wind tunnel.

"We have to get back to town!" she yelled, running for her bike.

Every instinct told Jake that racing into the jaws of the storm was the worst thing to do. Especially when it wasn't just a storm. It was the curse. But he knew exactly what was happening in town. Everyone was heading for the tornado shelter. Everyone but his father.

39   down the fraidy hole

Mr. Knight's attempt to dismiss the Plunger of Destiny as "an old stick and some buffalo hide" didn't satisfy Mrs. Bickers for a second. By the time the tornado siren went off, the siren of gossip had sounded all over town. The only townspeople who didn't know that the Plunger of Destiny had returned were the ones taking dirt naps on Temperance Street.

As the tornado siren knifed through the air, people rushed toward the town hall on foot, on bikes, on ATVs, and in cars and trucks. The KSF pickup arrived with the Knight family in the cab. They were all headed for the tornado shelter in the town hall basement.

Everyone called it the fraidy hole. It was where the citizens of Patience had ridden out thousands of thunderstorms pregnant with tornadoes. Over the decades, only two of these storms had given birth and dropped a writhing snake on Patience. Even though tornadoes weren't named like hurricanes, the old-timers called them many things. The devil's digit, God's bullwhip, and Medusa's braid.

A tornado can move as slowly as a walking man or as fast as an eighteen-wheeler barreling down I-70. Their rotating funnels reach wind speeds of 300 miles per hour. Strong enough to vacuum the feathers off chickens, suck the eyes out of geese, and drive a strand of straw through a telephone pole. They can cut swathes of destruction as narrow as a phone booth or as wide as a Wal-Mart. And they can last seconds or an eternity if you get sucked up in one.

While people funneled into the town hall, tumbleweeds rushed every which way. Oil Can Lockhart helped Mrs. Bickers out of her old Buick and led her toward the front door. Everyone gave them a wide berth. If Oil Can decided to spit, there was no telling which way or how far the wind would carry it.

As Mrs. Knight hustled toward the door, Mr. Olabuff caught up with Mr. Knight and Howie. He stopped Mr. Knight and cupped a hand against the wind. "What about Jim and Jake?"

Howie heard the question and spun around. "I saw Jake and Sira riding their bikes toward the highway."

"When?" Mr. Knight asked.

"About a half hour ago."

Mr. Olabuff's face crimped with confusion. He started to speak, but Mr. Knight cut him off. "You let 'em out after the EPA left town, right?"

Mr. Olabuff shook his head. "No, I went to the cafe. Then the siren went off."

Mr. Knight's eyes darted around, checking to see if

anyone was close. "Are you telling me they're still locked in the post office?"

Howie blinked in disbelief. "You locked Jake and Mr. Waters in the post office?"

"Shush!" his father snapped.

Howie went on, shouting over the wind. "Jake must've gotten out, I saw him, but Mr. Waters could still be in there! We have to go get 'im!"

"All right, all right." Mr. Knight scowled as he thrust a hand at Mr. Olabuff. "Give me the keys."

"They're on my desk in the store."

"Get inside," Mr. Knight ordered Howie. "And not a word to your mother."

Howie and Mr. Olabuff headed for the door. Mr. Knight steadied himself against the buffeting wind and held on to his hat as he struggled back up the middle of the street. He kept his head up to watch for flying debris.

He was halfway to the tire store when the wind ripped a section of tin off the sidewalk overhang. It slammed down on the street and slid toward Mr. Knight like a runaway toboggan. He saw it coming and jumped. The tin sheet shot under him as a blast of wind knocked him to the ground.

He struggled to his feet and looked up the street.

The sky looked as if a planet made of oozing black marble had descended and was hovering on the edge of town.

Something banged into his ankles.

The Plunger of Destiny skittered and bounced up the street toward the storm. The wind had sucked it out of the back of his pickup. The witch's ladle was racing to the cauldron.

When he looked back up at the roiling tarry mass of sky, there was a new color in the mix. A sickly green. He watched, transfixed, as a dark triangle stretched toward the ground. The devil's digit was reaching for Patience.

The question was this. Was he willing to die trying to save the man who had brought it upon them?

A wave of dust and debris swept over him. He turned and ran.

As the wind roared outside, Jim Waters pushed mail carts and boxes toward the southeast corner of the room. The plan was simple. Build a bunker to take cover in if the storm smashed through the roof.

While Mr. Olabuff squeezed down the narrow stairwell leading to the basement, Howie backtracked to one of the front windows. He wanted to make sure his father got back with Mr. Waters.

He strained to see through the thick dust and blowing debris that filled the street. His father emerged out of the dust, running toward the door. Howie looked for Mr. Waters to follow. No one appeared.

Mr. Knight never looked up as he ran inside and dashed for the stairs. Howie started to yell something but then ducked down so he wouldn't be seen. He knew his father would make him go downstairs. Someone had to get Mr. Waters.

He ran outside. The blowing dust filled his mouth with grit. He lifted his T-shirt over his face, creating a mask.

The stinging dust peppered his belly, but at least he could breathe. Something slapped him in the forehead so hard it rocked him back on his heels. He reached up and peeled a leaf off his forehead. He laughed. He'd never imagined a leaf could pack such a punch. He put his arms over his head and ran into the raging cloud of dust and debris.

By the time Howie reached the tire store, he was spitting dirt. His skin felt like he'd run through a car wash that sprayed sand. He slipped inside and grabbed the ring of keys on the desk.

Back outside, he was relieved to see the dust was letting up. Leaves and paper still churned through the air, but at least he wasn't going to get his skin sanded off. As he ran around a pyramid of old tires and headed toward the post office, he made one small mistake.

He looked up.

A thin, dark column rotated at the edge of town—Medusa's braid.

Medusa was the Greek monster with snakes for hair. You never wanted to look at her. If you did, you turned to stone. Looking at Medusa's braid was just as dangerous. It didn't turn you to stone, but it could stick you between a rock and a hard place.

Which was what happened to Howie when he saw the tornado. He stopped dead in his tracks, caught between the urge to watch and the urge to see tomorrow.

Except for a slight wag back and forth, the tornado wasn't moving. It was busy sucking up a section of road north of town. And it was growing thicker.

A spine of lightning almost as thick as the tornado

plunged down from the mother cloud, followed by a sonic boom that blew the lock on Howie's muscles. He ran to the post office door, fumbling with keys until he found the right one. He pried the door open and stole a last glance at the tornado.

It was moving now, kicking up what looked like great flocks of swarming bats as it glided toward Patience.

Howie lunged through the door.

40 six feet under

As they struggled to keep their bikes upright in the wind, Jake and Sira checked for cars at Gas & Goodies and the Tumbleweed. There were none. It meant Pearl and Sean and Sira's parents had already left. Turning off the highway, they couldn't see into town. Courage Street was obscured by a soaring curtain of dust.

A tumbleweed crashed into Jake's leg, leaving another patch of bloody scratches. Flying tumbleweeds had clawed them so many times, their legs looked like scratching posts for cats. Jake figured it was a warm up for the dust-grinder he would have to ride through to reach his father.

As the wind shifted and pushed them toward town, the curtain of dust suddenly lifted. Jake was the first to see the churning black column at the other end of town. "Sira!" he shouted.

When she saw the tornado, she instinctively hit her brakes.

He kept riding. "It's moving away from town!"

And it was. For reasons only scientists who have yet to be born will someday understand, the tornado had changed directions.

They leaned into their pedals, lowered their heads against flying debris, and sped toward town.

As they flew over the railroad tracks, the wind shifted again. A blast of cold air stood Jake up, almost blowing him off his bike. He clutched his handlebars and squinted into the wind.

The tornado might have backed up but now it was shape-shifting into another beast. "Digit," "bullwhip," "braid" no longer applied. The tornado was expanding like a great monster loosening its belt, making ready for the main course. The roar was deafening. A thousand freight trains couldn't drown it out.

Their bikes shuddered on the shaking ground.

When the ground shakes, instinct takes over. All you want to do is get down.

They leaped off their bikes and tried to stand. Along with the roar in their ears, the tremor surging up through them brought a wave of nausea. They fought the urge to throw up.

Then the huge tornado transformed again. It looked like invisible hands had grabbed the bottom of it and were slowly pulling it apart. It was splitting in two.

One tornado veered to the left, digging up the fields to the north. The other thrashed and whipped back and forth as it churned toward Courage Street. It hit Mange Field, scattering the outfield fence like a box of toothpicks. The wire backstop was yanked out of the ground like a weed and disappeared into the tornado's vortex. It moved across the top of Courage Street, churning up bricks like they were Styrofoam peanuts. Then it slammed into a home, slapping it away like a house of cards.

Jake yanked the bolt cutter off his bike. He ran up the street, straight toward a whipping carousel of flying debris.

"Jake!" Sira screamed.

But the wind swallowed his name.

———

Howie ignored the deafening roar and the vibration thudding up his legs as he tried another key in the padlock.

Jim Waters stood silently on the other side of the screen. There was nothing he could do but watch. He wasn't watching Howie. He was fixed on the window Jake had slipped through, monitoring a tiny patch of sky. In the last few minutes, it had gone from gray, to coffee, to black. Now it was ghoulish green. They were almost out of time.

"Got it!" Howie mouthed. He threw off the lock, pulled open the door.

As Jim felt his ears pop, he knew it was too late.

He yanked Howie through the door and threw him into the bunker he'd built in the corner. As the building shook and the roof banged up and down, Jim dove on top of the bunker and burrowed.

———

Like a nightmare in which you try to run but can't, Jake struggled against the blasting wind.

He watched helplessly as the tornado staggered down the street, taking ragged bites out of houses. Then it veered across Courage and slammed into the post office. The front half of the building exploded like a bomb.

Jake opened his mouth to scream, but he was silenced by a small projectile fired from the post office. It struck him in the forehead. He dropped like a stone. It was another first in the history of head bonks. Lying on the bricks beside him was the bonker. A rubber stamp. The red, ink-filled impression on Jake's forehead read, CONFIDENTIAL.

Sira saw him drop and struggled toward him. As she pulled his limp body to the nearest house, she kept an eye on the twin tornadoes. The one in town veered around what was left of the post office and uprooted houses as it moved east. An electrical transformer exploded in a flash of light. The tornado north of town was retreating, or stalled, she couldn't tell which. But it had grown squat and thick, and changed color. It was now jet black with a glossy sheen.

When she got Jake to the house on the corner, she set him down to open the door. He groaned and came to.

She helped him to a sitting position. "We gotta get inside!"

He turned and saw a window sticking up from the ground.

The coffin house.

"Nooo!" he screamed.

She pointed at the glistening tornado to the northwest. It was even thicker than the one that had split in two. And it had changed direction. It was heading for town. "Your pick! Get in the house or get sucked into that!" She disappeared into the dugout house.

Jake stood up and gaped at the massive tornado as it lumbered into Patience. It looked like a gigantic drum of spinning tar.

The Wizard of Oz it wasn't.

It was great.

It was powerful.

But there was no curtain.

He couldn't take his eyes off it. He was caught in the coil of Medusa's braid.

The door flew open. Two brown arms grabbed him and pulled. He tumbled into the house.

The wind slammed the door shut. Sira pulled Jake to the dark corner farthest from the tornado. They dropped to their shins and covered their heads.

The earth-shaking roar that rose around them made it feel like they were strapped to a jet engine taking off.

Jake reached over and grabbed Sira's hand. This was it, he thought. The final destruction. He was never getting out of Patience. He was going to die right here, in the coffin house, just like his nightmare predicted. The only bone the curse had thrown him was that he wasn't alone.

As the roar drowned out even thought, a scent curled into his brain. He had heard somewhere that people sometimes hallucinate smells before they die. Usually good smells, like baking bread or freshly mown grass. He wasn't so lucky. His last scent was rotten cow manure. Leave it to the curse to throw him a stink bomb.

He pressed close to Sira and sang into her ear. "Take me out to the stink farm . . ."

He thought he heard her laugh.

As the coffin house shook in the endless sonic boom, they squeezed out the beat in each other's hand and sang.

> *Take me out to the cloud.*
> *Buy me some cow pies and buff'lo chips,*
> *I don't care if I'm up to my hips.*
> *Let me root, root, root in the Knight soil,*
> *It's a smell with a charm.*
> *For it's one, two, three whiffs, you're out,*
> *At the old stink farm.*

41　slime city

It seemed like forever, but it was over in a minute.

Suddenly all the noise and shaking stopped. The world went silent and still. The odd thing was the total lack of light. The half windows in the coffin house were still black.

Jake thought maybe they'd been knocked out by falling boards or fallen asleep and now it was night. Of course, there was also the possibility that they were dead and whatever afterlife they'd landed in was having a blackout.

He realized he was still clutching Sira's hand. He felt his face flush with heat and pulled it away. "Are you okay?"

"Yeah," she answered.

They got up and shuffled through the darkness to the door. It was stuck. With both of them pulling as hard as they could, it finally opened, with a wet sucking sound. Their hands instantly shot up against the assault of light. And stench.

At first, as their eyes adjusted to the harsh sunlight, they couldn't figure out where they were. Then they understood why the windows had been blacked out.

The ground, the jagged shards of trees, the street, and the bashed-in houses on the other side were all covered in a wet blanket of muck.

Stinky muck.

The muck recipe included manure, manure compost, green gold, black gold, Dung Shui, and Pie-Agri. While the first tornado had been a wrecking ball, the second had turned into an aerial dump truck. It had picked up the entire inventory of Knight's Soil & Fertilizer and dumped it on Patience.

The big bang. An inside job. Death by a million cow pies.

Normally, Jake would have thought twice about stepping into such a mess, but he had other concerns. He ran into the muck, slipped, almost fell, and ran up Courage Street. At least, as well as anyone can run in ankle-deep sludge.

Sira followed, using his tracks in the green-black slime like sunken stepping-stones.

All the town hall needed was a few candles and it would have made a handsome chocolate birthday cake. The front doors were gone. The townspeople emerged from the fraidy hole with Mr. Knight leading the way.

He dashed out of the building and yelled "Howie!" as he hit the muck. He went down and slid several feet. It's not hard to imagine his next word. Hint: it was a factual statement.

Mrs. Knight marched past him without offering a hand.

Neither snow nor rain nor manure nor fallen husband will stop a mother lion from finding her lost cub.

The others stepped outside with a variety of reactions.

Mr. Olabuff was the first to notice it wasn't just the inventory of KSF that the town was under. There were tires everywhere. In the street, on rooftops, there was even one perched like a glistening chocolate donut on top of a utility pole. When he looked up the street and saw that Mr. Tired Tires Tire Company had been flattened and not one pyramid of tires remained, he put his face in his hands and cried.

Pearl and her baby, Sean, had opposite reactions. She let loose with a scream of horror and disgust. Sean let lose with a scream of joy and tried to wriggle out of her arms so he could play in the muck, like Mr. Knight seemed to be doing as he slipped and struggled to his feet.

Mr. and Mrs. Rashid were overjoyed to see Sira coming up the street. This time she didn't hesitate. She ran to their open arms and had a thank-Vishnu-we're-okay hug.

Oil Can Lockhart scanned the devastation as he packed a fresh chaw into his cheek. "That's the thing about tornadoes," he declared to no one in particular. "It puts a fine edge on life. Not everybody gets to live like this."

Mrs. Bickers and Lillian Huffaker clutched each other as Mrs. Huffaker held a handkerchief over her nose. "Well," Mrs. Bickers announced, "we won't be making ice cream out of this."

More than half of the post office was gone. The first tornado had ripped the building away as far back as the metal screen. The screen was buckled and impaled by a great tangle of barbwire. Behind the screen, the roof was partially collapsed.

By the time Jake got there, Howie was stepping through the bent hole in the screen where the door had been. He was dazed but unhurt.

"Is my dad in there?" Jake yelled.

Howie snapped out of his daze. "I don't know."

Jake jumped past him and started pulling rubble off the pile of boxes in the corner. "Dad?"

Mrs. Knight slid through the muck and gathered Howie in a bear hug. Mr. Knight wasn't far behind.

Jake heard a groan, turned toward it, and pulled away a soggy bundle of mailer boxes. Underneath was a blue work shirt with the Waters & Son Plumbing logo on the sleeve. He had never been happier to see it. He pawed away a layer of spilled mail and found his father lying on his side. Blood oozed from a deep gash in his forehead. "Dad!"

Jim's eyes opened. He tried to look toward Jake. He grimaced in pain. "Don't move me and don't step on me. I think my legs are broken."

Jake froze, unsure where his dad's legs were in the rubble.

"By the way," his father asked, "what took you so long?"

Jake leaned down and started to tell him when Mr. Knight barged into the rubble. "Is he okay?"

As he turned to stop Mr. Knight from coming closer, Jake's anger exploded. "No! And he wouldn't be hurt if he'd been in the town hall!"

Mr. Knight flushed with anger. "Oh, so this is my doing? None of this would have happened if he hadn't brought the Plunger back to town! He knew he was playing with fire, and he got burned!"

By now the others were arriving. As the mayor, and the owner of the muck that covered Patience, Mr. Knight wasn't going to miss the opportunity to make sure everyone understood who was to blame.

He started to deliver his next salvo but Howie stepped forward. "Dad, if it weren't for Mr. Waters," he said, pointing at the tangle of barbwire piercing the metal screen, "that wire would've cut me to ribbons."

Mr. Knight threw his arms wide. "If it weren't for Jim Waters, we'd still have a town!"

"Marvin," Mrs. Knight said with the calm of a stalking lioness. "For once in your life, shut up."

In the silence that followed, the wail of a siren rose in the distance.

42   be the fox

EMS workers pulled Jim Waters from the rubble and took him to the hospital in Sharon Springs. Both of his legs were broken, one required extensive surgery.

Jake was treated for his CONFIDENTIAL contusion and given a note by the doctor for the first day of school. The note explained that Jake was not trying to be a smart aleck or displaying the tattoo of some weird gang. In a week or two, the note promised, Jake's forehead would be as blank as every other kid's at school.

There was one other important development. The Department of Health and Environment and the EPA, in the form of Ms. Sandra Cass, returned to Patience to assess the damage and environmental impact of a town slimed by cow manure in various stages of decomposition. Because of the risk of *E. coli*, shigella, typhoid, and several other diseases, Ms. Cass declared Patience unfit for human habitation, ordered an immediate evacuation, and sealed it off as an environmental disaster area.

In the report to her regional office, the only thing she omitted was her final conclusion. The curse of her great-great-grandfather had finally delivered on its last promise. The only thing that remained of Patience, "the rose of the prairie," was its lingering scent. And it wasn't anything like a rose.

To ensure that the Cass family revenge was as painful as possible, Ms. Cass issued one more order. The citizens of Patience were subjected to a battery of shots protecting them from the diseases they might have been exposed to.

By the time Jake got his last shot, his arm felt like he'd been gored by a bull. The good news was that he was finally allowed to see his father in the hospital.

When he found his father's room, he opened the door and almost ran into Mr. Olabuff coming out. As Jake backed out of the way, he was even more startled by Mr. Olabuff's face. His eyes were red and puffy. Like he'd been crying. He gave Jake a sheepish look and kept moving.

Jake stepped into the room. His father was lying in bed with both legs in full casts.

Jim's eyes brightened when he saw his son. Then he answered Jake's puzzled expression. "Red came to apologize."

Jake moved to the side of the bed and checked out his father's casts. "Is he going to jail?"

"No, I'd have to press charges."

"Why don't you?"

"Good people do bad things, Jake. Sometimes you have to cut 'em some slack."

"It's my fault anyway, Dad. If I'd gotten you out when you told me—"

"Here's how I figure it," Jim interrupted, raising his lecture finger. "The thing about things getting worse before they get better is that you never know when the worse is over and the better begins." He smiled up at Jake. "Did the ranch get hit?"

"I don't think so. It looked like the damage stopped at the highway, but whether it got hit or not doesn't matter," Jake explained with growing excitement. "That's where I went instead of coming back to the post office." He pulled the rusty tin container from his back pocket and set it on his father's chest.

Jim stared at it. "The map?"

"Yep." Jake grinned. "But there's something I need to tell you." The door suddenly opened behind him.

They both grabbed for the tin. Jim got it first. His large hand wrapped around it just as Mr. Knight and Howie swept into the room.

Mr. Knight stopped at the end of the bed. He was all smiles and friendliness. Like nothing had ever happened. "I just talked to the doctor. He says you'll be dancing a jig in two months."

"He must be good," Jim replied, " 'cause these legs never jigged before."

Mr. Knight tossed him a laugh. "The other good news is that this whole thing isn't going to cost you a cent."

"Why not?"

"I'm paying for everything."

Jim started to protest but Mr. Knight wouldn't hear it.

"I insist. And it's not some stupid bribe like I tried last time. If you wanna press charges against me, go ahead. I deserve 'em, right, Howie?"

Howie nodded. "Right."

Mr. Knight grabbed a chair, planted it next to Jake, and sat.

Jake stopped breathing. The tin was still hidden under his father's hand. Mr. Knight's nose was practically over it.

"The thing is," Mr. Knight said, shifting from jovial to sincere. "I want to do whatever it takes to bury the hatchet."

Jim gave him a dubious look. "The hatchet?"

"Let me put it another way. The way I see it, that tornado solved a lot of problems."

"As in?" Jim asked.

Mr. Knight ticked them off on his fingers. "One, nobody has to worry anymore about nitrates leaching into someone's well. Knight's Soil and Fertilizer is gone, finished, kaput. Two, so is Patience. Which brings us to number three. Our families have been good neighbors for six generations, and for a hundred and twenty-eight of those years we've suffered under the curse. Now, finally, that's over too. And now it's time to move on. Time to go our separate ways and start over somewhere else. But you know what the greatest thing about this whole disaster is, Jim?" He reached forward and touched Jim's hand.

Jake's heart beat harder than the heart of a man who wakes up in a coffin.

Mr. Knight leaned forward with a rascally smile. "The last laugh is on the curse."

Jim raised an eyebrow. "How so?"

"I was talking to some tornado experts, and they told me that if Nature had its way the second tornado should have flattened the entire town and killed us all. But it didn't. Know why?"

"Why?"

" 'Cause it ran smack-dab into KSF. All that raw material got sucked up into the killer tornado, and it dragged it down like a pack of wolves pulling down a buffalo. It was a hammer looking to crush us, and KSF cushioned the blow with a million cubic yards of manure. That's why we got the last laugh on the curse. And that's why, by my reckoning, the slate between the Knights and the Waters family has been wiped clean."

Jim stared at him, trying to decipher his reasoning. "Maybe it's the anesthesia, Marv. I don't follow."

Mr. Knight stood up. "You saved my son, and, by a twist of fate, KSF saved us all. I say we count our blessings, go our separate ways, and be sure to send Christmas cards."

Jake dreaded what was coming next.

Mr. Knight reached toward Jim, opening his hand for a shake. "Is it a deal?"

Jake clicked into default mode. Do what all J. Waters do. When in doubt, don't move.

But there are times when you're pitched into the family gene pool and you don't swim the stroke your father and his father swam before him. There are times when you plunge deeper into the pool than you've ever plunged before. When you shoot to the bottom and stir up instincts that have been buried in the silt for generations. There are times when you go under and become the fox.

Jake stepped between his father and Mr. Knight, grabbed Mr. Knight's hand, and vigorously pumped it. "It's a deal, Mr. Knight!"

As Mr. Knight recovered from the surprise, Jake slipped his left hand behind his back. Jim pressed the tin into it.

"Well, aren't you the little man?" Mr. Knight chuckled.

"Yes, he is," Jim agreed as Jake tucked the tin into his back pocket.

Then Jake stepped out of the way to let the two men shake.

"No hard feelings?" Mr. Knight asked.

"No hard feelings." Jim turned to Jake and Howie. "You boys wanna know a secret?"

"Sure," Howie said.

"When we were your age, Marvin and I used to go to the quarry all the time."

"That's right," Mr. Knight interjected. "We were the best divers in Patience."

"We even named the diving rocks, Kennedy and Vandenberg."

Mr. Knight laughed at the memory. "Kennedy was mine, Vandenberg was yours."

"No, Marv, Vandenberg was yours," Jim corrected. "You're the one that always flirted with Last Crack Rock."

While the two of them quibbled and reminisced, Jake and Howie slipped out of the room.

As they left the hospital, the late-day sun cast long shadows across Sharon Springs's main street. They headed toward the high school, where everyone from Patience was being put up. They walked in silence.

Jake had a plan, but there was no way he was telling Howie about it. He couldn't trust Howie anymore. Not that it mattered. Like Mr. Knight said, the Waters and the Knights were going their separate ways.

Howie finally spoke up. "So?"

"So what?" Jake said flatly.

"What was that little thing between you and your dad?"

"What little thing?" Jake asked with not-a-clue cool.

Howie let out a scornful chuckle. "Hey, my dad may be blind and a little stupid, but I'm not. I saw your dad give you something."

Jake slid a sideways glance at his ex–best friend.

"C'mon," Howie pressed. "What's the big secret?"

"There's no secret, and even if there was, why should I trust you?"

" 'Cause I didn't blow the whistle on you right there. 'Cause I don't trust my dad to do the right thing anymore. I'm not even sure I trust your dad. They've been doing so many dumb things lately, I'm beginning to think they both did headers off Last Crack Rock when they were kids and they've never told us about the metal plates in their heads."

Jake laughed. Howie was back to being Howie. "I don't trust 'em either. But that doesn't mean I trust you."

"Why not?"

"Gee, Howie, let's see. You blabbed to your dad about the Plunger, then you stole it outta my house—"

"Yeah, and when I found out your dad was still locked in the post office, I tried to get him out. But you weren't there. You'd gotten out. I saw you and Sira ride out of town before the tornadoes. Where'd you go? What was more important than busting out your dad?"

Jake kept walking, but he couldn't run from the truth. Howie had a point. If things had turned out differently and his father and Howie had died in the post office, it would have been Jake's fault. And he never would have forgiven himself.

"Whatever it was," Howie continued, "wherever you went, I know that's your big secret. If you wanna keep it to yourself, that's your business."

Jake glanced over at Howie. There was a stillness in his friend's face he'd never seen before. All the mischievous bravado was gone. Even his eyes were different. Howie stared ahead with prairie eyes.

Howie jammed his hands in his pockets. "But here's the thing, Tweener. Tomorrow we could move to different towns. This could be the last day we ever see each other. Is this how you wanna end it? With secrets?"

Jake didn't need a long sit-down to figure out his next move. That's the thing about being the fox. You know when to turn on a dime.

"No, I don't wanna end it with secrets." Jake shot Howie a knowing smile. "But I'm warning you, this secret really stinks."

"I don't get it."

"How do you feel about going back to Patience?"

Howie stopped. "Are you nuts? The place is a cesspool."

"Yeah." Jake grinned. "A cesspool with buried treasure."

43   hunting and gathering

After Jake and Howie found Sira in the high school gym, they went outside and Jake walked them through his plan. They made a list of all the equipment they'd need and divided it into three categories.

- Transportation
- Search & Digging
- Safety

They each took a category and gave themselves twenty-four hours to beg, borrow, or steal everything on their list. The next night, geared up and good to go, they'd begin the hunt for buried treasure.

Then they held a little ceremony in which Jake made Howie swear on the grave of every Knight buried on Temperance Street that he would not breathe a word about their plan to anyone. After that, Sira and Howie went off to have dinner with their parents.

As dusk triggered the streetlights, Jake went back to

the hospital to check on his father and wait for the surprise he had arranged. His father was asleep when he got there.

When he woke up, Jim was famished. After the nurses ignored his third request for dinner, he started to get irritated. Then dinner arrived. It came through the door in this order:

- The delicious aroma of Fat Burgers.
- A familiar voice shouting, "Excuse me! Is this the room of a plumber who wanted to be a prince?"
- And Wanda.

Jim wasn't sure what to bite first. A Fat Burger or Jake, for calling Wanda and telling her what happened. "You didn't need to come," he protested.

"And not see you with two broken legs?" she joked as she handed him a huge burger. "Wouldn't miss it for the world."

As they ate, Jim and Jake filled her in on the whole story of what happened after she hopped in her red Mustang and wisely left town. With the two storytellers milking their material for maximum effect, they lifted their one-woman audience to the heights of comedy and plunged her to the depths of tragedy. All without telling her about the map, of course.

After they finished their account, she said, "You know what the most tragic thing is?"

"What?" they asked.

"Of all the things in Patience that got buried in sludge, the one thing that escaped was the collection of the American Toilet Museum."

Jim laughed. "Actually, Wanda, you may be in luck. We're still not sure what happened to the ranch."

The only person who did was exploring the ranch with a flashlight at that very moment.

Inside the old house, Sandra Cass slowly circled her flashlight beam around the ragged hole where the Dolphin Deluge Washdown Water Closet had once been. She knelt down and took a closer look. The splintered edge was a mix of colors ranging from dark to light. Her scientific eyes deduced the obvious. Some of it was freshly splintered wood. Whatever had crashed through this hole had done so recently. And it wasn't tornado damage, because neither of the cyclones had made it as far as the old Waters ranch.

She bent closer and cast her beam down the hole. She was startled as the light caught two darting shapes in the cellar. Rats. Then the beam found the Dolphin Deluge lying on its side. It was surprisingly white. Her scientific mind went to work again. If it had been lying there long it would have been covered in dust. Obviously, the ancient and cursed toilet had fallen to its new resting place in the very recent past.

She smiled with satisfaction. Perhaps the Plunger of Destiny's return had done more than turn Patience into the cow-poop Pompeii of the plains. Perhaps it had stirred up some new clues in an old mystery. An old mystery about the only thing buried under Patience that still had value.

Jake decided to leave the little reunion in the hospital before Wanda started the long drive back to Vegas, where she was working as a showgirl again. If there was any chance of Wanda and his father getting back together, they needed some alone time.

The next morning, Jake, Sira, and Howie began gathering the equipment they needed. Sharon Springs wasn't their hometown but they did go to school there. Where there's school, there's friends. Where there's friends, there's things to borrow. And where there's no friends with what you need, there's cunning.

- Friends loaned Howie a couple of ATVs.
- Friends loaned Jake shovels, rope, flashlights, two compasses, two bolt cutters, and muck boots.
- Cunning disguised Sira as a candy striper at the hospital, where she borrowed three chem-bio suits from the first responders' supply room.

Their activity went unnoticed because everyone's attention was on the new distraction that had come to Sharon Springs. The media. A plague of television crews had descended and was gobbling up stories from the victims of Patience in what was being billed as the "doodoo disaster," the "caca catastrophe," and the "cow-pocalypse," depending on which reporter you listened to.

The treasure-hunting trio didn't rate a second glance as they quietly procured their equipment and stashed it in a dense row of trees outside town. That evening they proceeded according to plan. They all had dinner with their respective parents.

When Jake visited the hospital, he was disappointed that his father didn't want to talk about Wanda as much as he wanted to talk about the map. Jake had anticipated the map part. He told his father that, after their close call with Mr. Knight, he'd hidden the map in a safe place. And there was no reason to retrieve it until Jim recovered from his broken legs, and then they could go after the treasure.

Jim fell for Jake's white lie but insisted on hearing a description of the map. Jake was happy to oblige.

Later that night, Jake, Sira, and Howie went to bed on their cots in the high school gym. A little past midnight, while the citizens of Patience dreamed of their faces illuminating TV screens across the land, the treasure hunters slipped into the moonless night.

44   back to the scene of the slime

With Jake and Sira on one ATV and Howie and the equipment on the other, they followed a county road back to Patience that kept them well north of Highway 40. The night was clear, with an endless sweep of stars.

Because the road was flat and straight, they didn't worry about being seen. They could spot headlights coming two miles away, giving them plenty of time to pull off the road and hunker down in the ditch. Not being seen was essential to the plan's success.

They didn't need light to know they were getting closer to Patience. They only needed their noses. As the smell invaded their nostrils, they killed their headlights to avoid detection by the manned checkpoint on Highway 40 to the south. And they throttled down so the growl of the ATVs wouldn't be heard.

When they reached an unmanned barricade across the county road, they drove around it and kept going. The putrid stench of Patience kept growing stronger.

Reaching the next crossroads, Jake drove his ATV through the intersection, stopped, and pointed into the darkness. "There."

Behind him, Sira flicked on a flashlight and the beam searched the corner of a field. It found a vertical block of yellowish stone.

Limestone fence posts are a common sight in the high plains. In the 1800s, trees and lumber were so scarce, the pioneers had to carve their fence posts from stone.

The threesome walked to the stone upright and made sure it was the corner post. Their light beams revealed two rows of stone posts. One line marched straight east, the other marched south. The barbwire between the posts had long since disappeared, making the vertical stones look like rows of tombstones in the darkness.

"This is it." Jake pulled the tin from his pocket and unfolded Jeremiah's leather map. Sira shone a light on the map as Jake oriented it to the fence. The two fence lines were marked in the northwest corner of the map as a row of dots moving east, and a row of dots moving south. The dots moving east ended with the number "37." The dots moving south ended with "31."

He traced his finger along each row. "We go thirty-seven posts east and thirty-one posts south. Then we follow two lines south and east into the field." He pointed to a small X on the map where the imaginary lines met. "And that's where it should be buried."

"If the tornado didn't dig it up," Howie cautioned.

"And if all the fence posts are still there," Sira added.

Jake folded up the map and tucked it back in the tin.

"Right, so be sure to check for fallen or buried posts, and if you hit a double gap, then figure the post was taken away and be sure to count it."

"Got it." Howie headed back to the ATVs.

They hid the ATVs in the ditch, put on their chem-bio suits and muck boots, and grabbed shovels and two bolt cutters.

"See you at the X," Howie said, starting down the fence line running south. Even without his hood on, the baggy white suit made him look like a ghost. He stopped and turned to Jake and Sira, who were following the posts running east. "Hey, Cricket," he teased, "thanks for sparing me 37 and 31 from your Book of Slumber."

Without skipping a beat, she whispered through the darkness. " '37. In 1937—"

"I'm not listening!" Howie shouted, covering his ears.

"Shut up," Jake whispered harshly. "Someone might hear us."

Howie's light beam bobbed away into the darkness.

Jake counted the third post as Sira caught up with him. "In 1937, Kansas had four thousand three hundred and sixty-eight newspapers, more than any other state in the country. In 1931, the football great Knute Rockne was the first celebrity to die in a commercial airplane crash. It happened near Bazaar, Kansas."

Jake stopped and shone his light in her face. "If I lose count because you're rattling off freaky facts, you're the one who's going back and recounting."

"Sorry, nervous energy." She pulled her fingers across her mouth and mumbled, "My lips are sealed."

For the next few minutes, they concentrated on not falling into prairie dog holes and making sure they counted every post.

"Thirty-seven," Jake announced as he patted a post. "It's an odd number to pick. I wonder why he picked thirty-seven and thirty-one."

"No-brainer," Sira said. "They add up to sixty-eight, and 1868 was the year Jeremiah founded Patience."

Jake shook his head as he pulled a compass out of his pocket. "Sometimes I wish you'd just skip a grade."

Her mouth dropped open in mock shock. "And miss a year of living in the stinkiest town in America? No way."

"Come on, Howie might be there by now."

She moved into the field ahead of him. "I'll lead, so you don't fall in a hole."

"Good idea."

As Sira walked into the field, he followed directly behind her, with his flashlight and his eyes glued to the compass. He had to make sure they headed due south.

They soon came to a high chain-link fence blocking their way. It surrounded what was left of KSF. So far, everything was just as Jake had predicted. They used the bolt cutters to cut a hole in the fence. If they found the trunk, they'd have to cut a bigger hole on the way out.

Now came the tricky part. No matter what they encountered, they had to keep walking on a perfect southerly line. If they wandered off course, they'd miss the exact location of the X.

Sira stopped at the edge of what looked like a deep ditch. "Hold up."

They pointed their flashlights down. It wasn't a ditch, it was one of KSF's settling ponds. Or what was left of it after the tornado.

"Wow," she said.

Jake's flashlight beam danced around the bottom of the pond. "It's empty."

"The tornado sucked it clean."

"Yeah, but not that clean. Time to hood up."

They pulled on their chem-bio hoods. Sira gingerly led the way into the empty but shallow pond. Jake followed, trying to keep an eye on the compass and not slip in the muck. Their boots made sucking sounds as they walked across the lagoon.

They walked through another empty pond before they heard the sucking slurp of Howie's boots off to the right. They signaled with their flashlights. He signaled back. They were on course to meet at the X.

A minute later, Jake and Sira arrived at the north edge of another settling pond. This one was empty too.

Howie arrived at the west edge and threw off his hood. "You've gotta be kidding. He buried the trunk in the middle of a pond?"

"The pond wasn't here when he buried it," Jake said through his hood. "It was your dad who turned this into sludge central."

"Hey," Howie said, brightening, "that means the trunk and everything in it belongs to my family."

"Nice try," Jake countered. "You know it belongs to everyone."

Sira started down into the almost empty pond.

"Enough stalling, guys. Nobody ever said digging up treasure was a walk in the park."

Howie threw his hood back on. "Yeah, but why did we get stuck with a walk in the poop?"

The trio slid down the four-foot bank into the settling pond and kept their compass bearings as they moved toward the intersecting point. They met a couple of yards from the pond's opposite bank.

"X marks the spot," Jake announced.

Howie lifted his shovel. Jake and Sira jumped back as he thrust it into the muck. The blade went in with a loud smack and stopped after a few inches.

"The good news is there's not a lot of sludge," Howie reported. "The bad news is there's solid ground under it."

They dug two at a time while the third took a break, held the flashlight, and tried to stop slippery blobs of muck from sliding back into the hole. It was hardly a break.

After an hour of digging, they had a hole five feet wide and four feet deep. They were soaked from sweating in their chem-bio suits. Whoever was out of the hole took off their hood to get some air. Not that it was fresh. So far, Jake's biggest regret was not bringing gas masks. And a backhoe.

Howie threw his shovel onto one of the piles of dirt next to the hole and yanked off his hood. "This is crazy!"

Jake looked at him through the foggy plastic window of his hood. *"Ad Astra per Aspera."*

"What?" Howie demanded.

"To the stars through difficulty." Jake dug his shovel into the bottom of the hole and started to sing. "Take me out to the stink farm, take me out to the cloud. . . ." He heard Howie laugh and the scrape of his shovel biting into dirt.

"Buy me some cow pies and buff'lo chips," Howie sang along. "I don't care if I'm up to my hips."

When they got to "For it's one, two, three . . ." they jabbed their shovels into the bottom of the hole. On "three," Howie's shovel went *thunk!*

They froze.

Howie pumped the shovel up and down.

Thunk-thunk-thunk!

A second later, three shovels chopped away at the packed dirt.

A minute later, the top of a trunk was exposed.

The ground was so dry and packed, it took another half hour of digging before they could get the trunk to shift in its prairie grave. But from the minute they heard the first *thunk*, the smell of rotting manure had disappeared.

It was an old wooden trunk with a bow-wood top and heavy wooden slats banded around all four sides. With Jake and Sira each on a corner and Howie on the other end, they squatted down and hooked their fingers under the trunk's top band of slats. Jake counted it down. "One, two, *three!*"

The ground lost its grip and gave up its treasure. They lifted it, bracing their backs against the sides of the hole. It wasn't as heavy as they'd imagined.

"What now?" Howie asked. Between the trunk and their bodies pressed against the walls of the hole, there was nowhere to go with it but up.

Jake jutted his chin toward the shortest mound of dirt and sludge on the edge of the hole. "Up here, on the short pile."

They lifted the trunk to shoulder height and gave it a hard push up onto the pile. A little too hard. The trunk slid off the top of the pile and toppled out of view.

"Oops." Sira giggled.

"Who cares?" Jake clambered up out of the hole. "We got it."

"Yes, we do," a voice said.

Jake only saw the dark silhouette before the light exploded in his eyes.

45   never play with guns

He shot a hand up against the blinding light and tried to make out who was standing above him at the edge of the pond.

"Do you know what they call people who take advantage of natural disasters to steal things?"

As he recognized the voice he saw the gun in her hand. Sandra Cass.

"Looters," she said. "You know what they do to looters in Saudi Arabia? They cut off their hands."

"We're not in Saudi Arabia," Sira piped up from the hole.

"And we're not stealing," Howie added. "This is my dad's land."

Ms. Cass swung her light to the two faces in the hole. "For your information, little Mr. Knight, we're not in Patience anymore. You're in a Superfund cleanup site, and everything here, from the hazardous waste to trunks that pop out of the ground, has been seized by the federal government. Now, you two, climb out of the hole, and the three of you lift the trunk up here, or I'll throw you all in jail for trespassing on federal property."

Howie and Sira climbed out of the hole, joining Jake.

As the three of them lifted the trunk to the edge of the pond, Jake's shock at their surprise visitor gave way to suspicion. "How did you know we'd be here?"

"I didn't. But next time you want to loot government property, you should do a better job of hiding your getaway vehicles."

It still didn't add up, he thought. Why was she prowling around in the middle of the night? "So you were looking for us?" As she stared down at him, he could just make out her sneer in the spill of her flashlight.

"Let's put it this way, Jake. I told you I was fascinated by history. Especially local history. And when I saw that someone had tampered with the old toilet out at the Waters ranch, I figured someone knew something, and they might be making a move before we brought in the heavy equipment and scraped what's left of Patience off the map."

Sira twitched with anger. "So you've been after the treasure all along!"

Ms. Cass answered with a disdainful laugh. "No, but it's turned into an unexpected benefit." She impatiently waved the revolver in her hand. "Now be good little children and get back in the hole."

They hesitated.

She pointed the gun. "Now."

They scrambled back down into the hole.

She examined the trunk with her light. There was a rusty lock on it. She set the gun and flashlight down, pulled out a pair of surgical gloves, put them on, and grabbed a bolt cutter. The lock broke between the cutter's jaws.

Jake, Sira, and Howie strained to see as she banged the bolt cutter against the side of the trunk. The old wax seal fell away like a crumbling donut. She lifted the lid.

"None of that belongs to you," Jake protested. "It belongs to the people of Patience."

"The people of Patience?" she echoed with mocking laughter as her flashlight illuminated the boxes, satchels, and leather bags in the trunk. "You mean the people who tarred and feathered my great-great-grandfather and rode him out of town on a rail?" She lifted a leather saddlebag. "I like to think of this as reparations. A fair settlement for the pain and suffering he must have endured."

"But you said it belonged to the federal government," Sira protested.

Ms. Cass opened the saddlebag and pulled out a sheaf of papers. "Little girl, I *am* the federal government." She shuffled through the papers and muttered, "Marriage license, land claims, railroad bonds." She tossed them in the air. "All worthless."

"That's history!" Sira yelled.

"It is now." Ms. Cass pulled up a fancy wooden box. "Oh, look, this one says 'Waldo Knight.' Now, I wonder what the richest shop owner in Patience had to hide from a bunch of bank robbers?" She opened the box and stared into it.

Howie couldn't stand the suspense. "What is it?"

She tilted the box and poured a few coins into her hand. "Some old coins, including a double eagle, and a wedding ring. Not great, but it's a start. Here"—she tossed the empty box at Howie—"don't say I didn't give you anything."

Jake didn't flinch as the box flew over his head and Howie caught it.

Inside, Jake was seething. The curse of Andars Cass had lived up to its terrible final words. Patience was no more. But now Sandra Cass was defiling the only thing that was left.

She lifted a fiddle case from the trunk and fixed her light on it. "And this one says 'J. Waters.' My, my, now what could the wealthiest man in all of Patience be hiding in a violin case?" The light beam danced wildly as she tucked the flashlight under her arm, closed the trunk lid, and set the fiddle case down on top of it.

She lifted the latches on the case and grabbed the flashlight from under her arm. "I'm thinking paper. As in stocks, bearer bonds, or just good ol' hard cash." She opened it.

Jake watched as her face froze in the glow of light bouncing out of the case.

"A fiddle?" she muttered in disbelief.

"A real fiddle?" Jake was equally stunned by what Regina Waters had put in the case. Then he saw Ms. Cass's face tighten into rage. "If it's just a fiddle," he blurted, "can I have it?"

She snapped toward him. "You already got your gift."

He recoiled with confusion. "What gift?"

"The Plunger of Destiny."

He gaped up at her. "What do you mean?"

She slammed the fiddle case shut. "Who do you think found it first? Who do you think put it on eBay and made sure your father bought it?"

"But—but why?" Jake stammered.

"Because I knew if the Plunger came back to town— curse or no curse—it would tear this place apart. But this," she proclaimed as she opened her arms to the surrounding devastation, "exceeded my wildest expectations!" She threw back her head and laughed.

From the moment he had been blinded by her flashlight, Jake's gut had tightened with fear. But now he felt the bone-cracking grip of terror. Looking up at her, as her maniacal laughter burst toward the stars like a volcano, he knew she was capable of anything. For the first time, he feared he and his friends might be standing in their grave.

He had to do something. Soon.

As her arms came down, the flashlight beam danced wildly.

Out of the corner of his eye, Jake caught the glint of metal. One of the shovels was lying outside the hole to his right. Ms. Cass was still standing above them, on the edge of the pond and behind the trunk. Her gun was some-where on the ground within reach. *Time to be the fox,* he told himself. *Time to hold your breath and go under. Time for the sixth J. Waters to have a vision.*

The vision came in a flash. Sandra Cass hated his family so much, she would do *anything* to twist the knife.

Jake stretched a hand up and pleaded, "Ms. Cass, please give me the fiddle! It's all my family has left! Please!"

She stared down at him.

He felt Sira's and Howie's eyes on him. He knew they were trying to figure out why he was acting like a total wimp. He just hoped they didn't call him on it.

Ms. Cass slid the beam of light to his face. "You're right, Jake Waters, it is all you have left."

He squinted into the light, trying to squeeze out tears. "If you give it to me, you can take everything else, and I'll never tell anyone." His face tightened as he sobbed. "Please, Ms. Cass! Just give me the fiddle! Please!"

Her mouth twisted in disgust. "How 'bout this? How 'bout I give your fiddle the same respect Jeremiah Waters gave Andars Cass?" She yanked the fiddle case up by its handle, took a couple of steps, and flung it into the darkness.

Jake didn't hesitate. His hand shot to the right, grabbed the shovel, and hurled it like a spear. The blade caught her in the shin. She screamed in pain. Her flashlight spun to the ground. She stumbled and caught herself on top of the trunk.

He scrambled out of the hole. She braced herself on the trunk with one hand while the other fished for the gun. He grabbed the trunk and pulled it over the edge of the pond. She tumbled after it, sliding into the pond face-first.

By the time she stopped sputtering, screaming, and flailing around in the muck, she looked like she was tarred and ready for feathering.

Jake didn't have any feathers, but he did have the gun.

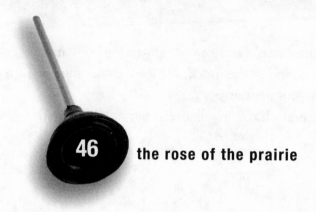

46   the rose of the prairie

In the year after Jake, Sira, and Howie foiled Ms. Cass's attempt to pilfer the community chest, many things came to pass.

The EPA Superfund:
- Razed every building in Patience except the town hall.
- Removed two feet of contaminated topsoil.
- Made sure the drinking water was safe.
- Repaved the original grid of streets.
- Sterilized the old street signs and put them back up.

The federal government:
- Built a new post office.
- Cleaned up and repaired the town hall.
- Provided the citizens with disaster relief to rebuild their homes.

- Moved Sandra Cass to the other side of the state.
- As in Leavenworth.
- Penitentiary.

Jim Waters finally made it "to the stars" when he:
- Opened the American Toilet Museum at the old ranch.
- Tricked his first patrons into coming by posting signs on the highway that read ATM—THIS WAY.
- Impressed history buffs and plumbers with his collection of sensational sanitary-ware and nuggets of toilet knowledge.
- Wowed everyone with the Dolphin Deluge Washdown Water Closet.
- Became one of the Points of Interest in the Kansas triple-A guide.
- And still had time to take care of the town's plumbing needs.

Inspired by the American Toilet Museum and Jim's pioneering spirit, the townspeople founded the Rose of the Prairie Restoration Society. With the rallying cry of "Homegrown!" the society helped make the following possible:
- Mr. Knight opened a big country store called Knight's Necessaries to Niceties.
- Oil Can Lockhart built a replica of the Silver Keg Saloon and now dispenses advice from behind the bar. He never chews tobacco on duty.
- Mrs. Huffaker opened the Thunderstone Ice

Cream Shop. She now sells Thunderstone Ice Cream in three states.

- Mrs. Rashid opened the Smoky Hill Hotel & Restaurant and won an award for the best Pakistani American food on the high plains.
- Mr. Rashid revived the *Patience Rose Petal Press*. Its first headline read PHOENIX RISES FROM FUMES.
- Mr. Olabuff opened the Mr. Sail-Car Sail-Car Company, which builds railroad sail-cars for racing on a ten-mile track of his own design, and for cross-country touring on abandoned railroad lines.
- Mrs. Bickers oversaw the rebuilding of Mange Field, which was renamed Cricket Field in honor of the last World Series of Workup champion.
- Pearl works behind the counter at Knight's Necessaries to Niceties.
- Sean has progressed from a jumper swing to a push car.
- The only time he turns blue is when he pitches a fit.

Wanda came back to Patience, but not for the reasons you might expect.

- She and Jim agreed that they were better at being friends than husband and wife.
- Jake liked this because now he always had a choice: to hang out at a quiet house or a loud house.
- At first, Wanda came back just to organize and

produce the first annual Curse of Cass Reenactment Festival.

- When it was a big success, the town asked her to stay and run the Patience Chamber of Commerce.
- She did.
- But she still travels a lot giving her popular lecture, "How to Home Grow Your Small Town."
- If you see a red Mustang with a new paint job, it's probably Wanda coming your way.

In case you're interested, the First Annual Curse of Cass Reenactment Festival:

- Drew thousands of tourists.
- Began with actors in nineteenth-century costume reenacting the fateful day the curse began.
- Included a classical concert and barn dance featuring the violin that made it all possible.

And if you're wondering, "How could a violin make all that possible?" the answer lies in what happened right after Jake turned the tables, and the gun, on Sandra Cass.

After putting Howie on guard duty, Jake and Sira found the fiddle case that Ms. Cass had flung into the darkness. The case was cracked, but the fiddle was nestled inside, undamaged. Under the beam of their flashlight, the fiddle's wood had a dark, lustrous glow.

As Jake lifted it from the case, his skin tingled. The last

person to touch it had been his great-great-great-grand-mother, Regina Waters. The last person to play it had been his great-great-great-great-great-grandfather. The presence of his ancestors rolled through him like a warm wave.

Sira was overcome with a different feeling. Curiosity. She pointed the flashlight into one of the sound holes and leaned in close to see if anything was hidden inside. Like diamonds and jewels. All she saw was a label.

She read the only word she could make out in the scattered beam of light. "Stra-di-var-i-us."

In the next few days, several key questions were answered.

Musical experts determined that the fiddle with the inscription *Antonius Stradivarius Cremonensis Faciebat Anno 1707* was not a fake. It was a real Stradivarius violin and worth several million dollars.

Antiques experts determined that, except for some nineteenth-century coins and bills, most of the other things in the trunk had limited value except as historical objects. Which is exactly what they became when they were displayed in Patience's new Rose of the Prairie Museum.

Jim and Jake Waters decided what to do with the family violin. Rather than sell it and become millionaires, they donated it to the Rose of the Prairie Restoration Society on two conditions. One, that it would never be sold. Instead, it went on tour. The violin instantly became a cash cow as it toured the world in the hands of famous violinists. The second condition was that the violin would return to Patience every year for the Annual Curse of Cass Reenactment Festival.

But the discovery of a Stradivarius in the Waters family begged a question. Why didn't Regina Waters and her grandfather ever tell Jeremiah, or anyone else, that they owned a Stradivarius?

The only other family story about the violin that had been passed down through the generations was how the old man had acquired it. Before he became blind and a fiddle player, Regina's grandfather had been a country doctor. His patients paid him with all manner of goods. The oddest payment he ever received was from a stranger whose life he saved, but not before having to amputate the stranger's left arm. Although the stranger was very thankful that the doctor had saved his life, he could no longer hold the violin he loved to play. So he paid the good doctor with what he called his "fine fiddle."

But this story didn't answer why Regina and her grandfather kept the Stradivarius secret to themselves.

Some believe Regina and her grandfather never knew it was a Stradivarius. But if that was the case, why did she consider it the most valuable thing in the house and put it in the trunk? Others believe they knew it was a Stradivarius and kept it a secret for another reason. Regina was a city girl and probably had doubts about becoming the wife of a pioneer in such a rugged place. So she kept it a secret because the violin was her insurance against things turning out badly. If she needed it, it was her ticket back to the city.

While this mystery may never be solved, two other loose ends are more easily tied up. Did Sira ever complete "Kansas: 100 Years of Freaky & Fascinating Facts"? Did Jake ever finish his over-the-summer school project?

The violin provided Sira with the fact that had been eluding her all summer. '07. In 1707 Stradivarius made the violin that would eventually save Patience, Kansas, from being wiped off the map. She got an A+ on the project.

In Jake's quest to find the project that took the least amount of time and paperwork, he finally settled on one. He did a poll and asked every citizen of Patience the same question. "Since Patience was destroyed but soon will be rebuilt, do you believe the curse was real or not?"

His findings were split right down the middle. Sort of.
- 33.33% said they didn't believe in the curse.
- 33.33% said they believed in it.
- 33.33% said they didn't believe in the curse on Tuesdays, Thursdays, and Saturdays, but on Mondays, Wednesdays, and Fridays they did.
- Which raised a follow-up question. "What about Sundays?"
- 100% of the respondents to this question said, "On Sundays, it's not polite to talk about curses."

Jake's teacher wasn't sure how much effort Jake had put into the project. However, the teacher was uncomfortable asking a lot of questions of a student with CONFIDENTIAL stamped on his forehead. So he told Jake that his project got a C on Tuesdays and Thursdays, but on Mondays, Wednesdays, and Fridays it got an A-.

Luckily it was Monday.

47 a year later

The morning after the First Annual Curse of Cass Festival, most of Patience was sleeping in.

Not Jake.

He sat on the porch in his baseball uniform. The letters across the front of his jersey spelled PIONEERS. He looked down Endurance Street at the two neat rows of wooden houses. Their yards were cinnamon-colored in the August heat. A tumbleweed rolled lazily across the street. A cottonwood at the side of the house warbled its phantom song of rain.

A lot of things had changed in a year, but some things would never change. In the summerlong war over the color of grass, August heat waves would always conquer the sprinklers. The south wind would always deliver tumbleweeds. And the lullaby of a cottonwood would always soothe a worried soul into sleep.

The creak of a screen door brought Jake out of his reverie.

His father stepped outside with a cup of coffee. "Sorry I can't make the game."

Jake shrugged. "It's okay. But you're gonna miss Thunderstone Ice Cream Day."

"And you're gonna miss the busiest day of the year at the museum. There'll be tons of tourists coming out to get their picture taken on the Dolphin Deluge Washdown Water Closet."

Jake grinned. "Yeah, I was thinking about it last night." He moved his hands up and down like scales. "Baseball, or watching people sit on the Dolphin Deluge? Baseball, or watching nut-jobs posing on the first flush toilet west of the Mississippi?"

Jim laughed as Jake got up and moved down to the yard. He swung a leg over his bike. "And I was thinking something else." He glanced up at his father. "I was thinking there's one thing worse than dying before you see what's over the horizon."

"Oh yeah?" Jim smiled. "What's that?"

"Dying before you see what's under your nose."

Jake rode down the street and stopped at one of the many changes in Patience. The yield sign at the corner of Endurance and Courage had been replaced with a stop sign. All the yield signs in town had been replaced with stop signs.

But the biggest change on the corner was the two-story house soaring out of the ground where the coffin house once hunkered in the earth. Yes, the coffin house probably saved his and Sira's life, but he was still glad it was gone. Along with the nightmare that went with it.

He rode past the town hall, which now doubled as the

tourist center, and along Courage Street. The commercial buildings on each side had been rebuilt in traditional high-plains style. Tall false fronts painted in cheerful colors, with a boardwalk and an overhang that ran down each side of the street. The street had been repaved in red brick, with plenty of room for diagonal parking.

Wal-Mart it wasn't.

When Jake reached Cricket Field there were already several players warming up. Sira and Howie were there in their Pioneers uniforms. A few other players belonged to the Patience Twisters.

The Pioneers and the Twisters were the only baseball teams in town, but the fact that the town had grown enough to field two complete teams was a huge change. The fact that they played each other every game and would both make it to the Patience World Series didn't bother anyone in the least.

During the game, Oil Can Lockhart rooted for the Twisters. The Pioneers' biggest fan was Mrs. Bickers, who still watched from her porch, rang her cowbell, and signaled outs with a gong.

Wanda was there too, rooting for Jake and the Pioneers almost as loudly as Mrs. Bickers. Rumor had it that when Mrs. Bickers passed away, Wanda was going to buy her house and take over her "luxury box" porch.

During the seventh-inning stretch, the violinist who had played during the festivities the night before played "Take Me Out to the Ball Game" on the Stradivarius. Everyone sang the real lyrics.

"Take Me Out to the Stink Farm" had been sung the

day before during the Reenactment Festival. A recording of it could also be heard on the *Curse of Cass* CD, which could be purchased anywhere in town. Another one of Wanda's moneymaking ideas.

Jake, Sira, and Howie stood shoulder to shoulder during the song. As Jake's eyes scanned the changes around him, his mind wandered to the changes on the horizon. In a week, they'd all be starting ninth grade. In the next four years, there'd be more changes than he could ever imagine.

But there was one thing that would never change.

His vow.

OOPS. He still planned to get Out of Patience Someday. But before he did, there were a few things he wanted to see. The horizon could wait. It's not like it was going anywhere.

48 the last out

Should you be wondering about one final mystery, it might be this. What happened to the Plunger of Destiny?

It was last seen by Mr. Knight as it raced toward the tornado.

After that, no one knows.

- Perhaps it was blown out of Patience and landed a hundred miles away.
- Perhaps one of the tornadoes sucked it up into its vortex and blew it into orbit.
- Perhaps one day someone will find it while they're walking on the prairie.
- Or walking in space.
- Perhaps one day it will come back to Patience again.
- Perhaps.

acknowledgments

I would like to effusively thank the "first responders" who braved the manuscript when it was a daunting and unwieldy mountain of paper dusted with a writer's dream. Their comments, criticism, and encouragement helped the dream come true. Thank you, Ryan Brandt, Kevin DuBrow, Cindy Meehl, Gerri Brioso, Leslie Garych, and Siegmar and Lois Muehl.

A heartfelt thanks to my editors at Delacorte Press, Michelle Poploff and Joe Cooper, whose pestering and persuasive brilliance infused the story with the kind of sensibilities a guy obsessed with plungers and toilets often overlooks.

I'm also grateful to Sara Crowe, my agent, for her visionary leap of faith.

And a profound thanks to my daughters, Holly and Kendall, and my wife for never leaving the dinner table when I insisted on sharing freaky and fascinating facts about the history of toilets.

Brian Meehl has been a paperboy, a dishwasher, a janitor, a garbageman, a dancer, a millworker, a mime, a bicycle messenger, a street performer, a Muppeteer, a dog, an actor, a playwright, a TV writer, and an author. He has no intention of deciding what he wants to be when he grows up.

Because he is a fugitive being sought by several high school guidance counselors, he can't reveal where he lives except to say it's somewhere in Connecticut country. He shares his hideout with four horses, three dogs, two daughters, one wife, and an angora bunny. They all wish he would grow up sooner rather than later.